Unexpected Love

A Benton Center Romance

David Allen Edmonds

Copyright 2022 by David Allen Edmonds

Published by Snowbelt Publishing Ltd.

All Rights Reserved.

ISBN-13: 978-0-9985-4667-4

Cover design: Julie Bayer, State by Design
Editing: Edits by Sue
Proofing: Barbara Kauffman

Dedication

"In the future days, which we seek to make secure, we look forward to a world founded upon four essential human freedoms. The first is freedom of speech and expression—everywhere in the world."

—Franklin D. Roosevelt, 1944, from his *State of the Union* speech.

Chapter 1

It was another one of those fall days that explained why people loved Benton Center, Ohio, so much: a clear blue sky full of crisp clean air, and the first batch of red, orange and yellow leaves lying on the deep green grass of Town Square. It was a Norman Rockwell painting come to life. Groups of volunteers were erecting the PumpkinFest booths along the eight paths that spoked out from the Gazebo, while others busily unloaded bales of hay and straw-filled scarecrows from flatbed trucks along Main St. Pumpkins and twisty, knobby gourds from another 18-wheeler were being distributed to every corner of the Square. Preparation for the weekend's festival were in full swing, and as every year Maggie McGrath and Brent Wellover were among the volunteers.

Brent grinned down at his girl as she tried to keep her auburn hair under her stocking cap and off her face. She always lost control of her hair when they argued, and the breeze today wasn't helping. Maggie was nearly a foot shorter than his six-foot-two frame, but to Brent it didn't matter. Her attitude more than made up the difference. The blush now rising up her face was obliterating her freckles, which told him she was nearing her 'stomp phase'.

"I swear to God, Brent." She nearly spat the words at him. "If you ask me one more time what my plans are I'm gonna tear your throat out!" 'Plans' meant how they were going to spend their lives now that college was out of the way, and it certainly wasn't the first time the childhood sweethearts had tried to figure it out.

Brent always found Maggie adorable, even when arguing. He let go of her hands and settled comfortably onto a bale of hay. "Nope." He kept his voice slow and calm. "You're way too nice to resort to violence, and you'd never put on a show for the whole town."

"Oooh you make me so mad!" She took two quick steps and leaped onto him.

Almost onto him anyway. Maggie missed her target as Brent moved slightly to the left, and she toppled face first into the straw. Stranded on the bale, she waved her arms and legs to regain her balance. Brent had anticipated her move, and as any gentleman would, helped her to her feet and dusted the straw from her clothing. Then he gathered her in his arms --God he loved this woman-- and held her until he stopped laughing and his ponytail stopped swinging. When she caught her breath, he spun her around to face him. "I know you don't hate me, Magnolia."

"Oh, yes, I do. I really do." She tried to free her hand. "Lemme go!"

"Not until you say it."

"Never. I am totally sure. I hate you."

He raised his light brown eyebrows skeptically. "Well, I didn't want to have to resort to this, and I know you're not really mad at me."

"Don't you dare." He dodged the glare from her green eyes. "Not in public. Brent. No!"
He slipped his hand under her elbow and tickled. She writhed and struggled but he kept tickling till she dissolved in laughter. Passersby laughed. Other PumpkinFest volunteers laughed. The crowd gathered now in the front window of the coffee shop across the street laughed as they always did at their antics. Taking a deep breath, Maggie playfully slapped his arm, Brent took her hand again, and they sat back down on the hay bale.

"I have to ask about the future, Mags, because I love you."

"I know. I love you, too." She leaned her shoulder into his. "I want to be with you forever, but how are we going to do it?" They had been dating since junior high, and he had always been her rock, but now their careers were pulling them in different directions. The frustration of not knowing their future was threatening to turn their usual bantering into something more serious.

Brent noticed the crowd observing them from the sidewalk. Several held iPhones and hopefully were taking videos of the decorations, but probably recording their every move. Like they always did. "Maybe we should wait until we're alone."

"Ben Cen is a small town. We're never alone." Maggie stood and turned to the gawkers in front of them. "Nothing to see here," she said as unsarcastically as she could manage. "I think we're fine. Thank you for your concern, but my friend here has stopped his ass-like behavior." She waved her hands as if parking an aircraft until the sidewalk slowly cleared, then turned to him with an exaggerated sigh. "You know, Brent, it would be easier if we just asked them what to do with our lives."

He had always felt gossip a harmless irritation and let the ignorant words skip off his back. But Maggie had been hurt in the past, especially by allegations about her father. He relaxed the ridge on his forehead and widened his eyes. "Yeah, but would even be easier if you didn't care so much about what other people thought."

"I mean, I don't, not really, you know that. The main thing is I know we'll be together."

As an adolescent Maggie had been devastated by rumors of her father's drug abuse and infidelity. Brent didn't think the gossip was intended to hurt her, rather an irritating reaction to her father's fame, but it was the basis of her insecurity. "It's just that you do, Maggie, you do care what they think."

She gestured at the passersby. "Not these people. I don't know them."

"Maybe." He nodded at the Coffee Pot across the street. "But the folks in there."

Her head spun to face him. "Of course I do, they're my friends. Our friends."

Brent took a breath; they'd had this conversation before. "But it's our life. Yours and mine. We'll decide our future, not anybody else."

"They're not telling us what to do." She furrowed her brow. "Of course not."

"Then why do you pay so much attention to what they say?"

"I don't." She bounced her weight on the balls of her feet and glared at him. "It's so easy for you. You've made your decision. You're going to Ethiopia and dig water wells. But do you even know when you're leaving? How long you're going to be away?"

He wanted to stand up but kept himself at her eye level on the hay bale. "You know I'm all registered and have my shots. I just don't know when the placement will come through or exactly how long I'll be in-country. That's why I don't think we should get married right away."

Maggie crossed her arms across her chest. "And I don't want to wait."

"I don't either. But the advantage in waiting is, we'll both get our careers started, so when we settle down, we'll stay settled down."

She jammed a lock of wayward hair under her cap, and her neck flushed. "You don't think I want that too?"

Brent saw her face and heard the warning in her voice. "That project in Chicago will be great for your career. It's exactly what you want to do. Urban development with professors you know, which should lead to a job in Cleveland."

"As you've said before. Several times." She glared at him. "But if I do that, we'll have to wait to get married even longer. Maybe a whole year." Her voice increased in speed again. "Idon'twannawaittobewithyou!"

Her words ran together but Brent knew what she meant. He managed to speak calmly and keep the snark out of his tone. "When we marry, I want us to be in the same city. The same continent at least." He reached for her hand. "Look, I don't want to do a long distance thing for even a day. It will be hell not being together."

Maggie shrugged free and threw her arms into the sky. She took half an exasperated step to the right, then to the left. "I don't know what to do!"

It seemed simple to Brent. Get her work project and his volunteering out of the way this year, then get married next year. They'd been over it way too many times. He slapped his forehead and snapped, "Wait. I got an idea. Just lay it out to Teddi and girls across the street and get their opinion. You won't even have to ask; they'll tell you what to do."

Her eyes widened and her freckles disappeared in a wave of red. "I hate it when you're like this." She knocked over the hay bale with a magnificent swing of her leg, turned her back on him, and rushed across the Square toward the Dress Shop.

It always struck Brent that she ran like Godzilla stomping Tokyo to smithereens, each foot placed deliberately to cause the most devastation. This wasn't the first time they'd had this argument, and it usually made him grin, but this time their voices were harsher, and their words bitter. It made no sense to keep re-hashing the same argument.

He thought they had passed the test of their relationship; four years of college in different cities hadn't reduced their love, but strengthened it. They were secure with their own lives, and they were deeply committed to spending them with each other.

He slapped his work gloves across his knees and turned to head to the Coffee Pot for his shift. Brent checked the traffic and thumbed the crossing lights before cautiously setting foot in the crosswalk. He'd restrained his frustration as long as he could, but let it out in the end, and now they were both mad.

Chapter 2

Maggie burst through the door of the Dress Shop and plopped into the depths of the overstuffed davenport before her friend Sammi Patel could even open her mouth to greet her. Sammi's mother, Riya, nearly dropped the tea pot and cups when she realized who their visitor was and the state the poor thing was in. Riya handed her daughter the tray without a word.

Sammi kissed her cheek and gestured toward the devastated lump of her friend. Riya nodded and swished through the beaded curtain leading into the work room. Sammi set the tray on the low table and squeezed onto the sofa by Maggie's feet. Samantha's parents were first generation immigrants from India. They started their tailoring business in a tiny building off the square. The Patels were expert craftpersons with outgoing personalities like their daughter, and were able to purchase a better building across the square from the Coffee Pot several years later. They used the expanded space to add retail as the name over the door suggested.

Maggie's eyes fluttered open at the sound of clinking pottery. "It's like I passed out."

"Stress," Sammi said, pouring the tea. "Comes from fighting."

"You saw that?" Maggie stretched the kink from her neck.

"Pretty obvious. Right in the middle of the Square. Probably live now on the Interwebs."

Maggie didn't smile at their usual joke. "Did Teddi see? And the others?"

Sammi sipped the tea. "Probably, but--shoot. They didn't really see it, you know what I mean?"

Maggie squinted. "No, I don't."

"Probably thought it was your normal fun fighting. Typical Brent and Maggie. Teasing each other. Tickling you into oblivion."

"It was." Maggie sighed. "Started that way."

"Yeah, that's how it looked, but it turned ugly, didn't it."

Maggie wrapped her arms around herself. "It did. I just snapped."

Sammi grinned. "Don't know if the ladies at the Coffee Pot noticed, but I've seen that foot stomp before."

Maggie didn't return the grin this time either. He made her crazy, then complained about her temper. It wasn't fair. "Brent is being such a pill. Says it's an easy decision. It's not, it's the most important decision of my life."

Maggie watched Sammi's eyebrows form black frowny faces above her dark chocolate eyes. "Our lives. The most important decision of our lives. You know what I mean. What I meant."

Sammi nodded and raised the teacup to her lips.

"And he's so calm about it." Maggie loved that about Sammi too, but at times her silence was infuriating.

"He's letting me, forcing me, to make the decision myself." Maggie looked for confirmation from her friend, but this appeared to be one of those times.

"So, you're arguing once again about getting married now or later, right?" Sammi peered at her over the lip of the fragile cup.

Maggie dropped her feet to the floor and sat up. "Why can't we just get married? We can deal with the other stuff later, it's not important."

Sammi nodded, her face blank. "That's one way to look at it."

"You're not being particularly helpful, Samantha."

Now Sammi grinned. "You can't get this wrong, Margaret Mary. I know he loves you, and I know you love him. It's only a matter of the timing."

Maggie knew in her heart that was true. She discarded her doubts in a sigh. "Well, I'd rather not go to Chicago without him, but darn it, this is a great opportunity for me. I'm not going to blow it."

Sammi nodded over the rim of her cup as her friend continued. "Brent doesn't have to go to Africa to volunteer, he can do that anywhere."

"He could. Or you could stay in Ben Cen and marry him when he comes back."

"But I may not get another opportunity like this again." She swiped hair from her forehead. "Besides, what would I do if I stayed here?"

"Do what's best for you." Sammi reached over to hug her, then said, "You do you, Margaret Mary."

"But we may have to wait a year to get married. A whole year."

"Yeah, one whole year, then you'll be together forever." Sammi's eyebrows arched again.

Maggie brushed away a tear. "You think?" She was sure the rumors of her father were untrue. Her parents' marriage had been stressful because of the time spent apart, but loving. And committed. She hated that the rumors bothered her. She hated that the rumors made her doubt even the tiniest bit.

"I know. You and Brent are made for each other."

"But can I be without him that long?" Maggie smiled thinly and stood up. "Can I even text him in Ethiopia?"

"You're the strongest woman I know, Maggie." Sammi clasped her friend's hands. "You can do it, you made it through college, right? Have faith."

"Thank you Sammi." Maggie pulled her friend into a long hug. "Sorry for the drama."

"Don't do that to yourself." Sammi nodded confidently. "And don't worry about Kennedy, either. I got that under control."

Maggie's eyes popped open in shock. She broke the embrace and dropped back into the sofa. "Perfect. I finally make a decision, and she comes back home? My enemy, my nemesis?" She felt warmth rise up her neck.

"Not to worry. The airhead's only going to be in town for six weeks." Sammi waved her hands as if brushing away Maggie's words. "Even if she gets the job."

"That is not very encouraging." Kennedy Philips' goal in life in high school was to be more popular than Maggie. They had competed in everything from cheerleading to student council to the homecoming court. Including Brent.

Sammi spoke faster. "It's just an interview with the Town for an internship. What I hear is she needs something on her resume before even her father's company will hire her. Even if she gets it, it's temporary."

"OK, sure. I get that part. Kay Kay gets something out of the deal, she always does." Maggie's brows knitted together, her freckles disappearing in the flush. "But what in the world does Benton Center need her for?
She's got no marketable skills." She was a climber and a suck-up. A dilettante. Worse, she'd always had her eye on Brent.

Sammi took a breath. "The mayor and council think the town's economy is falling apart. We're losing business, and we don't have the money to fix things up. Especially around the Square."

"Kennedy Philips is the answer? Come on." Maggie rubbed her hands over her eyes as it came to her.

"Her father, right? Big shot executive at that insurance company."
Sammi brought her hands together and nodded. "Bingo. If we hire his daughter, maybe BiggInsCo writes us a big check."

"You're on town council, you could vote against her." Maggie raised her eyebrows hoping her friend wasn't offended by her horrible suggestion.

"An internship is like getting free labor. The town is broke and there's no way she won't get it." Sammi's palms opened. "In a financial sense, it's really not a bad idea. It's worth a shot."

"Great news for the town, but Blondie flouncing around when I'm not here, not so much." One more thing to worry about, Maggie thought. She loved Brent and trusted him, but Kennedy was a player. She enjoyed the hunt and had tried several times over the years to take him away from her. "You'll keep an eye on her?"

"Absolutely. Nothing will happen." Sammi looked

closely at her. "Besides, Brent's leaving shortly anyway, so don't worry. They won't be in town at the same time for very long."

"OK, I guess." Maggie sighed and climbed out of the sofa. "It actually makes it easier to leave."

"You don't mean that."

"Well, if he wants to get everything out of his system before we get married, I kinda do." Maggie pursed her lips. "But I'll kill him if he even looks at her."

"Stop that." Sammi reached for her hands. "Have you talked to your dad yet?"
Maggie returned her squeeze. "No, I'm going to talk to him now."

"Give him my love." Sammi kissed her cheek. "And call me from the Windy City."

Riya reappeared and gathered both of them in a hug. Maggie knew she had been eavesdropping and loved her for it. She wished her own mother were still alive to worry over her. Maggie turned at the door to the shop and saw the two Patel women lost in conversation on the sofa. She missed her mother more than ever and yearned for her words of encouragement.

The door tinkled happily as she left, but that didn't match her mood. Hopefully her father would give her advice that she could believe in. She loved and trusted him, but not very often had he been present to offer her advice that she could use.

Chapter 3

The Coffee Pot bell tinkled behind Brent as he exchanged his fleece for a green apron and exchanged himself for Teddi behind the counter. "Tag, you're it," he said and kissed her cheek.

"Bout time you stopped flirting with that girl out there in front of everybody in town—"

"—and dragged myself in here to do some honest work," he mimicked. "Theodora, you aren't really my mother, you know." He ducked as she snapped the counter towel at him.

"Good as." She enveloped him in a hug, then stood back to examine his face. "Hmm," she said after a moment. "Glad you finally got here, my feet are killing me."

"Sit down." Brent noticed the concern on his substitute gramma's face. "I got you covered." He swirled some cinnamon into her coffee mug and tapped the rim with the spoon. "It's not like you're done working." He nodded to her table in the front bay window.

"My second job." She dropped her voice to a whisper. "Gotta keep my finger on the pulse of Benton Center. You know that."

"Other folks might call it gossiping." He smiled deviously and jumped back as she took another swipe at him with the towel.

"Somebody has to do it." The timer binged in the kitchen, and she hurried away.

Brent had been working the counter since he was in grade school and his parents owned the Coffee Pot. It was a family business and never really felt like a job. Theodora 'Teddi' Burns had been there forever, working her way from sweeping floors and bussing tables to managing the shop. The Black woman became his second grandmother as well as business partner after his parents died and they each inherited half of the business. He especially enjoyed the afternoons after the lunch rush was over. He could keep up with the customers and still have the time to research the water crisis in Northwest Africa. Today the work would keep his mind off Maggie.

He bookmarked a website on his laptop and scanned the room. Except for Teddi and the gossip girls the shop was nearly empty, which reminded him it was time to sit down with Teddi and take a look at the books. He noticed scuffed paint on the wainscoting and a place where the wallpaper was peeling. In several other places as well. At some point they'd have to spend some money and freshen the place up. Maybe he should add that to the list of decisions he was facing.

Brent began college as a highly recruited all-state linebacker. A step slow for high tier D-I, he accepted a full ride scholarship from Kent State. Typical of many athletes he planned to get his teaching degree in history and become a coach. Brent was heading for all-conference honors as a freshman when he blew out his knee. He made the tackle and was congratulated for his heart and his desire, but the injury ended his career. Fortunately after his grueling rehab, KSU renewed his scholarship. Equally fortunate, he was able to walk normally and do most everything except compete in football at a high level.

He'd graduated on time last June and had several interviews for teaching jobs, but declined the offers. He wanted to do something worthwhile and, well, exotic, before he settled into life as a teacher and small business owner. The lack of clean water was a global crisis, people were dying, and he was researching how he could get involved and make a tangible and visible change in the world. This would be a good time to go overseas, especially if Maggie decided to accept the project offer. He closed the computer and picked up the towel and spray cleaner.

Brent liked spritzing the tables and wiping them until they shined. It had been the first job Teddi had given him as a little kid. He stood back and admired how they looked, then grabbed another load of the dirty dishes and stacked them next to the washer. The Coffee Pot had always been a part of his family, and he'd never really considered running it as a full-time job. His friends Irving and Sammi both ran family businesses. He wondered if it was what they wanted to do or what their family expected of them.

Irving Yoder was the eldest of five boys, and Brent's best friend. They shared the gridiron and the basketball court and a lifetime of lame jokes, but personally they couldn't be more different. Where Brent was charismatic and popular, Irv was as invisible as a 6'-7" person could be. Loyal and good-hearted, but painfully shy. Where Brent could easily converse with anyone and enjoyed it, Irv was reduced to a red-faced babbling wreck at the mere sight of a girl. He had a great sense of humor, but apparently only Brent was able to entice the jokes from his mouth.

The Yoders owned a farm on the outskirts west of Benton. Soybeans mostly, and as the eldest it would one day be Irv's to run. He hadn't needed a college degree, but Irv had gone to the community college for two years to pick up new methods in organic agriculture. If he wanted, Irv could stay right in Benton Center and have a happy productive life.

In that respect, Brent thought, Irv was a lot like Sammi Patel. Maggie's bestie was finishing up her M.B.A. at Kent State University's School of Fashion, and would be taking over her parents' boutique whenever she wanted to. Sammi's personality was both the complete opposite of Irv's and the perfect charisma for a career in marketing anything. She had even run unopposed for a seat on Town Council. Quite simply, she was a born saleswoman and the friendliest person in a very friendly town.

Brent loaded the tray of dishes into the washer and punched the button. He carried the towel with him back out front, realizing that, like him, both his friends were happy and had established businesses in Benton Center. He stopped when it struck him: but I have love, too. He must have laughed out loud, for Teddi and her friends forgot their gossiping for a moment and spun in their chairs to see if they had missed something good.

"See you tomorrow, Teddi," he called as he hung the apron on its hook. Teddi raised her hand and waved but kept her head facing her Gossip Club friends. Brent grinned at her devotion to all things gossip.

He paused on the sidewalk. Maybe what the shop needs to do is stay open later and serve dinners. Sandwiches, nothing extensive. We'd have to hire a cook, at least another server, and hope there would be a market for another restaurant. Probably wouldn't work without a liquor license. He took a couple steps toward the square then stopped again. The afternoon was fading and lights warmed the windows of Sammi's Dress Shop. He wondered if Maggie was still there, and thought about crossing the square to see.

No, he told himself. It's better for her to cool off before we talk. She'll figure out, eventually, that my idea to postpone the wedding is our best plan. It will be awful to wait to marry her, but we'll make it work. I'll talk to her tomorrow.

Chapter 4

Maggie pulled off the road at the crest of the last hill to clear away the confusing thoughts of Brent before talking with her father. Her home spread out in the valley below, the clear pond in the meadow reflecting the front porch, the brown logs and green metal roof, and the forest of pines and vibrant leaves enclosing it all in a hug. The scene she loved from her childhood recalled the memories of the three of them together. When they were a family.

It was also the picture on the album cover that changed their lives. Dad had transformed the love of their family into song. Warm music from the heart, and lyrics that spoke to the heart. Sales skyrocketing, gold, then platinum, regional fame then national, from the front porch to the bus tour, and Dad was gone. Rich, famous, and in every major city in the country. Her family was reduced to two, Maggie and her mom.

Maggie hadn't felt his absence the first couple of years. They were rich and Maggie was famous for being

Terry McGrath's daughter. The single 'Butterfly Pond' was the hit on the album 'Butterfly Meadow.' That led to the 'Butterfly Springtime Tour.' All of this came from his pet name for her: she was Butterfly. Maggie was his muse and also the reason he was never home.

Maggie was popular in junior high. She knew the new songs before they came out. She knew Jocko and Mick, her Dad's bandmates. She got autographs for her friends, snagged pictures and swag, even tickets and backstage passes. The only kid in the county, maybe the whole state, to take a bow at the Grammies. In the fan-zines and on-line she was the teenage source of her father's inspiration.

But her Dad was never home. Terry and the Love Pirates played to small intimate crowds, refusing the large arena venues. The smaller attendance demanded more gigs, more weeks on tour and fewer days at home. Her teen popularity came from her connection to him, but that connection faded in his absence. Before long she saw her popularity as a poor substitute for her father's presence.

Maggie grew closer to her mother as the two of them shared the misery of his absence. They were firm in their love for him and his for them, and enjoyed his infrequent visits, but nothing could replace the time they missed being together. The few days a month he was home were frustrating; interviews, promotions and exhaustion left even less time for the three of them to be a family.

What little time they had together was precious. Quiet, pleasantly boring, close. Hiking, cooking, and simply being in the same room. They would sing together like they had when Maggie was little, but as an adolescent she refused to play the guitar despite her father's encouragement. It was enough to be with him and sing with him, but not play. The guitar is what took him away, and she would never do that to her mother.

Her mother did it to her instead. Lindsay died when Maggie was fourteen. Heart attack with no prior history; she fell to the kitchen floor, dinner on the stove, the carrot peeler in her hand. Maggie shook her head as she remembered how she'd expressed her grief in anger and resentment. And in self-pity: everything happened to her. First her dad left, then her mother. When her father postponed the tour and returned home, she spent the anger on him. His words could not console her, his actions infuriated her.

Terry and the Love Pirates disbanded. Terry cancelled the rest of tour and returned home to take care of his daughter. His popularity at the time was such that this was seen as the humble, heroic and probably temporary act of a loving father, determined to take care of his 'Butterfly.'

Eventually Terry's presence and devotion convinced his daughter of his love. She realized his own hurt, and they grew from an uneasy peace into a deeper caring. It was then she'd determined that she needed to be her own person, not only the daughter of Terry McGrath. She was glad when he'd finally started playing his twelve-string on the porch and hoped that someday he would ease back into performing, and maybe compose music again.

Maggie took another long look at her home in the valley and smiled. The gorgeous October day matched the happy memories of her family. She slid the car into gear and wound down the slope into the long gravel driveway. She heard the thunk-whack and smiled again. She didn't have to turn and see to know that her Dad was chopping and stacking wood.

She hopped out of the car and ran to him like she always did. He dropped the ax and opened his arms as he always did. "Butterfly!"

They hugged, then walked toward the house. "Quite a pile of wood you got there." She checked to be sure he was wearing gloves. His fingers were calloused from playing the guitar, but he needed to protect them. "Winter's not gonna get us this year."

"Looks like you got enough for several winters, Pops."

Terry stopped halfway up the steps and looked at her closely. "You OK?"

"Not really." Somehow he always knew. "I need to talk something over with you."

He nodded. "Cinnamon cider sound like a plan?"

She smiled and followed him into the house. Whether his advice would help or not, it was good to be with him.

Chapter 5

Brent couldn't wait till tomorrow to talk to Maggie. Six rings later his call went to her voice mail, and he tossed his cell onto the seat beside him. He kept speeding along the dead straight country road toward Irv's farm and asked himself again if she was mad or busy or both.

The Yoder farm sprawled across a gently undulating, nearly flat, piece of land southwest of Benton Center. They raised mostly soybeans, and some cows, chickens, and pigs were penned near the barn for family use. He parked near the rambling white monstrosity of a building, smiling at the family name spelled out in the roof tiles.

His footsteps raised plumes of dust as he made his way up the earthen ramp into the barn. Irv had set up a quarter of the main floor as his workspace, and Brent found him there, hunched over his workbench. "Got her about done?"

Irv continued rasping the lip of the first cylinder in the inline four engine block. "Pretty near."

"Just have to reinstall the engine, huh?"

"Yup."

Brent walked around the table and peered closely at the Ford 8N tractor. "Paint job looks nice. Red and gray."

"How it looked 70 years ago." Irv stopped rasping, ran his finger over the cylinder head, and selected a different rasp from the rack.

"I remember how it looked when you found it."

"Dad wanted to scrap it. Mal thought it was stupid." Irv rubbed the new tool over the rough spot. "They rented a tractor instead of paying to fix this one. Had to do it on my own time."

"I thought your brother was smarter than that. I know your dad is."

"They take a longer view." Irv gave the metal a last rub with an oily rag. "They're farmers."

"Wait. You're not?"

Irv tossed the rag aside. "Look outside. What do you see?"

"Beautiful fall day. Not a cloud in the sky."

"Perfect weather?"

It was Brent's turn. "Yup."

"Not if you're a farmer. Hasn't rained in almost two weeks."

"But your soybeans are already in."

"Land still needs rain. Is it in the forecast? Will there be enough rain? Enough snow this winter?"

Brent watched his friend carefully clean his tools and put them away. He'd come here for advice about Maggie, and instead he was learning what a farmer was. Or wasn't. "Where are you going with this?"

"It's about control. Lack of control. Dad, Malcolm, most of my brothers are OK with that."

Brent was glad his friend was talking, but hoped he'd get to the point. "The weather?"

"Yup. Can't control it. They know it'll work out in the long run."

It looked like Irv was grinding to a halt again. "But you?

"Nope." Irv gestured to the tractor and the workbench. "I can control theses with my hands and good set of tools. I changed a pile of rusty metal and some worn-out rubber tubing into something useful."

Brent wondered if Irv had more to say, but his friend pointed to a four-foot-long wooden propeller hanging from a nail on the front edge of the hayloft. "Next project."

"WWI?"

"Bi-plane. Gotta do some research."

Brent watched Irv wipe down his workbench, hang the rag on its peg and turn toward the door. "Oh yeah. What were you here to talk about? Probably not my issues." Irv extended his boot from the leg of his Oshkosh coveralls and toed the rough wooden floor. "Sorry."

"No, but you gave me my answer anyway."

Irv looked at him blankly. "Maggie?"

"She's the weather, like you said." Brent laughed as he continued. "You thought you were talking about yourself, and your family and the farm."

"I was."

"Yeah, but I heard you tell me that Maggie is like the weather. You can't control either one, it's stupid of me to try, and it'll work out in the end."

"Yup, well—"

"You're brilliant, Irving! I shouldn't tell her what to do, I should let her decide!" Brent shook Irv's hand vigorously and bolted down the ramp to his car.

Irv spit once into the dust. "Yup. You should."

Chapter 6

Part of what Maggie loved about autumn was the ritual of talking with her dad over a mug of cinnamon stick cider. She watched him pull his finger from the pot warming on the stove to his lip, then shake his head no. Not quite warm enough. Terry used the wooden spoon to stir it, then crossed the kitchen to the cupboards next to the sink. She saw him pause as he pulled out two heavy mugs, one engraved with a scroll T, the other a scroll M.   His shoulders slumped a bit as he left the mug with the L in its place on the shelf. He shut the cupboard door, then rummaged the pantry for the cinnamon sticks. He put on a smile as he stuck one in each cup and returned to the stove. "Hot enough," he announced. They inhaled the sweet steam as he poured and swirled the cinnamon sticks to add that flavor. Almost as good as drinking it, she thought.

The warm afternoon sun was guiding shadows across the pond toward the front porch. Her father toed the inside door and used his backside to pop open the screen.

"About time to replace it with the storm door, Butterfly."

"Probably, but it's heavenly out here now," she replied. Maggie sat down sideways on the swing, her back on the pillow against the arm, and reached her feet into the waning sunlight. Terry handed her the M mug and sat down on the rocking chair.

Maggie slurped too much of the hot liquid and fanned her face with her fingers.

"Little hot, darling daughter?"

"Oooohhh." She'd always done that as a little girl, and now felt it was part of their ritual. Maybe not the first time you burned your tongue, huh?" Her father kept his eyes on the peaceful ripples playing across the surface of the pond.

"But it's so good, Daddy. So good." She blew across it and took a smaller sip. She loved their time together. "And it smells wonderful."

Terry waited a beat, still looking at the water. "It reminds me of your mother."

Maggie stopped in mid-sip. "She always made it after we raked leaves."

He sipped some more. "We're missing the smoke. The cider and the smoke are supposed to be together."

"A big pile of burning leaves." Maggie sighed. "When I smell one, I remember the other. I miss it."

"I miss her." Terry reached his hand to hers. "Eight years."

She squeezed his hand in return. His eyes remained on the pond. "That's why I don't think I should be leaving you again, Dad."

He didn't look at his daughter as he spoke to her. "I will always miss her."

Maggie set down the cider and picked up the large

white envelope. "I'm not going to accept this."

Maggie knew her dad knew without looking she was holding the paperwork to participate in the Urban Planning Project. "Honey, I will miss your mom every day of my life whether you are sitting next to me here or working in Chicago."

"But I can't help you if I'm 350 miles away."

He turned his face to her. "Margaret, without your help I would not have made it. Absolutely." He smiled at the irony. "I came home to take care of you, and you ended up taking care of me."

Maggie's eyes filled with tears. "We took care of each other. Now I'm leaving you alone. Again."

"You can leave now because you helped me then." His face pulled taut as he concentrated. "It's like a pearl in an oyster, I guess. It still hurts, it'll always hurt, but I've surrounded the pain, isolated it."

"You need to get back to writing songs, Dad. I don't think that's an original image."

Terry laughed. "Might have heard it elsewhere, but hey, we had a deal, didn't we?"

"Deal?"

"We had very nearly this same conversation before you started graduate school, remember?"
Maggie set the empty mug on the table. "And I was right, wasn't I?"

Terry shook his head. "No, you were right about college. I couldn't have handled four years. Probably would've gone back to drinking."

"That's why I lived at home and went to Akron."

"But I made it without you during grad school."

"And I said I'd never leave you again. Now this opportunity comes up." She slapped the envelope on the table.

"Maggie, I'm stronger now and besides—" His voice fell away.

"Now it is time for me to spread my wings." He had said the words so many times before that Maggie repeated them as a zombie mantra.

Terry nodded and his eyebrows rose. "You may not believe me, but I ask you to trust me."

"That is so, I don't know, corny."

He had told her many times before that she needed to define herself as he had needed to tour with the Love Pirates when he was young. She also knew how guilty he felt at leaving her and her mom, and how much of her childhood he had missed. He would not prevent her from following her dreams even if it hurt, as she was sure it would. He turned to her. "What does Brent think?"

"This is my decision, not his," she said too quickly. "I'm not waiting for him."

"But—" Terry began, then appeared to think better of it. "I'll stay out of that."

"Thank you." Maggie relaxed her face a little.

"Well, here's how I think the two of us should handle this." He held up the large envelope in front of her.

"Go back and work with your professors in Chicago. For me. It'll be good for both of us."

She turned her glare from the paperwork to him. "What are you going to do when I'm not around to take care of you?"

"I'll manage." He turned his face back to the pond. "I did the last time."

"No, this time you'll start writing music like you used to do. Like you were born to do." He didn't respond. "Like you promised you would last time."

He looked down at his empty mug, refusing to meet

her eyes.

She put her hand on her father's arm. When he looked at her, she said softly, but clearly, "You were, you are, a world class musician, but you haven't written a thing for years."

"I can't write music anymore." His glance left her again.

"You still play your guitar."

He shook his head. "I can't write, can't create. Since——"

Maggie watched her father's shoulders shake. "I hear you," she said.

Terry slowly turned to her. "Lindsay was my inspiration."

Maggie brushed a tear from her eye and steadied her breathing. "I'll make you a deal."

Her father's eyes narrowed into a squint. "Another deal?"

"Yeah, and this time we have to trust ourselves, and trust each other." She reached for his hand. "I'll call the University of Illinois in Chicago and accept the placement. You go into your studio and write some music. If we both do our jobs by PumpkinFest next year, you'll have your creativity back, and I won't ever be afraid to leave you by yourself. Maybe you can even think about playing in public."

"I don't know, Maggie."

She could see the lines of guilt etched across his forehead and around his eyes. "I don't either," she said. His hands felt limp in hers. She squeezed them.

He pursed his lips and fought his face back under control. She said, "Let's give it a shot for five or six months. You and me."

"You are so much like your mother." A small smile

escaped his face. "So, what you're saying is, if I get back on my wings, you'll fly to Chicago on yours?"

She reached across and hugged him. "See, you're writing a song right there."

Chapter 7

The next day, Brent sat down at the counter of the Coffee Pot and opened his laptop. Another advantage of working in the afternoons was his chance to overhear the Gossip Club. He snickered to himself thinking he was doing precisely what he had accused Teddi of yesterday. He watched Teddi approach from the kitchen with a tray full of four-toed bear claw pastries. She placed several in the glass case on the counter next to him. He kept his eyes on his screen and his ears open.

Teddi set the rest of the bear claws in the center of the front table next to the carafe, the silverware, and the good cloth napkins. Gena Cobb, Mary Jane, and several other ladies greeted her; Sammi Patel pulled out a chair for Teddi to sit down. Soon their heads had drawn together like flower petals at night or the fingers of a fist. The Ladies Gossip Club meeting was underway.

Brent knew The Gossip Club of Benton Center to be faster than social media. Whether it was more accurate or not was another question, but faster definitely. Barely a day after Maggie and Brent's argument, the ladies had concluded that what they had seen in the Square was simply another example of Maggie and Brent's normal behavior: all was well with Ben Cen's Favorite Couple. Brent felt as if he and Maggie had dodged a gossip bullet, for the ladies had accidently arrived at the right conclusion without the benefit of any facts.

"She's the planner, I've always said that." Gena Cobb nibbled the finger of a bear claw. "Left on his own, that boy would wander around clueless."

Mary Jane's head and the others bobbed in agreement. "He does have his head in the clouds sometimes," she said. Brent kept his eyes down and the smile off his face. They were clueless.

"I think that's one of the things that make them a great couple." As the youngest of the women, Brent knew that Sammi rarely spoke, and did so now hesitantly. Teddi smiled and nudged her with her elbow.

"Opposites attract?" Gena's eyes narrowed as she snapped off another piece of the cinnamon frosted pastry. "Is that what you young people think? Seems old fashioned to me."

"I don't know, I don't think that, it's just--"

"--he does fly by the seat of his pants." Gena continued despite Teddi's warning look. "We all know that, don't we? He waits for the last minute to do something, while she has a plan in her hand weeks ahead of time."

Wait, Brent thought. I'm the stomper? He tamped down his urge to laugh out loud. As usual, the ladies were oblivious.

"However they do it, they've been getting along since grade school." Sammi looked from Teddi to the others. It looked to Brent that Teddi was ready to change the subject.

Mary Jane set her coffee mug on the table and tapped the rim with one of her black lacquered fingernails. "You guys have known each other for what, 20 years?"

Sammi grinned and dared a peek at Brent over her shoulder. "Not quite, but let's see, 15 at least. Teddi has known Brent his whole life."

"Everybody knows everybody," Gena said dismissively. "It's a small town."
Mary Jane took another sip. "We've only been here ten, since Meredith was born. I feel like a tourist." The ladies laughed. "No, really not, but I don't have all the details on their big plan."

Brent checked the Square beyond the Ladies to see if Irving had arrived for their PumpkinFest shift. He thought Teddi would respond, but before she opened her mouth, Gena said, "It's pretty simple. Maggie's off to Chicago Saturday night, right after the fireworks. Brent's going to drive her and help her settle in. Probably fly back."

"That's not exactly what Maggie told me." Sammi looked for encouragement from Gena to continue, but the older woman looked from her to Mary Jane. Brent shook his head. They had no idea.

"They can't leave before midnight, that's when they get crowned King and Queen of the Fest. They get to set off the fireworks this year."

"But, she just ran away from him. Didn't you--"
Mary Jane ignored Sammi. "Their typical foreplay." Brent coughed to dislodge the pastry stuck in his throat. "He'll do what she wants, like he always does." The black-clad woman checked to be sure everyone was listening and dropped her voice. "The King will follow his Queen to Chicago."

The others laughed in appreciation as Sammi furrowed her brow. Brent took a slug of coffee. Before the young woman could speak, Gena declared, "They're in love. They'll be married as soon as they both get back home."

Brent tried to focus on his NGO's, non-governmental organization, website but couldn't. *We pay so much attention to other people's opinions, and they think I'm the crazy one and Maggie's the planner. And PumpkinFest Queen? She won't even be in Ohio.* He wished the door would tinkle and a customer would distract him.

After leaving Irv's farm yesterday, Brent had searched Benton Center in vain. Maggie wasn't with her dad, not at Sammi's, the Bookstore or any of her normal haunts. She hadn't answered his texts or calls. Nothing.

Brent looked up from the counter and noticed again, how rarely Teddi spoke to the other gossipers. She was engaged, but an active listener not a speaker. He checked the door and refolded his arms across his chest.

*   *   *

Brent had slumped onto the top step of the gazebo. Not being able to share his decision with Maggie was killing him. It had been a long, silent day not seeing Maggie after their fight. He'd pushed aside the thought of many months without her, and it came to him. RiverPark. He ran through the square, across the street and down into the municipal park. His feet pounded the cinder path, the river rushed along beside him. There was a thin flow of people enjoying the twilight, and several waved as he thundered past. Finally the arched stone bridge rose over the flowing water; he raced up and down, around the bend and there she was.

The first bench past the river. The one hidden from view by the heavy foliage and curving path. The bench where they'd kissed the first time.

Maggie looked up, startled at the sound, then grinned. "Brent."

"You're a hard person to track down." He took a deep breath and settled onto the bench beside her.

"Worth it though."

"I hope so." She kept her eyes on the small portion of the river visible through the bushes.

"So, I've been thinking."

"A rare and novel concept." She kept her eyes averted, but a small grin tugged the corner of her mouth. "Thought I'd give it a try for once."

"What were you thinking about?" Maggie uncrossed her legs and re-crossed them the other way.

Brent gave her tight jeans and leather boots a second look. "The only thing I ever think about."

"Football?" The word exploded from her mouth as if she'd been holding the punch line to a joke. She turned and sprang up into his lap.

"But, what? Hey." This was quite an improvement.

She pulled back onto his knees. "Listen. I've decided. I talked to Sammi and my father."

Brent's eyes narrowed. She said quickly, "No, they didn't tell me what to do."

"But that's what—"

She kissed him quietly. "I think you were right."

"But I, wait. What?"

"That's what you were in such a hurry to tell me, wasn't it? Go do my work while you're in Africa and we get married later." She grinned. "Beat you to it."

"No, well yes, I was, but. Shoot. Now you got me all mixed up."

She leaned back and adjusted her tam. "OK, now

you get a turn to talk. Go on."

She was clearly enjoying this too much. "Yes, I think that's the right decision," he said. "But no, that's not what I was going to say."

"Yes, you were. You so were."

"Like totally," he grinned and reached to tickle her before thinking better of it. "But no, I figured however it went, Magnolia, it was your decision, not mine."

Her eyes focused on his as he continued. "Look, I've made my decision. I agreed to the posting in Africa. I'll go when they send the airline tickets." It was hard to concentrate this close to her sparkling jade eyes. And the freckles. "You can either take the deal in Chicago or not."

He really wanted to kiss her but needed to finish. "I came to tell you that whichever way you decided was good with me." He didn't have to wait, as she buried him in a wonderful hug.

*   *   *

That evening had turned out just the way he'd planned it. They were both happy with their decision. He looked up at the gossip club again and covered his laugh with a cough. They just kept on talking as if they had a clue.

Teddi turned to see if he was OK, then said to the ladies, "Maybe they get married, and maybe they don't. I do know they're in love, but you never know how these things will turn out."

Gena waved her away. "We've been watching these two their whole lives, Theodora, you know they will. Probably announce their engagement in the gazebo after he crowns her."

Several of the women twittered. Brent shook his head.

"I expect they will." His foster grandmother leaned

back from the table and folded her arms. When the others finished fantasizing and began deciding the next topic, she stood and cleared a tray full of dishes away from the table.

Brent heard her use the word 'expect' and knew what she meant by it. The power of expectations. What the town thinks will happen often morphs into what the town wants to happen. Expectations cause stress. She'd explained to him that trouble happens when expectations are not met. There's blame. Someone always pays for not meeting the expectations. Someone is judged to be the victim, the other judged to be the villain.

Brent helped Teddi deposit the dirty dishes in the bin and re-fill their drinks. Although the ladies often got the details wrong as they did now, he knew the women loved him and Maggie. The two of them had been judged worthy years ago, but the Gossip Club wasn't so lenient on everybody.

Like Kennedy Phillips, for example. High strung, wealthy and beautiful, she had not made the grade. She could be arrogant, self-centered and rude, but what adolescent didn't have a whole host of obnoxious qualities? He knew he did.

Benton Center in general and these ladies in particular had decided that he, Maggie, Sammi and even Irving, were beyond reproach: local kids with proper mid-western values. Kennedy? As far as Brent was concerned, she had chosen to go to college out of state to avoid the criticism the town had determined was her due.

Brent knew that Teddi was not really a gossip. She had his best interests at heart. He watched her return to the table with the drinks and rejoin the group.

Gena, the Mayor's secretary, held their attention for a beat, then said, "Oh, and one other thing I heard today.

Did any of you ladies hear that Kennedy Philips is interviewing for a position with the town?" If there were one thing the manager of the Coffee Pot had taught him, it was that good gossip required a good villain. It was even more important than the truth.

Gena continued, "The mayor thinks she's the answer to our--" She dropped her voice to a whisper. "--financial crisis."

Brent caught himself before gasping out loud. He hoped Gena was wrong as usual, for Kennedy back in town was the last thing he and Maggie needed.

Chapter 8

In addition to his title of King of the PumpkinFest, Brent's official duties this year included working on the Decorating Committee. That consisted mostly of transporting bales of hay, scarecrows and pumpkins to various points on the Square and displaying them as the Chairwoman of the Committee saw fit. His brawn was required, not his artistic sense, and certainly not his opinion. He was fine with that, because Maggie held the position this year, and that allowed them extra time to be together. That had been the case anyway.

Irving Yoder's official title should have been Chairman of the Construction Committee, but he'd refused that honor. Chairmen had to go to meetings, file reports, and worst of all, discuss matters with the Chairs of other committees. He would re-assemble the game booths and the various stands like he did every year, he liked the work, but he didn't want the authority. Besides that, Sammi Patel was the Chairwoman, and Brent knew Irv was more than happy to be her faithful, if silent, assistant.

Unofficially, Brent was Irving's assistant, or assistant to the assistant if the organizational flow chart were to be followed accurately. This year, Sammi was happy to have Brent's help, Irv was too, and Brent was happy to give it.

What was uncommon was Brent and Irv's current working relationship. Throughout their long friendship, Brent had been the leader and Irving his loyal wingman. Brent had been the captain of the football team, surely, but also captain of the basketball team although the tall and lanky Irving was the leading scorer and rebounder. Now Brent stood in awe, his role reduced to holding things, carrying things and bracing things. Irv was in his element; his tools were extensions of his hands, seemingly hard-wired to his brain.

"I thought our job was to assemble the Pumpkin Toss booth," Brent said.

"Hold it straight." Irving slammed the bolt through the matching hole and ratcheted it tight with the impact wrench. "That's what we're doing."

"We had this one put together a half hour ago."

"Wobbly."

Brent moved to the other side of what would be the counter of the booth, and realized he hadn't seen his friend's eyes the whole time.

"Hold it." Brent held it.

Slam. Ratchet. "Needed bracing."

"Sammi tell you to do that?" Brent watched the tips of Irv's ears redden. He couldn't resist.

Irv removed the ratchet head from the drill and gestured with his own head at the wood pile. "2 x 4."

Brent laid the ten-footer on top of the counter, and Irv marked the length with a pencil he'd plucked from behind his ear. He muttered something, but Brent saw Sammi coming down the path towards them and didn't hear it. "Oh, oh, the boss is coming."

The flush descended down Irv's face from his ears to his chin, the reverse of Maggie's, Brent realized. Irv's head jerked back and forth seeking a hole to climb into.

Brent avoided Petey and his crew of kids chasing their kite down the path and waved. "Sammi, what's the haps?"

She pecked his cheek, glanced at Irv and said, "Just doing my Chairwoman thing, dawg." She was wearing jeans and a fleece and held a clipboard. "Did I say that right? Dawg?"

Brent smacked her palm as she giggled. "Spoken like a true urban guerilla."

"Hold it." Irv adjusted the 2" x 4" and readied the circular saw. He didn't raise his eyes to either of them. Brent steadied the board, and Sammi watched Irv cut it.

"Oh, Assistant," she said cheerfully as the saw blade whine down to a stop. "I need your report."

Irving was now completely beet red. He might have mumbled "Coming along. Fine. Almost done."

Sammi looked to Brent. "As the assistant to the assistant, Mr. Yoder is reporting on the improvements he's making to the booths, this one in particular," he said.

Sammi looked to Irv. "Well, I, erm, last year." He swiped at a bead of sweat rolling down his face. "I, um saw, that a little girl, and, and it almost, um, fell down. Collapsed. On her." He let out a breath, exhausted.

Sammi looked to Brent. "Mr. Yoder is expressing his concern that last year this booth nearly collapsed and squashed a kid." He squatted and pointed to the brace they'd attached to the underside of the counter. "Assistant Yoder has strengthened the structure so as to not endanger anyone this year."

"No one told you to do that, Irving." Sammi beamed.

Before he could think, Irv spoke. "Is, is that OK?"

"OK? No, Irv, It's brilliant. Thank you." She kissed his cheek as quickly as a ninja, and was gone down the path before he could run away.

Brent looked from her happily sauntering legs to his friend's deliriously shocked face.

Irv stuttered, "She, she--"

"--she did indeed." Brent completed Irv's thought, led him to the rear of the pickup, and propped him against the tailgate.

"Whoa." Irv's eyes widened as his face slowly approached its normal color.

"You know, she's not that scary. Just a little bit of a thing." Brent knew better than to expect his friend to say anything about Sammi, and he changed the subject when his friend's dopey expression relaxed. "Hey, I need some advice."

Irv's eyes returned from a galaxy far, far away from Benton. "What can I do you for?"

Brent grinned, not knowing if the tall drink of water had intended the quip. "Our shop. Teddi's and mine. I'm worried about it."

"How so?" Irv's eyes narrowed.

"It needs some work inside, paint, wallpaper; it's starting to look a little worn out."

Irv looked closely at the Coffee Pot and other businesses lining the Square. "Not the only place that needs help."

"I guess the question is whether it would be worth putting money into it."

Irv considered. "Do either you or Teddi have the money?"

"We can scrape some together and get a small business loan for the rest. I want to know if we should take the gamble."

Now on firmer footing than romantic relationships, Brent watched his friend's mind leap into action. He pivoted around the Square again. "I'll have to take a look at the specifics, but--"

"Is that a good but or a bad but?"

"Good, mostly good anyway. The Pot has good bones. The building is sound, but yeah, it needs some sprucing up."

"You can do it?"
Irv smiled. "We can do it."

"Great," Brent said. "It's been in my family a long time. I'd like to keep my hands on it. I love the place."
Irving didn't return Brent's wide smile.

"What?"

"You know, in the long run nobody is going to make any money around here if we don't get the whole Square in better shape. It's all looking a little shabby. A couple empty storefronts, too."

"We can fix our place, but what can we do about the rest of the Square?"

Irv's eyes focused. "I'll think about that, too."

Chapter 9

At that very moment on the opposite side of the Square, Brent noticed Kennedy Phillips smiling as Mayor Grieselhuber and Nate Richardson vied with each other for the right to hold the Town Hall door open for her. In the true spirit of Benton Center bipartisanship, it appeared as if they had found a compromise: Mayor Tom stood with his back against the door and beckoned her to exit the staircase, while the Councilman gestured for her to follow him toward the crosswalk.

Irv elbowed Brent, and they watched the blonde pause in the doorway before stepping between the men.

"What is she doing?" Irv asked.

"Making sure they get a good look at her?" Brent shrugged.

"Maybe she can't find the crosswalk without their help." They watched her link her arms with her twin escorts as the traffic stopped for her, and the three marched into the Square.

"Same old Kay Kay," Brent said as the three toured the PumpkinFest preparations like Dorothy between the Cowardly Lion and the Tinman.

"The girl loves her flounce." Irv nodded to Brent, and the two men stood the counter upright. They both grinned as Kennedy pulled the men to a stop, opened her enormous purse and arranged large dark glasses on the bridge of her slightly upturned nose. She re-looped her arms in theirs and continued processing toward the gazebo.

"But the girl does know how to make an entrance."

Kennedy glanced at Sammi and a group of female volunteers, and steered Tom and Nate around the Victorian structure the other way, toward Brent and Irv. She dropped her escorts' arms and hurried the last several steps to Brent just as he turned back to the booth. She encircled him from behind and squealed in delight. The mayor and the councilman exchanged surprised, then disappointed looks.

"What, who?" Brent managed to swipe a thick hank of her hair off his face and wriggle free. "Kay Kay."

She buried her face in his chest. Over her shoulder Brent watched the big farmer turn his face away in embarrassment and the mayor smile weakly. Behind them, Irv muttered something and banged a spike into a beam more forcefully than necessary.

Brent held her at arm's length. "Pretty dressed up to be working on the Fest." He looked at the smart tweed suit, jewelry at her throat and wrists, and 4" heels.

"No, silly." She swiped his arm then nestled closer to him. "Job interview." Brent put some space between him and the sweetly scented woman. "How did it go? I'm sure it was fine."

"I was so worried, Brent, but I got the *job!*" Irv giggled at the sound of her voice, and several starlings burst from the gazebo eaves.

Brent looked at the two grinning politicians. "What did you have to be worried about?" Behind him Irv grunted something that sounded like 'don't get her started.'

"Thank you, kind sir. But you know, most people went to these *massive* state schools and have these tremendous resumes. I just have a degree from a small college, not even in Ohio. I was *hoping* to put something special on my *curriculum vitae* to impress BiggInsCo. These gentlemen offered me an internship."

Kennedy focused her beaming smile on the two older men. They didn't say 'aw shucks' out loud, but Brent was sure he heard it. Behind him Irv fired a half-dozen nails into the wood with his pneumatic tool.

The mayor grinned shyly in return. "We're happy to have a young woman of her character working for Benton Center."

"We even kicked in a small stipend," Nate added.

"So how long will you be with us?" Brent hoped he'd be safely away from her in Africa.

"BiggInsco initiates a new cadre in the spring, so at least through the first of the year. *Cadre*, isn't that a cute word?" She aimed her radiance at the councilman. "Although Mr. Richardson did mention something about a vacancy on the town council."

"That's great. You could work for your father at BiggInsCo and still have time to work for the town." Brent felt her hand in his and extricated his fingers. "Hey, Irv and I have plenty to do here if you've got the time."

"If only I had some skills, like you big, strong men." Kennedy put her hand over her mouth and giggled. "Except for this guy." She toppled a scarecrow off a hay bale with her toe. "He's your more typical male. Not like you and your friend Irving."

If she were wearing lacy gloves, she'd be on the set of *Gone With the Wind*, Brent thought. Spending a little time with her field hands, before moseying off with the higher ups. "I'm sure you've got more important folks to talk to, Kennedy, and Irv and I got to get this booth set up."

"Nobody is more important to me than you, Brent." She darted close and kissed him before he could react. Then she linked her arms to her two companions to continue her review of the Square, twiddling her fingers at him as she sashayed away.

"Mr. Yoder, there is something else going on here." Brent watched Dorothy, the Scarecrow and the Cowardly Lion prance down the yellow brick path. "Why does she need an internship to get a job at BiggInsCo? Her dad's the CFO, isn't he?"

"Yup. But that's not what bothers me." Irv wiped his hands on a rag as his eyes followed the three-person parade. "She sweet on you, Brent?"

"No, that's just a game she plays to get under Maggie's skin."

"A competitive game with you as a prize?" Irv shook his head. "Say what you want, but I'd rather be shy and alone than play that game."

"You're a poet, my friend, a veritable bard."

Irv shrugged and tossed the rag onto the now sturdy counter. "I don't know about that, but I do know you shouldn't be playing any games with Maggie. She loves you."

"I love her."

"Then marry her." Irv spat onto the grass. "Seems pretty simple to me."

"This from a guy who can't speak a whole sentence

in front of a girl?"

Irv returned his friend's grin. "Not deflecting today. We're talking about you and Maggie."

Brent wedged a hammer and the socket wrench into Irv's toolbox. "Simple? I should marry her when I'm in Africa and she's in Chicago? How does that work?"

"Got to be simpler than dealing with her." Irv hooked his thumb over his shoulder at Kennedy leading the two politicians into the Coffee Shop.

"You think I'm interested in her?"

"Doesn't matter. She's interested in you." Irv unplugged his impact wrench and began coiling the cord.

"Look, Maggie didn't want me to tell anybody, but we decided last night what we're going to do."

"Last I heard you couldn't find her."

"Finally did, and she trusts you, we both do. So--"

"--so she's on her way to Chicago now, and you'll be leaving shortly."

Brent's mouth gaped open. "How did you know?"

"Only logical decision to make." Irv loaded his toolbox into the storage locker in his truck.

"Really, Irv? It might have been logical, but it wasn't simple."

His tall friend turned around. "You'll miss her."

"Hell yes," Brent said. "I want to be with her every minute of every day."

"And you'll stay away from Little Miss Flouncy-flounce."

"Yes, mom, of course." Brent snorted a grin. "You sound like Teddi. Besides, I'll be out of here as soon as they send me the flight info."

"The Gossip club is not always wrong. And unless we went to different high schools, you know Ms. Kennedy works fast." Irv tossed the coil into the bed of his truck. "You know, I kinda envy you and Maggie."

Brent's face opened in amazement. "Irv, you have got to be kidding. All this was making me crazy. Still is. Maggie, too."

"Yeah, I know, but it'll work out." He stretched his two-meter frame and sighed. "You got expectations. Me, nobody even knows I'm in love."

Chapter 10

Maggie knew she was doing the right thing, but it still felt like she was running away. She had spent the last day packing her car, driving west, getting lost in downtown Chicago, finding the apartment the University was providing her, getting somewhat settled and sleeping ten hours like a dead woman. She knew her decision was correct, both her best friend and her father supported it, more importantly Brent supported it, but from a corner of her heart, a tiny doubt nagged her.

She yawned and tossed the covers off her bed. The Urban Planning and Policy department of the University of Illinois at Chicago had provided her and the other team members an apartment on S. Throop St., walking distance to the campus. It was small, in a four-story building and surprisingly comfortable. Better than the flat she'd rented as a grad student. She glanced at her phone and knew a shower would help her mood.

Deep in her heart she was sure. Sure of her love for

Brent, and sure of his love for her. Sure of her talent and sure of his desire to help others. Sure of it all, but still. She worked the last of the conditioner from her hair, gave it a squeeze and final rinse, and stepped out of the shower. She had completed all her duties as Queen of the PumpkinFest except one.

Maggie dressed quickly hoping to find a nearby place for coffee before her first meeting with the project group. Ella's Corner on W. Jackson looked promising, and she settled into a booth. The scone was delicious, but it reminded her of Teddi as she ate it. She wished she was as confident in all her decisions as she was in choosing a restaurant.

She copied Sammi's link from her iPhone, pasted it onto YouTube, and opened the video of last night's coronation at the culmination of the Fest. The weekend had been a success, Sammi's organization efficient, and her committee chairs competent. Sammi had assured Maggie that she could leave to make the Monday morning meeting in Chicago, and confirmed it in several texts. But she hadn't been there to be crowned.

Maggie opened the link to the coronation. The video was jumpy, probably handheld from someone in the crowd, but there was Brent on the top step of the Gazebo. He wore the royal ermine cloak, held the scepter with a pumpkin on the end, and balanced the crown designating him as the King of the PumpkinFest. The Square was filled, and at his feet hundreds of people chanted his name. His smile was false like a mask.

The crowd to Brent's right was parting to admit the royal pumpkin carriage. It always reminded her of Cinderella's, but instead of a rat, the driver was Irv. The round orange coach was bearing the Queen to the gazebo, where shortly she would be crowned and take her place beside the King. Together they would conclude this year's Fest by joining their hands and igniting the traditional fireworks display.

Maggie jabbed the pause button. A Pumpkin Queen stood smiling next to Brent, and it wasn't her. She hadn't imagined there would even be a Queen if she weren't there. Some years there had been only a King or only a Queen. There didn't have to be both. Sammi promised she'd take care of it or pretend to be the Queen herself.

She re-started the video. The committee had planned the ceremony this year to resemble a marriage: the groom waiting nervously at the altar as his bride processed down the aisle. The other Queen alighted from the pumpkin carriage, skipped up the stairs, embraced Brent and took her place at his side. Took *her* place at *his* side! Who was it? Tall, shapely, color of her hair reddish brown, like her own. No. It can't be. It could not possibly be. *Kennedy!*

Maggie frantically raised the audio level and moved closer until her nose practically touched the screen. It looked like, maybe, hopefully, Brent pushed Kennedy away as she nestled into him, but he did take the crown off the pillow, raise it over her nemesis and crown the imposter Queen of the PumpkinFest. She checked the time and stopped the video. She'd have to contact Ms. Samantha Patel after her class.

Maggie took a long breath and carefully released it. She loved city planning for several reasons, but mostly it was the combination of the practical with the creative. Her career was good for both her head and her heart. She finished her coffee in the booth at Ella's and organized her things. She was still on time for her meeting at the University. She told herself again she had made the right decision. She was sure that there must be a rational explanation for replacing her as Queen. Emotionally it was tougher. Her heart longed for Brent. She wanted to be with him, she wanted to be his Queen.

Chapter 11

Brent tried once again to find a comfortable way to cram his legs under the seat in front of him. The tourist class seats in the Lufthansa version of the 747 were larger than most carriers, but too small for his frame. He was jammed in with three hundred other economy passengers, it was the third leg of his journey to Ethiopia, he wasn't sure what day it would be when he landed, and he felt alone.

He'd expected to be alone on the trip to New York, and Frankfurt, and Addis Ababa. What he hadn't expected was the feeling of loneliness he'd experienced at the PumpkinFest the night before. Was it only last night?
Brent hadn't been alone. Hundreds of people had chanted his name. He'd held the scepter, balanced the crown and worn the cloak. The Square was filled for the culmination of the PumpkinFest, and his popularity was off the charts. He was King of the PumpkinFest and king of social media, but he felt alone.

The loneliness came from expectations, he realized.

When he had finally found Maggie, and they had finally come to a decision, nothing else had mattered to him. Their problems were over, and they had a plan. Living apart would be miserable, they both admitted it, but they were in love and they had a plan. A plan they had worked out together.

But he hadn't considered the expectations of Benton Center. He'd stood alone on the top step of the Gazebo next to Kennedy. She nestled against him and pecked his cheek. "How do I look? Like your wildest sexual fantasy?"

"Dammit, Kay Kay," he mouthed while smiling at the adoring crowd.

She waved wristy-wristy, elbow-elbow --like royalty --, and said from the corner of her smile, "I must look great! They think I'm Maggie herself."

"Maggie, Maggie," the crowd chanted.

"Yup, it's all about you." Brent took the crown from the pillow Mayor Grieselhuber held before him and raised it over her head. Several clumps of blond hair tried to escape from the back of her wig.

The crowd stilled. "With this crown, I name Thee Queen of the PumpkinFest!"

Kennedy smiled radiantly, rotating from her King to her subjects to the mayor like a lighthouse. The crowd burst into frenzied applause, then began counting down from twenty. Brent clasped her hand and when the crowd reached zero, they hit the button to release the fireworks. Booms and crackling jolts of light joined the applause and the PumpkinFest was officially concluded.

The town expected a King and a Queen, Kennedy had said, and offered to help. The mayor said it was an existential necessity. Nate figured it was a win/win. No one would get hurt. Sammi thought dressing Kennedy as Maggie would be clever and fun easy to explain to her friend. Irving was his monosyllabic self in front of the committee, his only comment was 'Halloween.' Now as Brent squirmed to get comfortable and recalled the hasty meeting, Teddi hadn't said much either. No one had a better idea, and he'd gone along with it.

Brent wished now he hadn't. He and Maggie had postponed their wedding plans, and he had 'married' her rival Kennedy. In public. On the internet. In the minds and hearts of Benton Center. Maybe the deception would hold; the town would see what they expected to see and it would die out in a few days. Knowing the town, it probably wouldn't, and he didn't want to pin his hopes on his deceitful behavior.

On one hand it was kinda funny. The auburn wig and the crown. Sammi thought so too; she'd help plan it. But how would Maggie react? It'll be on YouTube for sure. He looked out the window, but the bright sky and the white clouds didn't answer him. He'd done this to help, but he'd probably screwed it up again.

It was no wonder he felt alone. Brent tried to fit the tiny airplane pillow into the crick of his neck. He missed her, he longed to be with her. He was sure of her love, but not being able to see her and explain himself was killing him. He squirmed to stretch the skimpy blanket over his torso and cursed the airline for its lack of Wi-Fi.

Maggie was probably feeling worse. He was sure the video of the coronation was somewhere on social media, and she had seen it and been hurt. He didn't know when or even how he was going to be able to contact her. Hopefully Sammi had reached out to her and explained it. His emails from the plane had bounced back; maybe the hotel in Addis Ababa had better service. He fell into a fitful, lonely sleep.

Chapter 12

Maggie and the other dozen members of the project team spent most of Monday filling out paperwork, synching their devices and participating in team-building exercises. Her sadness at being 7000 miles away from Brent didn't leave much interest in cheerful bonding, but she knew several team members from grad school and the others seemed friendly enough. And they did end the day with a nice meal at a trendy Chicago restaurant. Back in the apartment, she tried unsuccessfully to reach Brent, then fell asleep over her required reading.

Now Tuesday morning the team was assembled on the Adams St. Bridge spanning twelve lanes of traffic on I-90 84 feet below. She pulled her coat tighter against the wind off Lake Michigan and strained to hear the project leader's voice over the sound of the traffic.

"This is part one of our project, ladies and gentle-men." He smiled and opened his arms. "Come on, I know it's cold, but this is just a October breeze. Come closer."

Maggie shuffled a few paces forward where she could both see and hear. "It'll get lots colder, and before you ask, yes, the Edmund Fitzgerald did sink in Lake Michigan." Several groaned and he continued. "This bridge here and what you see below is how Chicago solved their problem." He pointed behind them to the west.

"Housing, small businesses. Lots of people." He pivoted to the east. "Over there, the lake in the distance and the Loop in between."

He paused as the sound of the cars and trucks below drowned him out. He pointed over the side of the bridge. "It's obvious what the issue is. How do people get to the lake and to their offices while thousands of cars pass every hour? How do you keep north-south I-90 from cutting off the east-west flow?"

"Is this just a rush hour problem?" a blond-haired man asked. Others in the group laughed; it was late morning. "Yes, but the thing of it is, it's always rush hour on the Kennedy Expressway. 24/7." After more knowing nods, the leader continued. "So you see this is one of several bridges leading to the Loop, pedestrian and vehicular. And they've made an effort to dress them up a little bit." Maggie forced the image of Kay Kay from her mind and noticed the red hand railings and the groups of blue six-pointed stars worked into the metal fence-work. The design resembled the city of Chicago flag.

There were several more questions and answers, then the group moved on to the second portion of their project. Maggie was glad she'd worn her Asics joggers, as they continued eastward over the bridge toward the lake. She'd worn them in the hopes of getting a run in sometime today, knowing how the exercise would keep her mind off Brent.

Twenty minutes or so later, Maggie recognized the triangular pediment over the main entrance of the Art Institute of Chicago. They crossed Michigan Avenue and stepped out of the stream of passersby to admire it. One block later they turned onto Monroe and passed Millennium Park. The weak October sun reflected off the mirrored surface of the Bean in the distance, where she planned to take selfies for Sammi. Her friend was entranced by the massive stainless-steel sculpture, claiming it was roughly the same size as fifteen adult elephants.

Several blocks nearer the lake, there was no bridge to cross the ten lanes of Lake Shore Drive, and with the group strung out, it took two cycles of crossing lights to manage it.

Their destination was Monroe Harbor. The team leader pointed southeast into Lake Michigan. "That's Northerly Island. The site of the second part of our project." As the group caught sight of the island just east of Soldier Field, the leader continued.

"Richard M. Daley, the former mayor of Chicago, wanted to develop Northerly Island, but Meigs Field stood in his way. One Sunday night in 2003 he sent city crews with bulldozers to tear up the runway. No authority, no legislation, and contrary to Federal Aviation law, he simply took the land. The Chicago Park District held the title, but he had enough political power to pull it off. The busiest small airfield in the country, and he made it unusable.

"Now you're asking yourself what in the world this has to do with our project." The group huddled closer. Maggie was glad she was inside and protected from the wind. "Cleveland has the same two issues that Chicago had. Access to the lake and what to do with a small airport on the lakeshore. Interestingly enough, the same I-90 is the culprit in both cities. Our project goal is to come up with solutions. And, before you ask, no, we are not using the Daley method. We'll keep it all legal, shall we?"

There were several questions and comments. A half an hour later the group spread out while retracing its steps west, and Maggie noticed a sign reading "Maggie Daley Park." It was too much of a coincidence, so she followed the winding downhill path and found a bench overlooking the children's park. Running kids, loud and laughing kids, worried mothers, and contented grandparents. Despite the weather all were enjoying the climbable, hands-on playground equipment: tubes to slide through, ropes to scramble up, swinging bridges to traverse and padded hills to race up and down. The happy noise made her think of Brent. Her cell tweedled and her heart rose.

"There you are. Finally."

Maggie tried unsuccessfully to keep the disappointed look off her face.
Samantha."

"Not Sammi? I must really be in trouble."

Maggie flinched at the sound of a kid in the park screaming. "You said not to worry about Kennedy. That you'd take care of it."

"I did, everyone was fooled. The whole crowd. Coronation went off without a hitch. Every expectation met. The mayor is happy, council is happy." As her friend's voice sped up, Maggie knew there was more to the story: the town was blaming her for the whole thing.

"Is Miss Kennedy happy too?" Maggie peered into the small screen as the excitement drained from Sammi's face. "That's really important to me."

"I'm sorry, Mags, but it seemed the best solution. We got them out of there before anybody thought of an actual engagement. Only a couple people even mentioned the ring."

"People in the crowd mentioned an engagement ring? My engagement ring?"

"No, no, I said only a few. We were so worried that it would become a thing and the crowd would demand a proposal, but no. Irv worked it all out, and we got the carriage out of the square, and Brent made it on time to the airport and—Hey, girlfriend, are you OK?"

Maggie swiped the tear from her eye and swallowed. "Yeah, I am. Brent and I made our decision, and I know it wasn't real, but I never expected the whole town and every social media platform to see he was marrying *her*."

Sammi looked down. "I never thought of that. We, I was so concerned about keeping the Fest traditions going, and I knew you were safe and-- Shoot, I blew it."

"It's OK, Sammi." Maggie put on a valiant smile. "Time to put on my big girl pants."

Sammi's eyes narrowed. "You sure?"

"Not really," Maggie said and terminated the Face-Time call. As much as she trusted Brent, if she'd known that Kennedy would be her Doppelgänger, she'd have stayed in town and clawed her face off.

Chapter 13

Brent had been smart enough to listen to the training video and pack his Imodium, but he hadn't realized what drinking so much coffee would mean to his stomach acid level. He belched into his fist again and reached into his backpack for his Pepto-Bismol tablets. He tried again to fall asleep in the back seat of the Dodge Ram, but either the jarring rutted roads or his longing for Maggie made that impossible. His eyes jerked open as the truck finally jounced to a stop.

The NGO had picked him up at the airport yesterday and assigned him to a well repair team in the mountains of the Tigray region of northern Ethiopia. Hundreds of simple and efficient wells were sprinkled across the mountains, but when they needed parts or maintenance, it was the team's responsibility to bring needed tools and equipment. Brent had agreed to this assignment thinking he could handle the physical labor and hoping the hard and productive work would be a good way to avoid thinking about Maggie. What he hadn't planned on was how hard it was to breathe at 7,000 feet and that Irv was the one with the manual skills, not him. As this was his first day, his only duty was to observe. He staggered to a low stone wall and dropped down. Fifteen steps and he was gasping for breath.

Melaku and the two other members of their team carried the testing supplies across the hard packed reddish clay to the well in the center of the village. The first step was to monitor the water for cleanliness and volume. The crowd of people, Brent thought it must be the entire village, closed around them. So much for observing, he thought.

He looked away from the village to the arid, grayish green rolling hills. Their ascent hadn't been through mountains, even low ones like in Pennsylvania, but the Tigray Province lay well over a mile above sea level. He took another long breath and wiped the sweat from his face. Hot, too.

His cell vibrated and he jabbed his hand into his pocket to grab it. Maggie! Brent had tried to call from the airport and again from the road, but the calls had failed.

"Brent, you finally picked up," Irv said, his voice surprisingly clear.

"How did you get through?"

"Just lucky. Whatcha doing?"

Brent grinned like his friend was sitting on the stone wall beside him. "You know, obliterating pain and suffering, saving the world from drought. The usual."

"Same old, same old." Irv cackled a laugh. "Heard from Maggie?"

"Nope." Brent looked up at the sound of the villagers singing.

"Then I guess I'll have to tell you."

Brent re-focused on the call. "Tell me what?"

"The coronation fallout." Irv paused. "Ben Cen has

spoken."

"Wait, let me. It's my fault, right?" Brent squinted against the harsh sunlight. "Something like, no ring, no proposal, no marriage, we fought, and I'm to blame?"

"It's only the Gossip Club, you know how they are."

"And?"

"And you're right, mostly, but here's the best thing. You can't hear all the noise from thousands of miles away."

There better be another best thing, because he couldn't do anything about it anyway. He watched the villagers, young and old, male and female, link their arms and sing. "Give me some good news."

"Great news. I got a job offer. Possibly."

"You have a job offer. Re-doing the Coffee Pot."

"Oh, then I have even more great news."

"Irving, you sound like a man in love. Or a lunatic."

His string bean of a friend laughed. "We're putting your reno on the back burner till you get home. We should do it together anyway, and besides, your idea is too small. I got a better one."

"Look, Irv, that's fine. I'm jet-lagged, and altitude sickness is kicking my butt. Get to the good part. It's Sammi, isn't it?"

"Um, uh, erm." Brent thought he could hear his friend blush over the phone. "It's, yeah, I guess, but I, it's not official. She wants me to take a look. And." Irv's voice ran out of gas.

"Good luck, my friend. You work with her, and we'll do our project when I get back."

"Thanks, B, I hoped you'd say that. Oh! One more thing."

Brent shook his head but couldn't keep the grin off his face.

"The best part. I forgot. I got to thinking of Sammi. Well anyway. You're not being blamed anymore. You were, but then Kennedy flounced in and bragged about how she pretended to be Maggie, and that she's the actual Queen."

"They're blaming Kay Kay?"

"No, they're blaming Maggie, but you're off the hook. Bye. Gotta go."

The call ended. Brent looked at the cell in his hand. Great, I'm not to blame, but Maggie is. The gossipers in his hometown were assessing blame for something that wasn't any of their business. The villagers in front of him here were faced with a life and death crisis, and they were hugging the NGO team and singing together. There wasn't a frown among them. It certainly put things in perspective. Maybe Maggie would, too.

Chapter 14

When the Skype call finally went though and Maggie could see and hear Brent, and he could see and hear her, their problems were still not over. All they had thought about since they'd parted last Saturday was seeing their favorite face, smiling, and hearing their favorite voice. But it was like a full hose with a tiny spout: they talked at the same time, they paused at the same time, they hesitated, they started to speak, they waited for the other to speak. Then they laughed.

The laughter did it. More accurately what broke the tension and awkwardness was Maggie snorting and Brent losing control as she scrambled to wipe the snot away without him seeing it.

"I love you, Maggie," he said between gasps. "You're one classy broad."

Maggie scrubbed every corner of her face. "Is it gone?"

"You're here," he said. "And you look perfect."

She took a long breath. "I love you too."

He reached his finger to the screen, and she touched it with her own. "If only."

Brent swam in the depths of her green eyes. "If the rest of my time here is like today, we'll be together before we know it."

"Tell me about it."

Brent did so, from the tiny airport, to the bumpy road, to the base camp, to the villagers dancing with joy and splashing in the water. He ended with, "Yeah, it's been great, except I can hardly breathe, and my language skills are non-existent." She laughed along with him. "They're giving me a video recorder, kinda like a glorified cell. I can document their work and we'll use it in advertising and fundraising."

"Great, but my big burly man is not getting his hands dirty?" Maggie's eyes twinkled.

"Oh, no, I'm still a beast of burden. Lots of stuff to haul around. When I get so I can converse a little better they'll let me do some of the repair work."

"My little volunteer is moving up the ladder." Maggie's nose crinkled like it did when she made a joke.

"And, Smarty-pants, I can use the video at home to help them fundraise." Brent tried to ignore her eyes and nose. "Your turn."

"I am really psyched about this project, it's so interesting, and it could land me the best job ever. Right in Cleveland. We'd be together, at home." Maggie slumped. "It's just that the whole thing is a competition."

"How so?"

"We need to design approaches to these two problems, we'll present them to the Cleveland people, and the team members with the best plans will get the jobs."

"They'll actually go forward with the designs you guys propose?"

"No, they'll pick the three or four of us with the most feasible, that's the word they used, the most feasible solutions." Maggie looked away.

"Hey," Brent said sharply and waited for her eyes to come back to his. "You got this, Mags."

"These are very creative people I'm in with. Some with more experience. Most of them."

"Creative? Maybe, but you're tougher. You'll eat them up and spit them out."

Maggie grinned as her heart brimmed. "Little old me, from little old Benton Center?"

"That's the one, now get in there and kick some butt!"

His eyes narrowed like they did when he competed. She narrowed hers and rasped, "City planning is not really a contact sport."

When they stopped laughing, he said "How about gossiping? Is that a contact sport? I heard from Irv."

Her face clouded. "I FaceTimed Sammi. Apparently it is."

"I hear I'm taking the blame."

"No, it's my fault I wasn't there to marry you. That's what Sammi told me."

"But then Irv said everyone is mad at Kennedy. She deceived the whole town."

They were quiet for a bit, then Maggie said, "Blamed for what? Mad about what?"

Brent looked up at her. "We're the only thing they talk about, but you're right. What is it exactly we, or even Kay Kay, did wrong?"

"Well, darling, you did crown the wrong girl." She

watched confusion fill his face, then burst out in a laugh. "No, we did nothing wrong. You and the blonde bombshell were playing parts in a play." Her eyes left his for an instant. "It's not like it was when I was a kid. That hurt."

The small town had been jealous of Maggie's proximity to her father's fame and had expressed it by spreading rumors about him. Brent gave her some time. "Are you OK?"

She let out a long sigh. "Yeah. I think this time they're just having fun."

Brent frowned. "Well for sure they aren't limited to any facts. They just make stuff up." The town had made it hard on her, somehow blaming her for her father's indiscretions. Supposed indiscretions.

"That's the fun part. It's not really about us; the gossip has a life of its own." Maggie noticed indignation had replaced the confusion on his face. "We're simply the host for their virus."

"Maybe that would have been funny before the plague," Brent said. She was the strongest woman he knew, but he didn't want her hurt anymore. "I hear you saying you're fine, but I think we should talk more about this. I've got a couple ideas."

Chapter 15

The first time that day Sammi FaceTimed, Maggie was on a Zoom call with her project team and simply ignored the call. The second time, 45 minutes later, Maggie was working on her own and punched the red button without looking and accidentally hung up on her. By the third call it was getting dark in Chicago, and Maggie could practically feel Sammi's energy pulsing though the ringtone. Her irritation, too.

"Just don't tell me you were working so hard you couldn't *pick up!*"

"Actually, Samantha, that's why I'm in Chicago and that's what I was doing."

"Not Sammi again." Her brown eyes squeezed nearly shut as one side of her face bunched up. "That means you're still mad."

"No, that is *so* last week." Maggie held her grin until her friend's face exploded in happiness. "I knew you couldn't hold it in much--"

Sammi let loose a string of rapid-unintelligible-high-pitched-circuitous-redundant sounds that may or may not have been words.

Maggie couldn't help but laugh. Rarely had she seen her BFF so filled with joy that she couldn't even speak. She held up a water bottle in front of her cell. "Take a sip and tell me what happened. All the details, but slowly so I can follow along."

Sammi took several calming breaths. "It was like Irv just floated across the Square and appeared to me in the Dress Shop."

"But you had spoken to him about doing the renovation before, right?"

Sammi nodded several times. "Sure, but just like when you talk to him, you're never quite sure he's following, you know?"

"He's male."

"Yes, he is." Sammi's eyes unfocused and floated away until Maggie snapped her fingers. "OK, I won't interrupt you again. Go on with your story."

Sammi blinked, shook her head clear, and began. "The doorbell tinkled and suddenly Irving was in the shop. Mom made a big fuss about him and Dad shook his hand. I had to lean my head back to see his face. He's a good foot taller than me."

Maggie smiled, seeing the scene in her mind.

"He got all flushed and mumbled something, but I couldn't understand it, and when Dad said something about the renovations, he looked like his life raft was floating away, and I thought he would run out the door, so I started talking."

Maggie grinned. "I bet."

"Mom dragged Dad into the back room, and I said,

'I want to pick your brain. If you're sure you can get the time away from working on the farm,' and he nodded, so I listed all the repairs we needed to make, asked how much they would cost, told him how long it should take to do the work, and of course, I asked him for his opinion."

"Did he say anything? In words?"

"Not the first time, he just looked at me blankly, so I asked him again."

Maggie settled back in her chair. Sammi was giving her the long version and it was going to take some time.

"Irv turned all red and tried to talk, but it sounded like his throat hurt, so I told him how much Teddi had liked the quality of the work he did for her, and she wants you to do more, and I know Mom and Dad will approve our project."

"He agreed?"

"Not exactly. I wanted to hug him he looked so lost. After an excruciatingly long pause, he blurted the *cutest* thing!"

Maggie had tons of work to do, it was getting late, and it looked like this story would never end, but couldn't keep herself from grinning. "Wait. He spoke *and* he said something cute?"

Sammi got her hands under control and took a breath. "He said, Irving, he said that our store looks like a beautiful woman in old-fashioned clothing!"

"That *is* good!"

Sammi's voice sped up as she continued. "I stared at him, Mags. My mouth just *fell open*. Mom was leaning so far out of the back room, she almost pulled Dad down to the floor. Irv looked like he wanted to run away. That's exactly what it looks like! I told him and wrapped myself around him so he couldn't escape. He has like *no confidence*. Mom dragged Dad into the show room and joined the hug."

Maggie had to interrupt. "You're saying Irving, goofy Irving Yoder, solved the Patel Family Squabble? You guys have been arguing whether you're American or Indian, or immigrant or home-grown ever since I met you."

"You know it. Now we decide to re-decorate and Irving." Sammi sighed. "Sweet Irving comes up with the perfect plan to tie it all together. A place for beautiful women to wear unique clothing. That's what he meant by 'old-fashioned'."

"You think so?" Maggie said doubtfully.

"Absolutely, I can read him like a book." Sammi beamed. "And that's not the best part."

"Tell me the whole thing, girlfriend, and don't skimp on the details."

"Well, when we finally got out of the shop, my parents just kept *talking*, he walked me to the Square and we sat down on a bench. I filled him in on a few more details of the renovation--I know how hard it is for him to talk, so I did."

"Very noble, Sammi."

"Thank you. When he finally responded, he took a deep breath and asked about you."

"Me?"

"You and Brent, yeah, I was surprised he had brought it up; I didn't have to pry the words out of him." Maggie felt her back tighten and her hands clench. She didn't need any more commentary about her life.

"What'd he say?"

Sammi caught her friend's eyes through the screen. "Irv said the controversy is nothing new, you guys have always been popular around here. He said he was tired of the blame game."

Maggie's eyes narrowed. "Me too. We both are."

"We all are. Anyway, he said there really is no blame, because you guys just changed your plans. You compromised and you both agreed, so that should be that."

Maggie took a chance. "Your Irving is a pretty smart guy."

Sammi didn't hesitate at *your*, she beamed. "He is so smart."

"Then he said something about being the only one of us not to go to college, didn't he?"
Sammi's face widened. "How did you know?"

"He gets on Brent about that all the time. He's a pretty funny guy." Maggie watched her friend's eyes glaze over. "And he's cute, and tall, and sexy--"

The last word snapped Sammi out of her reverie. "No, I mean yes, but we, we didn't, I, I thought...Drat, I sound just like Irving!"

The girls both laughed, before Sammi changed the subject. "No, there'll be time to talk about that later."

"Right." Maggie watched her friend's face regain its normal color.

"He did have one real concern, Irv did." Sammi made sure Maggie was listening. "He's worried that when you guys get back, Ben Cen is gonna break into Team Maggie and Team Brent. He says that's really stupid, because you guys have been perfect for each other since 9th grade."

Later than that, fall of 10th, after Mom died, Maggie thought. Right after Brent had faced down the bullies in the lunchroom. "Anything to keep the controversy slash gossip machine running," she said.

"Exactly, then he went on about which one of you is the planner--"

"Not that old canard, Samantha, really." Maggie held up a stop sign hand. "You're avoiding the most important thing. Did he kiss you goodbye?"

"No, I waited, and I, I thought he--"

"But you two do seem to be making progress." Maggie watched her friend relax and knew she felt the same.

"I hope so. There's so much more to him than anybody sees." Sammi's eyes focused elsewhere again.
Maggie let her dream for a bit longer. "So, back in the real world, is there anything else going on in Ben Cen?"
Sammi woke up with a grin. "You ready for the Kay Kay report?"

"No, but yes, I guess."

"Ambivalent much?" Sammi beamed. "Our girl, the phony Queen of the Fest--"

"Ouch!"

"Too early, huh? OK, so the financial crisis for the town is a *real thing*. The Square is looking shabby, there's not enough people visiting and buying stuff."

"Uh-huh. I know all that. We need more tourists."

"Yeah, but what you don't know is that Kennedy, the intern, has solved the crisis. She is behind the push to renovate the shops. And you probably didn't know that it was *her* idea for Brent and Teddi to re-do the Coffee Pot and for Irv to renovate the Dress Shop."

Maggie shook her head. "The mayor and Nate must be so proud."

"They're like love-sick puppies." Sammi's face clouded. "But the issue is serious. Council needs to get to work on this."

"How about Teddi? How's she doing?"

"I love her. She's like this wise old soul. Sometimes she's the only adult in the room."

Maggie furrowed her brows. "What's her take on me and Brent? Who is she blaming?"

"That's the thing, Mags. The more I watch her with the ladies, the more I notice that she doesn't say much. She's more of a listener. Kinda moderates things, makes them actually explain what they mean. She doesn't blurt her own opinions."

"Then she's not automatically against me."

"No. Absolutely not. She loves you both. I haven't heard her pick a side."

"And she can bake." Maggie grinned. "I miss her bear claws."

Sammi agreed with a smile. "Oh, yeah, one bad thing. Kinda bad."

"What's that?"

"Teddi's little nephew, Petey. You know?"

"Little guy, what, 11 or so?"

"Yeah, that's the one. Runs around with Meredith, Mary Jane's daughter, and a bunch of kids. They've been getting in trouble, and she's worried about him."

"Anything serious?"

"Little vandalism things. Minor fights. Teddi doesn't know how to help without stepping on her sister's toes."

Maggie glanced at the time. "Sammi, I gotta get going. Got a small group meeting."

"I'm back to being Sammi?" She grinned mischievously.

"You always were, my dear." Maggie returned the smile. "Keep me up to date, hey?"

"Will do." Sammi ended the call.

Maggie leaned back in her chair. I need to be in Benton Center, she thought. Brent too. We need to be together to help our friends.

Chapter 16

It was finally cooling off a little bit. Brent was exhausted, but the slight breeze now coming through the window of his room in the NGO building was better than nothing, and the small fan wasn't only circulating hot air. It ought to be cooling off, he thought, it's after midnight.

Darkness covered the village and the surrounding hills, disrupted only by scattered pinpricks of light. He stretched to catch the breeze on his skin, dropped to the chair in front of his laptop. Irv's a farmer, he's surely awake by now.

Irving answered the Skype call on the third ping. He was indeed awake, dressed in his usual overalls, a smile on his thin angular face. "Dude!"

"Dude yourself!" Brent had to grin. "That better not be 'The Age of Aquarius' you're humming."

"Not me. By the way, you look awful." Irv jammed one squinted eye nearly to the screen. "You sick or something?"

Brent recoiled from the enormous orb. "Back off, no I'm fine. Just a long day." He explained how his role on the team had expanded and now he was doing some of the water testing as well as recording and schlepping.

"It's the heat and the altitude."

"Sure it is." Irv nodded as if he meant it. "And you've been there a month so you're getting used to it."

"I admit I'm not a farmer like you, and I'm soft and lazy from living in a town, but, man, we were in this village today. They didn't have a well at all so we're digging one. What they have to do, what the *women* have to do, twice a day, is haul water from a stream. Down the side of a hill, maybe a half mile. I think I can help."

"My friend Brent, the Great White Father."

"I thought I was anyway. Yeah, so I see this girl, she's maybe 10, and she's carrying a jerry can down the hill from her house to the stream. I make it down the hill no problem. The water is muddy, there's barely a trickle and it's where the cattle drink."

"That's why they need the well." Irv nodded thoughtfully.

"Right, so I help her fill it and start up the hill. I get about halfway, and she tries to help me carry it. I assure her, I'm a varsity athlete, right? But it's hot and heavy and steep. I get closer to the top, I can see their house and a crowd is watching me, but I'm on my knees. I can't breathe, I'm dizzy, done. She grabs the can and scampers the last 100 yards, then comes back and helps me."

"That means you're *not* the Great White Father," Irv said seriously. "That's OK. Are you getting any better with the language?"

"I'm OK in Amharic if the conversation is about soccer or water wells. I can play with the kids and demonstrate the testing process. Otherwise, I just catch random words." Brent pursed his lips. "When they're talking in their local dialect, I have no chance. Good thing most of them have some English."

Irving paused several seconds. "That's all you've got to tell me? You're tired?"

Brent stifled a yawn. "Of course not. I miss her. A lot. Every day."

"At least you won the battle of the plans. You're not married yet." Irv didn't smirk much, and only with his best friends, but he smirked now.

"Low blow. Worst part is, I don't think her plan would've been any better."

The lanky farmer thought of a quick rejoinder but saw his friend's face. "Enough about you, I've got a story."

"Good," Brent said, "I need one. Maybe it'll help me sleep."

"Least I could do. OK, so I was working in the barn at your father-in-law's place--"

"Irving." Brent's voiced raised menacingly.

"Oops, sorry." Irv grinned widely. "Yeah. Terry wants to turn his barn into a recording studio. He's getting back into writing music."

"Maggie said something about that."

"No interrupting, young man, this is a bedtime story."

Brent swiveled the laptop and laid down on the narrow bunk.

"Good, now get yourself comfy cozy and I'll tell you all about it."

Brent stretched out and Irv continued. "The thing about playing music in a barn is that it sounds like you're playing in a barn. Acoustics are terrible. The first thing we're doing is fixing up the stage. I know, Terry and the Love Pirates used to play on the little stage they have, but they never recorded there so the sound quality didn't matter as much."

Irv glanced at his friend's drooping eyelids. "We're building a back wall to focus the sound. Almost got it done. He's pretty handy for a musician. We set vertical pieces of hardwood, and a little overhanging roof. Cupped the wings inward. Like those partition thingies the choir used to sing in front of at school. We'll stain it all, so it'll look much better. Match the wood in the barn. The recording stuff will run along the side of the barn. I just have to frame it. He's bringing in guys to do the wiring."

Brent's breathing slowed down with a sigh. "You're probably asking yourself how I can be working at Sammi's and helping Terry with the barn while managing the family farm. Darn good question, my friend. Well, I had a conversation with my Paw and Mal, and I'm easing away from the farm. Mal can manage it, he wants to, and I'm thinking of incorporating as a renovation service. Sammi's helping me with the paperwork.

"I know, it's a change. That's my name on the barn roof too, and I'll help them with seeding and harvesting, but this is something I really want to do. I love it." Irv glanced at his sleeping friend and added, "And I love her, too.

"Terry's job will be done about the time you get back home, and he's thinking about giving music lessons to kids. Teddi gave him the OK to use the back room at the Pot, so he doesn't have to wait to get going. I think Petey and his band of ruffians are signed up. Hey, you could get out your old guitar and join them. Just a thought."

Irv's brow furrowed. "You probably know, Maggie told her dad to get back to music, but she meant writing, I think." Irv glanced at Brent although he knew he was asleep. "But he's working on recording equipment and teaching little kids. I think maybe I'll speak to him about that."

Brent snuffled and rolled onto his side.

"I'll let you go now, buddy. You've been a great audience. We'll talk again soon." Irv grinned and broke the connection. He had a full day of work ahead, and part of that would be with Sammi.

Chapter 17

Maggie felt like a goldfish swimming alone in a clear glass bowl. Not even the tiniest scrap of seaweed or a gurgling diver with his chest of treasure to hide behind. Just eyes. Blurry eyes from every direction, evaluating her every move. The door buzzed as Maggie closed the lid on her laptop. She didn't exactly slam it shut because it wouldn't make any noise if she did, but that was her intent. She realized once again that scrolling through messages from her friends in Benton Center was as far as she should have gone. Opening the last one put her in a bad mood.

That wasn't true either: she was often in a bad mood. The last month without Brent had been hell. It was a struggle to keep her negative feelings in a box and bury them under the weight of her city planning project. For the most part that had been successful; she was doing well and had found a kindred spirt who shared her dedication and design concepts. But it was only the professional part of her life.

Emotionally Maggie was a wreck. Opening e-mails from gossipers was like picking an itchy scab, and she should know better. She considered deleting the messages, but that was wrong, too. Her contacts in her hometown represented the full range of well-meaningness, and they were her acquaintances and friends. She didn't want to hurt them. Instead, she picked the scabs and hurt herself. The last message claimed that she wasn't in Chicago at all: she was at a clinic in the Upper Peninsula of Michigan having an abortion. To think she would have an abortion hurt more than the inane comments and were harder to ignore.

The buzzer sounded again. The voice was garbled but Maggie hit the intercom button twice, their code for 'On the way. Stop buzzing'. Brenda Brittain was like her in a lot of ways, the most important being a compulsive study nerd. Maggie didn't know if she was also hiding sadness and wouldn't pry, for the two got along well in shared isolation and when working together. They didn't need to delve into each other's personal life, and they didn't have to entertain each other. Except tonight. Maggie left her notes and computer on the desk, stuffed her wallet and phone into her jacket, and took the stairs to the foyer. Tonight they had declared a holiday.

Brenda held open the door of the Uber, a dark red Nissan, and followed Maggie into the back seat. "Music tonight!" she exclaimed. "Beats the back booth in Viaggio's," Maggie said as they made a left onto Madison and passed the stylish Italian restaurant that served as their study lounge most nights.

Brenda was a tall, slim Black woman from Cleveland, who had received her Masters at UIC. The two women had made progress on one part of the project and were rewarding themselves with a night away from their books and maps and computers. Brenda and her sisters sang in the church choir back home in Cleveland, and she had been excited to learn that Maggie's dad was Terry McGrath. "Have I got a surprise for you, Maggie girl," she said and grinned. "Actually two."

It was a clear, cold night in Chicago, the moon reflecting off Lake Michigan and the lights in office towers and apartments twinkling. Maggie gave up trying to figure out where the Uber was headed and lost herself in the feeling of the great city at rest. Brenda had told the driver to take Lakeshore Drive so her view was unrestricted, and they could enjoy the wintertime view of Lake Michigan.

At the next exit the driver headed west away from the lake and soon Maggie was completely lost in the narrow, taxi-filled side streets. In a two-block long area of bars and restaurants and clubs, they jumped out and joined the parade of young people. As she stood gawking, Brenda grabbed her hand and led her down a short flight of stairs under a pink neon sign blinking 'Gerard's Down Under'. "You'll love this place," she said.

Maggie did. It was a narrow, low-ceilinged space with a bar along the left side, tables lining the right, and a small, raised stage at the far end. A guy with a handlebar moustache and a watch cap was perched on a stool strumming a guitar and singing "Leaving on a Jet Plane." Brenda led her through the small tables toward a young man waving his hand.

Brenda's younger brother Benjamin smiled warmly and held out his hand. Taller and skinnier than his sister, he radiated a similar confidence, but his eyes betrayed a larger dose of merrymaking. He would be capable of shenanigans, Maggie thought.

Brenda's first surprise hadn't been her brother, rather the other young man with him. Maggie raised her eyebrows at Brenda, who blithely ignored her. She shook Michael's hand and took the open seat between the two men.

Maggie hadn't suspected she was being set up by Brenda, for her friend was meeting her brother, not a date. Still it was awkward; she hadn't hung out with anyone except Brent in forever. Literally. She re-arranged her smile, ordered a Moscow Mule, and dove into the standard new-person questions.

Soon the music washed over her, and she relaxed. The two young men had met at their first jobs, a mortgage company in the Loop. Michael was from Detroit. Came from a large Polish family. He had a deep, reassuring voice like the Allstate guy, and a great laugh.

Michael turned to her. "What about you? You from Cleveland, too?"

Benjamin, on her other side snorted. "No way, man, she's from a little blue dot in a county that's all red." Brenda shook her head at her brother. "Really?"

Maggie turned to Michael. "Little town called Benton Center. It's the county seat, true, but it's very unique."

Benjamin leaned across her. "What she means is Conway County is just like most of rural Ohio."

"No, that's not--"

"Are you guys talking about race or politics or what?" Michael sipped his beer. "I'm just here for the music."

"Sorry, guys, my brother sometimes talks before he thinks."

"I get that," Maggie said. "But since he brought it up, may I say a few words?"

"Brendy," Benjamin said to his sister. "Your friend is one tough lady."

"That she is," Brenda agreed. Michael nodded.

"What the eminent sociologist Doctor Brittain said--"

Michael saluted her and Brenda nudged her brother in the side while laughing with Maggie.

"--is true. Basically. Most of Ohio is farmland, most of the farmland is Republican. Cleveland, where you all are from, like Detroit, is usually Democratic. That's why Benton Center is unique."

"Come on, you guys have what two Dems who hold County positions?" Benjamin said.

"That's the county, yes. The town is different. We have more diversity in race and in politics than any other place in the county. Our town council does a great job of giving all sides a voice and finding consensus."

"I don't know, man." Benjamin narrowed his eyes and dropped his voice into a growl. "I don't know. Not what I've heard."

Maggie's face brightened. "And we have the best festivals. Everybody works together, no one is left out. It's really fun."

Brenda put her hand on her brother's arm. "Why don't we visit Maggie and check out Benton Center for ourselves."

Michael grinned at his friend. "Yeah, give it a shot."

Benjamin's brow closed, nearly covering his eyes. "I don't know. Maybe we should."

Maggie looked at the three in turn. "You've never been there, have you? You should come down to the PumpkinFest."

"We will." Brenda's soothing tone calmed the waters. "We didn't come here to talk all serious. How about you boys getting the next round?"

When the men left, Brenda leaned across the table. "So sorry for that. I had no idea."

"It's OK, *Brendy*," Maggie said with a smile. Her

friend laughed and Maggie continued. "That's what people expect in a rural county. Just come and see and bring your brother along."

"Michael, too?" Brenda tried to grin innocently and failed.

"You trying to arrange my social life, lady?"

"Who, me?"

"I can handle that myself." Maggie also failed to find a convincingly irritated tone and expression.

"Hope it's OK. You're not offended?"

"No, nice guy. Just not interested." She grinned. "Now I can't wait to find out what your second surprise will be."

After Ben and Michael returned and settled over their drinks, Brenda gestured to the man in the spotlight on the stage. "That guy look familiar to you?"

Benjamin glanced at his friend. "Watch this."

"When we first came in, he reminded me of--" Maggie's voice trailed off as she half rose to see over the crowd.

Brenda laid her hand on her brother's forearm. "Should be familiar."

"It's Jocko!" Maggie squealed and shot fully to her feet. It was good that he had just ended the song, because she zig-zagged through the maze of tables, burst onto the stage and wrapped him in a hug.

The musician struggled to stand up under her embrace. The crowd applauded and the bouncers stepped closer.

"He played in her father's band," Brenda explained to the two men. "My parents loved them," Michael replied.

Jocko extended his arms and peered into her face. "Butterfly, you are a grown-up lady." He pulled her back in for another hug. "Haven't seen you--" He stepped back, and his smile faded.

"Since my mom died." Maggie clasped his free hand in hers. "Too long."

Jocko waved away security and guided her to the wings. The MC stepped to the mic. "Give it up one more time for Jocko, the last of the Love Pirates."

The next act was a three-piece blues group. As they set up, Maggie took the old folk-rocker's hand and lead him to their table. After introductions and handshakes, she said, "Brenda, that was some great surprise.   How did you manage it?"

"Pure accident. The day after you told me about your dad and the Love Pirates, I saw an ad in the paper." She grinned widely around the table. "Yes, an actual newspaper. The entertainment section."

"I remember those," Jocko said. The five settled into an easy camaraderie, based mostly on Jocko's road stories from concert tours, and jokes about his age. "It's great," he said with a wry smile. "First tour, girls are throwing underwear at me, now their mothers. Wait. Their mothers were the girls!"

Maggie sat close to him, happy to see him, but not daring to ask the question. Michael asked it for her.

"OK Jocko, when is the band getting back together? I'd love to see Maggie's dad and the whole crew one more time."

Maggie saw the sadness in his eyes as Jocko looked slowly from one to the other. "That's up to Terry. He's the boss."

The evening ended shortly after that. Jocko was dragged away by other fans after exchanging contact information and hugs and promises with Maggie. She took Brenda's hand. "Thank you, my friend. Seeing Jocko meant the world to me."

"I thought you could use a good memory." Brenda waved to the approaching Uber. "The way things have been going for you."

Maggie gave her friend's shoulder a squeeze as they piled into the ride and headed for the next bar. "I didn't think you'd noticed."

"Girl, you are not all that subtle." Brenda flashed a wide smile. "Like I said it was an accident."

"No, I think it was fate." Maggie smiled mysteriously. "And you've given me an idea."

Chapter 18

Brent folded up the portable soccer goals and tossed them into the truck bed. He wrestled the balls into the net bag and yanked the cord snug. He climbed onto the gate with the balls and sighed. He was not fully happy for his heart ached for Maggie. He had been able to run with the kids most of the game only having to stop and catch his breath a couple of times. He was making some progress with the heat and the altitude, but as an athlete he had never been unable to perform at a peak level.

Brent had changed his focus from himself to the work of the NGO and the people they served. In exchange for his time, his effort and his meagre skills, Brent had gained a precious insight that he would take back home. These people placed an enormous value on their community. Willingly, tirelessly, happily. He didn't give them these values and he wasn't their savior. They worked because they enjoyed working together. They didn't need him to do the work for them. But they did need money for tools and equipment. They could use the pipe, pumps, drills, and generators, if they could get their hands on them.

In Benton Center there was a strong community spirit, but it wasn't as deeply held as in the Tigray Province of Ethiopia. The PumpkinFest proved the town could work together; Brent wished that feeling would last the whole year. Restoring the store fronts around the Square might help. Getting more people into the downtown certainly would.

But thinking about the people back home in Ohio dragged him unwillingly back to the part of Benton Center he really disliked: gossip. Everybody wanted to know everybody else's business. Normally he'd let it wash over him, but now he and Maggie were Topic #1. Every text and email he received had a new 'fact' about him, her or the nauseating *@MagBrent*. He meant every one, not most, not some, every damn message he got, contained something he had never known about himself. Heard something he'd never said. Discovered things about Maggie that he knew weren't true. The latest was that she was pregnant and hadn't gone to Chicago to work, but was having an abortion at a clinic in Vermont. Most of the stuff was trivial, some almost funny, but the idea that their personal lives were everybody's to share galled both of them.

Brent shook his head to clear his mind. He had contacted the banker who handled the Coffee Pot's business and set up a savings account to handle donations for the water project. Soon he would use his social media platforms to get the word out. He had no problem with asking people for money. He had personal capital and now the notoriety that he could use for a good and just cause. In some ways he envied these villagers. At first glance they had nothing, especially compared to the citizens of Ben Cen. But that feeling of shared community was something he'd love to promote in his hometown.

He liked the idea of a large number of people giving a small amount of money. More involvement, more ownership. Skin in the game Teddi called it. She also said that a couple of large donors could prime the pump. He chuckled now realizing what that meant to well diggers. BiggInsco, he thought. The largest employer in Conway County. That's who he should hit up for a donation to get his campaign off the ground. He decided to start answering Kennedy Phillips' emails instead of deleting them.

Brent slid off the tailgate and hit the video button on his cell phone. He had become the semi-official videographer of his team. It was one skill he had. The NGO used the videos to promote their goals on their website. Maybe he could use them to promote his fund-raising at home. They'd look good on a Go Fund Me page.

The sun dropping behind the hills caused shadows to race across the valley. The repair team was packing up the last of their equipment, and the villagers were preparing a meal for everyone to share. It would be nice for them to have a house or pavilion-like structure that the whole community could use. But there he was thinking like their savior again. He was here to help them execute their plans, not make plans for them.

The only good thing about the gossip storm was it kept him from thinking how miserable he was being 7,500 miles from Maggie. The people of Tigray didn't need him to plan their lives. Maggie needed him to find a way to combat the wagging tongues of the Gossip Club. If he didn't do that, they would always be @MagBrent.

Chapter 19

There was no good time for Brent and Maggie to Skype or FaceTime. The nine-hour time difference meant one of them should be asleep while the other was wide awake. This chat was scheduled after Brent's full day of exhausting volunteer work in the heat, while Maggie was just stepping out of her morning shower.

Maggie wrapped her robe around herself and raced to the sound of the gong as the Skype call came in. Brent's face popped into view, and she smiled.

"So, how's the pregnancy going?"

"According to the Ladies of Ben Cen, our love child is the size of a pomegranate."

"Wait, what about the abortion?"

"You wouldn't pay for it, remember?"

"No, it wasn't that. I heard I was afraid of commitment."

"No, that's me. I'm never leaving Chicago."

"That will make them happy. They say you're too

good for O-HI-O."

Maggie shook her head and tried to keep the hurt from showing. "You know, Brent, this kinda sucks."

"No kinda about it. Only thing to do is find the humor in it."

"It's not funny."

Brent saw her face tighten in pain. "Wait, this is. Kinda."

"Kinda?"

"Yeah, we're not actually thousands of miles away."

"We're not? Seems like it. You can see Chicago behind me, and that certainly isn't Illinois in your background."

"Silly girl. No, the last email I got said we're together on an alien spacecraft."

"Wait. We've been abducted?"

"Don't worry, no mention of probing." He laughed and she didn't.

"Brent, that's not even remotely funny."

"Then why the grin, Magnolia? You want to laugh, you know you do."

Brent's tactic worked. Maggie snorted out a breath and cackled hysterically. Brent joined her, and soon both had runny eyes and red cheeks. "But it's really not funny," she managed.

"Then explain the green stuff running out of your nose."

"Brent! You said that last time!" She pulled her head out of camera range, then returned. "I do not!"

"No, you don't." He composed his face and loved her even more. "It's good to see you laugh."

She saw the love in his eyes. "I want to hug you, you big dope. Smack you a good one, then feel your arms around me."

"Me too. We're getting there, Mags. My flight home is six weeks at most."

"I won't get back to Ben Cen till the end of the summer." Maggie's eyes lost their sparkle. "You better come visit me."

"Won't be able to keep me away."

They held each other's gaze, until she said, "We need to do something about the gossiping. We really do."

"And miss all the levity?" When Maggie didn't laugh, he said, "I agree, Maggie. What do you have in mind?"

"Not a plan, really—yet."

"Will it help stop the flow of gossip? Can anything stop it?"

"No, nothing will help that."

"Then, what?" His eyes clouded in misunderstanding.

"Look," she said, "gossipers gotta gossip. We've known them forever and that's what they do. It's who they are."

Brent knotted his brow. She loved his man-face. "I suppose you're right," he said. "Most of them aren't mean. Uninformed and crazy, but I don't think they're trying to be hurtful. It's the hangers-on, the followers. The people who don't know us."

"I agree. Some people just like a Twitter fight." Maggie's shoulders slumped. "But several are our friends. Irv and Sammi. Teddi of course."

"You can't count Irv, he's out to lunch." Brent laughed a little. "I did hear he's helping Sammi re-do her shop."

"And he's helping my dad turn the barn into a studio."

"How does he have time for his family's farm?"

"Don't know, but my dad says he can build anything." Her voice sped up. "He's sweet and Teddi, she spends her time distracting the Ladies. She won't let them get away with saying the really mean stuff."

"But that doesn't stop them from forwarding it to us." Brent leaned forward as if she were actually in front of him. She did the same. "What about your plan?"

Maggie's face brightened. "Yes! Guess who I met in Chicago? Jocko! Dad's bandmate."

"Your plan is to get the Love Pirates back together? That's great, but how does that help us?"

"I don't know if that's the whole plan. I'd like to keep it secret from my dad. I'm still working on the details, but the main thing is to give Benton Center something to gossip about, right?"

"You think if they're busy enough gossiping about your weird plan, maybe they'll leave us alone." Bent nodded. "Is that what you're thinking?"

"We can't stop them, maybe we can divert them." Maggie cocked her head to the side.

"Well, nothing would be better than getting Terry and his band back together. We've all been waiting for that. It would certainly be big news in our small town." His face clouded.

Maggie noticed. "But there's something about it you don't like."

"Not the band, I love that." He centered himself in the screen. "But something isn't quite right. It's like we're playing by their rules."

"Like it's OK to say whatever you want even if it isn't true?" Maggie's face clouded. She'd been thinking the exact same thing. Years ago when Terry had been touring and the two of them were in junior high, the gossip mill had been relentless. Constant rumors of Terry's drug and alcohol abuse, his liaisons with various women and his run-ins with the police. As much as Brent tried to make light of it now, Maggie and her mother had been terribly hurt by it. The final straw had been the totally erroneous rumor that Terry somehow caused Lindsay's death. It had taken Maggie most of a year to even speak to her father, let alone trust him.

"Yeah, by playing along with them are we condoning it all?"

She noticed the concern in his eyes, smiled and said, "Don't worry, I'm fine."

"Good, then I gotta go, I have a meeting. We can talk about this more, right? I need some time to think about it." Getting Jocko and the Pirates together to play with Maggie's dad wasn't a bad idea at, all actually a very good one, but encouraging more gossip? We need to find a way to stop it all completely.

Maggie nodded and held the palm of her hand in front of the camera. Brent did the same, their palms touched, and the thousands of miles between them shrank. "I love you," they said at the same time.

*   *   *

Brent clicked out of Skype and turned off the computer. He was constantly amazed at her resilience and the way she had re-built her relationship with her father. He loved her and couldn't wait for them to be together and married in Benton Center. He slapped the desk in frustration. Most of his tenure in Ethiopia was complete, and she was nearing the end of the first stage of her project. The gossiping would stop, or at least slow down, when they returned home. It was silly gossip, not hateful, but it was still irritating.

The dwelling he shared with the other volunteers

was finally cooling down; now the sun was dropping behind the hills. He watched the few lights twinkle on as the shadows reached across the town. He thought about taking a light jacket but left it hanging on the peg. It would be good to be cool, a little cool anyway. At the bottom of the iron stairs attached to the outside wall, it struck him that what he wanted to do was punish the gossipers for hurting them.

The relatively cooler evening was coaxing people out of their homes. Small, brightly lit shops offering everything from CDs to pottery lined the narrow street. He stopped at several, mostly to convince himself he could actually speak a little Lingo. Melaku had called him to a meeting at a restaurant a bit farther down the street. He had no idea what the meeting would be about, but it would involve tapas and drinks. He waved to his boss and his team members seated under a striped Cinzano umbrella. Melaku stood up as he reached the table and extended his hand. "Mr. Wellover, how would you like to go home?"

Brent's face opened into a broad smile.

Chapter 20

Brent reached up and held the clapper while he shut the door to the Coffee Pot soundlessly. Teddi Burns was loading a batch of cookies into the display case with her back to him. He faced the ladies at the gossip table and held a finger across his lips.

"What's a guy got to do to get an oatmeal raisin cookie in this burg, be a member of council or something?"

"One moment, I'll be right with you." Teddi glanced through the wavy glass for an instant, then returned to stacking cookies. "Just one more second."

Brent grinned to Gena and Mary Jane and the other ladies. "I heard these cookies are famous. The folks in Ethiopia love them, so they say."

Teddi popped out from the display case holding her hand on the back of her head. "Brent! It's you!" She bounded around the counter and wrapped the other arm around him. He laid his chin on her curly gray head.

"You, OK?"

She looked up, still clutching him. "Fine. I smacked my head on the case. Got up too fast." She frowned and stepped completely away. "Brent Wellover, you cut your hair."

He took her hands. "That's why you didn't recognize me?"

"You had that darn ponytail for as long as I can remember. I told you not to let it get so long."

"But I've had the same face the whole time." He arched his eyebrows. "Oh, they forget so quickly."

Teddi smacked one arm and grabbed the other. "Come on, sit down and say hello to the ladies." She dragged him to the oval table in the front window and hurried to get him a coffee.

Brent hugged them all in turn, sat down next to Gena, and sighed. "OK, what's Benton Center's verdict on my hair?"

It looked to him as if they weren't really sure he had asked for their opinion, but as soon as one answered, they all joined in. When Teddi returned with his coffee it was oral pandemonium, or an exercise in rudimentary democracy. "They're all agreeing with me, aren't they?" Teddi's eyes smiled at him over the lip of her mug.

"Can't tell which way the vote is going, but they're loud."

Teddi clinked her mug with the spoon several times. "Ponytail or not, please. Hands up for yes, hands in laps for hideous." She didn't face him, but Brent knew she was grinning. "Let's see, 5 to 2. Mary Jane and Brenda, you have awful taste. Brent, grow it out."

Everyone laughed and Brent felt as close to being at home as he could without Maggie. The ladies peppered him with questions about the heat, his work, water, the language, bugs, kangaroos and his love life. He answered most of them with a smile, and several of them reached for their checkbooks when he finished.

"Thanks, really, but I'm not quite set up for donations yet. I'll be putting collection boxes, hopefully, in the shops around town." He made eye contact around the table and smiled at the Gossip Club. "You guys have been so kind, sending me cookies and letters and texts. It made me feel like I was home. I appreciate it."

The ladies bobbed their heads and congratulated each other. "Oh, and the fantastic stories you guys created about me and Maggie. They were the perfect way for us to forget our home sickness."

The women kept their eyes off him and away from each other. Brent opened his mouth to let out his frustration but felt Teddi's hand on his arm. "Irving's here, dear, working in the back room."

He formed his lips into a smile and slid his chair away from the table. "Haven't seen him yet. I'll see what he's up to."

Gena was the first to lift her head. "Working? He better not be working in the back or anyplace else in here. The building permits aren't complete."

Teddi glared at the mayor's secretary. "I signed that form weeks ago."

"Yes, dear, you did, but his name is on the deed as well as yours, so you both have to sign."

Now Brent comforted Teddi with a pat on the arm. "No problem, or as they say in Tigray Provence, *nolo problemo.*"

Mary Jane grimaced. "Sounds to me like Spanish."

"Maybe. But in any case, we don't want to run afoul of the law." Brent excused himself and strode through the tables to the back room. He and Irv had been discussing the project in emails, but he wanted to see how it was coming along.

Years ago the space had been a dry goods store with its own entrance from the alley. A previous project had opened a door to link it with the café; now he and Irv were giving it new life as a wine bar and music venue. The Coffee Pot was becoming the Pot & Flagon. Hopefully the renovated property would generate income during the evening as well as the day.

The room itself was long, with dark shelving lining the red-brick walls. One set of shelves was actually a series of small drawers where buttons and threads had once been stored. A trap door in the ceiling held a large wheel which had been used to hoist loads into the storeroom above. Irv liked the look and planned on replacing the rope and keeping it open. Tables were stacked along the side with a handful of music stands. Several booths were on order, but they hadn't decided how to arrange the seating area.

Irv was on a ladder adjusting lights. "Look OK?"

"Me or the lights?"

Irv scampered down and embraced him. "It's great to see you, but you do look a little ragged. What was all the yelling about out there?"

"Voting on my hair. You could have come out and saved me."

"Hair? What about it?"

Brent chuckled and high-fived his friend. "Apparently, I wasn't supposed to cut it. Anyway, Gena tells me I need to sign some forms. Looks like you started without the proper paperwork."

"Get that done, then get back here. We got a lot to do." He gestured to the music stands. "Maggie's dad is holding his music lessons here, and we need to fix up the space."

"Be back as soon as I can." Brent strode quickly from the room. It was great seeing everybody, but the one person he wanted to see the most was still 350 miles away.

Chapter 21

Brent hadn't really expected Benton Center to have changed in the months he'd been gone, but he felt somehow reassured that everything was in its place, and he was home. The Square was green and vibrant, his friend was hard at work, and the gossip club was still gossiping. He thought of Teddi always having his back, and his smile widened. If only Maggie were here.

A pack of kids, 11 or 12 maybe, raced down the gazebo steps and nearly bowled him over. One of them was Petey, Teddi's nephew and another was Mary Jane's daughter. They had been racing around the Square like wild people the day he left, too.

He reached the top of the stairs in the town hall and found it empty. Gena, he realized, was probably still in the Coffee Pot. He sat in one of the office chairs and pulled out his phone. Maybe Maggie had texted.

Several minutes later Brent clicked off the device and wondered how long Gena's coffee break was. He glanced out the window to see, and noticed the conference door room was open. He recognized Sammi's voice and the mayor's. It must be a council meeting. He pulled his chair closer and listened.

"I want to get your input on one more thing," Mayor Grieselhuber was saying.

"What's on your mind, Tom?" Brent recognized the deep, nasally drawl of Nate Richardson.

"The future. I'm worried about the future of Benton Center."

A sharp, high-pitched voice spoke next. Kennedy Phillips? She's on council? "It looks great to me and the members of the business community. We're all making money."

"You represent the business community?" Sammi's voice rose in disbelief. "What business do you own?"

"Have you heard of BiggInsCo?" The other voice snapped back. Yeah, that was Kennedy.

"We are doing well now, that's true." Mayor Tom spoke in calm, measured tones, unlike the two women. "But will we in five years? In ten?"

"How can we know that?" Kennedy's words were neither calm nor measured.
Brent heard the shuffling of papers. The mayor said, "Look at these figures." He paused. "The trend is down, clearly down. In terms of gross revenue and in foot traffic, we are consistently losing ground. Each year a little more."

"Your projection?"

"Nate, in three to five years we will be closing businesses on the Square. From what I hear, several store fronts are available now."

"I've only been in office two months, and I've heard this doom and gloom several times already," Kennedy said.

"BiggInsCo is in great shape. So are many of the shops on the square."

"What is *your* plan, Mayor?" Samantha said quickly. "I'm sure you have a plan."

Outside the room, Brent heard something drop onto the table. A pen? "Wait, I know," Kennedy said with a heavy dose of snark. "More traffic."

The mayor's voice sharpened. "Actually, yes."

"You've talked about this before. Many times."

Sammi said, "Tell us about your plan, Mayor."

"Ladies." Nate's voice was a soothing warning.

"Business is the lifeblood of this community," Grieselhuber said. "If business goes away, the town goes away. We do indeed need more people spending money in the Square."

"Go on," Kennedy demanded. Brent was familiar with her spoiled brat tone.

"We can get more people with improved access from the Interstate. The new interchange is about to open, and the traffic will flow away from us if we don't improve route 7."

Nate agreed. "Uh-huh. It will be easier to take 7 into Hartfield than working your way here on the old county roads."

"Exactly. If we widened the road from Benton Center to I-71, they'd spend money here instead of there."

"Our Uptown is so much better than anything they have in Hartfield. In terms of shops and restaurants. All they have is strip malls."

"Ms. Phillips, I agree. As things stand now." The mayor was beginning to sound exasperated. "That's why we're looking at all the possibilities."

"If Hartfield gets more business, they can improve

their town center. Maybe some of our businesses would move there."

"No way, Samantha," Kennedy hissed. "They wouldn't leave Benton Center."

"If they're losing money, they might have to." Brent imagined Nate looking from one of the women to the other.

"Maybe yes, maybe no." From her tone, Brent could envision the condescension on Kennedy's face. "But I do know for certain they will leave if Benton Center loses the special feeling we have worked so hard to establish here." No one interrupted. "But more traffic will change us. We'll need more lanes for the cars, and we'll lose the bike lanes. We'll have to tear down buildings and pave over green space for more parking. We'll need overhead lights for safety. And pollution. Just think of the costs for keeping the historic buildings clean, let alone the air quality." She looked around the table. "What I'm saying is, we could gag on too much traffic and lose our identity. That would cause us to lose our business."

"This is like reading tea leaves and consulting crystal balls," Sammi said. "You're projecting, Kennedy, guessing."

Kennedy started to speak, but Sammi spoke over her. "Hear me out. The one thing we do know is what we have now in Benton Center is working well. I say we should do *more* of it. If we stop growing, we start dying."

The mayor's voice dropped, and Brent strained to hear. "Looks like there's more than one way to lose our business community. If we preserve what we have, we could lose one way, and if we change, we can lose another way."

"Damned if we do, damned if we don't," Nate said.

"I agree." The mayor's voice was sharp. Did he slap his hand on the tabletop? "This is clearly too big an issue for this committee to deal with."

"Too big for the town council itself," Kennedy challenged. "Let's put it on the ballot."

"It looks like we have consensus on that at least," Mayor Grieselhuber said. "It's best to let the people decide in November. We'll discuss a ballot issue at the next full council meeting."

"What are you doing, young man?"

Brent flinched as Gena Cobb marched past her desk and shut the conference room door in his face.

"Eavesdropping is a crime."

"You need a roof to do that, Ma'am." He used his best sheepish grin.

"I have no idea what that means." She spun around and yanked open a file cabinet draw, totally dismiss i n g Brent's play on words. "I thought you were here about the building permit."

"Yes, Mrs. Cobb, I am, and I want to thank you for reaching out to us, Teddi and me, so we can avoid prosecution." Brent smiled again and pulled his chair closer to her desk. You catch more flies with honey than with vinegar, he thought.

She softened and sat down. "It's about the paperwork, Brent. Trouble always follows missing paperwork."

"Yes, Ma'am, I agree completely."

"Well then, you and Mrs. Burns are co-owners, as I believe I mentioned, and as such you must both sign this form, and this other one, before--" Her eyes focused on his. He smiled back. "Before *any* work can begin. Is that clear?"

Brent wondered how she had managed to not notice Irv or his tools in the back room. "Absolutely." He signed where she indicated, and folded his copies neatly, before dropping his voice. "Is there any chance you can tell me what the meeting in there was all about? I didn't hear much, but they sounded, I don't know." His eyes searched vaguely at the ceiling. "Mad at each other?"

Gena glanced at the door. "I don't know what was said in the actual meeting, and I wouldn't share it if I did." It felt to Brent that she was willing him to believe her. He didn't, but he narrowed his gaze and nodded.

"But I can tell you this. Mayor Tom is an unusual politician." She checked again to be sure the door was still closed. Brent had to clamp his mouth shut not to laugh at the irony. Gena, the queen of gossipers, worried about speaking out of turn.

"Most local politicians fight their way through elections for school board, zoning commission, and village council in order to run for mayor. They ascend the ladder and spend the money, then relax when their name is finally stenciled on the office door." She kept her eyes on Brent as she jerked her thumb over her head at the mayor's office door.

"No more mountains to climb," Gena continued. "No more opponents to slay, no more speeches to stumble through. Once you're the mayor in a small town like Benton Center, there's nowhere else to go. But Mayor Tom is not like that.

"He can see the future. Our future. And he doesn't like it." Gena shook her head sadly. "His fear is our friendly, homey, independent town will become irrelevant. Then forgotten. Then unknown. It will be nothing more than a dot on a map. Who even reads a map anymore? No one will even bother to google a town that's been lost."

Brent shook away the thought that maybe Gena was in love with her boss. "This is what the meeting was about? Benton Center closing down?"

"No," Gena said sharply. "Haven't you been listening? It's about how he's going to *save* Benton Center." Her brow creased and she let out an exasperated breath.

"I think it's time for me to leave." He reached across the desk. "Thank you so much for your help, Ms. Cobb, and for your insight."

She shook his hand, then turned to the conference room door and sighed. He trotted down the steps to the street.

Might have dodged a bullet, Brent thought as he waited in the crosswalk for the traffic to stop. There's always some kind of controversy. Whether it's following paperwork rules or right of way laws, someone is always bumping up against someone else. An SUV braked to a skidding stop, he waved to the driver, and crossed the street into the Square. He found a bench in the sun and plopped down.

It's always controversy. It's me getting around the building department forms or the guy in the pickup not stopping at the warning lights, or those kids over there squabbling over a kite. He looked closer as Teddi raced out of the Coffee Pot and pulled two of the kids apart. He couldn't hear what she was yelling but didn't have to. Petey and his pals were in trouble once again.

So am I, he realized. Stepped right in the middle of it the first day home. I'm going to have to pick a side. Expand the road or keep Ben Cen as it is. Team Sammi or Team Kennedy. Not really much of a choice.
Either way we go, this town is pretty great. Why do we have to fight about it? The villagers in Ethiopia barely have any clean water, and instead of blaming each other and fighting about the money, they work together to find a source. And they don't argue, they sing about it.

Brent plucked a weed from the grass, carefully including the roots. I'm not being fair. The gossip ladies took sides, but they sent me boxes of cookies and wrote me letters. Sent treats to Maggie, too. And Gena could have been a hard ass about the forms.

Teddi had disappeared back into the Coffee Pot, and now the kids were trying to get two kites airborne. There is always controversy, he thought, always a difference of opinion. Like Mayor Tom says about voters in Benton Center: we fight like crazy, we express our opinions, we vote, and we agree on the results. And we believe in the *Pax Cucurbitas*, the Pumpkin Peace: no politics during the PumpkinFest. We've handled other crises before, now that I think about it. His phone tweedled and he opened the text from Maggie. His heart leapt: he hadn't seen her in two days.

Chapter 22

Two days earlier...

Maggie forked a spinach leaf through the runny egg into her mouth. Across the table in Ella's, Brenda grinned. "I don't know anyone who eats as much breakfast as you do."

"Most important meal of the day. May I?" Brenda nodded and Maggie grabbed a piece of wheat toast from her friend's plate. "Besides, we got a big day ahead of us. First day of presentations."

Brenda's thin face contracted. "Not our presentation. We're sometime next week. We don't even have to be there."

Maggie wiped up the last bit of yolk with the toast. "It's the competition. I want to see what we're up against."

The two dozen participants in the Chicago to Cleveland planning project had formed into ten small groups. Each would present their solutions to the I-90 corridor and lakefront problems. The best presentation would land jobs with the actual developers of the project.

"Well, if it comes down to eating, girlfriend, we have got it in the bag." Brenda handed her credit card to the waitress.

Maggie got up from the booth and backed into a tall man. "Hey!"

"Hey yourself," he said. He had a scruffy beard and short blondish hair, and he stood like a statue in the middle of the aisle.

Maggie looked across the table. "Rude," Brenda said.

Maggie turned back to the man. "Excuse me. Could you please get out of my way?"

"Could you please be my wife?"

"What? Brent!" Maggie screamed his name and burst into tears. He wrapped his arms around her, but she stood stiff as a tree and bawled.

"This is Brent?" Brenda settled back down to watch.

"I didn't, you didn't, when, your hair." Maggie's tongue could not keep up with her racing mind or her rampaging tear ducts. She had no idea Brent was holding her as tightly as he could, rubbing her back and breathing her in.

Maggie stopped crying, pushed him away and glared at him. "You didn't tell me when you were coming back."

"I didn't know myself, I--"

She smacked his arm. "I wasn't expecting you until next week."

"Yeah, they decided that I--"

She smacked his other arm. "I was going to make a banner, buy balloons, and meet you at the airport."

"I thought it was better to--"

Maggie felt herself flushing and controlled the urge to stomp. "I had it all planned, a welcome home party, a nice dinner, some alone time, and you just show up at 7:00 in the morning like something the cat dragged in."

Brenda giggled and Brent said to her, "Hi, I'm Brent. The boyfriend."

She jutted her chin out and gave him a Maggie-like glare. "You sure about that?"

"Absolutely, her face isn't completely red yet."

Brenda snorted and lifted her hands in surrender, as Maggie pulled his head around to face her. "Hey, over here."

"So, is that a yes? You'll be my wife?"

"No way." Maggie dropped her hands from his face and stepped back. Brenda stifled a gasp.

"May I ask why?" Brent took her hands in his.

Maggie controlled the urge to kick him and to say yes. "For one thing, you cut your hair."

"Uh-huh. The average daily temperature in Ethiopia was 98. It'll grow back."

"For another, we both look a mess. I need to wash my hair."

"I've been in and out of airplanes for 31 hours. I don't know what day it is. You look perfect."

Maggie's heart pounded in her chest, and she couldn't pull her eyes away from his. "Um, this is not how we planned it."

"It isn't." Brent nodded. "But you're willing to discuss it at a later date?"

"Perhaps. If you behave yourself."

"That'll do for now." He pulled her toward him.

They kissed deeply, then she burrowed her face into his chest. Their heart rates blended, her foot finally relaxed, and they sighed as one. Brent peeked over her head at Brenda and winked.

*   *   *

Brent smiled at the memory and typed his response to Maggie's text. From what he could tell, it had been positive: either they'd hate her presentation and she'd be home next week, or they'd love it, and she'd be working in Cleveland a week or two later. Things are looking up. He strode a few steps toward the gazebo and noticed the door to town hall open.

Nathan Richardson was holding the door for Kennedy Phillips and gesturing with his arm. Probably going for coffee, Brent thought. She looped her arm through the older man's as they crossed the street toward him. Brent sat back down on the bench with his back to them as they walked along the path.

"Miss Phillips, you shouldn't let Miss Patel get you so riled up," Nate said as they passed him.

Kennedy's heels clattered on the hard surface. "Yes, I should let her words wash over me, like--"

That's all the dialogue Brent heard. They continued arm in arm through the crosswalk past the Book Shop and Bernie's Blooms and into the Coffee Pot. He waited a bit, then followed them. He held the door for someone struggling with a cake box, and saw Kennedy speaking to Teddi at the counter.

"Miss Phillips." Teddi was trying to adjust her head scarf while balancing a tray of pastries. "It's so nice to see you twice in the same day. Is everything OK?"

"Oh, sorry to bother you, Ma'am. It's just I'm upset, a little upset, and really need to talk to Brent."

The laugh-lines deepened as the older woman's eyebrows arched. "You think he'll calm you down, do you?"

She popped two enormous blueberry muffins from the tray to a bag. "Usually you two rile each other up." When the younger woman blushed, Teddi said, "Sure, darling, he'll be back--wait, here he is now."

Brent let the door tinkle shut and stepped inside. Kennedy turned to him with a latte in one hand, a dark roast in the other, and a frown on her face.

"Kay Kay." He looked at her closely. "You're upset?"

She smiled at his use of her nickname. "Actually I am." She stood up straighter. "With good reason."

Brent took the two drinks and followed her to a table. He shook Nate's large, calloused hand and sat down. "Nathan, she's got two members of her support system here. This must be serious."

The councilman hid his smile behind his coffee cup. "You just entered the eye of the storm, son."

Brent grinned back. Before he could speak, Kennedy said, "It's not just me. You're going to be just as mad as I am about this."

She laid out the gist of her disagreement with Mayor Grieselhuber and Sammi, finishing with, "See, you're mad about it, too, aren't you?"

This was the conversation Brent had overheard. "If what you're saying is true." He glanced across the table. Nathan's nod confirmed it.

"I am," Brent continued. "Definitely. We have worked too hard to preserve the character of this town, especially the Square, to have it over-run with congestion and pollution." Brent's voice sped up, nearly matching hers. "It'll ruin us. First the small businesses will suffer, then the house values will fall."

"Then we have a ghost town." Kennedy put down her latte a little too hard. He covered her hand with his.

"What do you think, Nate, you're the wise old owl?"

"Well now, I can see both sides. The town could die from lack of business and it could die from too much business. Kinda gotta hit the sweet spot."

Brent frowned. "You're in favor of putting the issue on the ballot."

"Let the people decide their fate, pick their poison." The farmer drank some coffee. "It's their town for goodness sake, and it's how we've always done it." A grin filled his weathered face. "The campaign should be a real doozy."

Brent faced Kennedy. She finished checking her face and closed her compact with a snap. "Well, sir, I respect your opinion, I do. I am going to do everything I can to convince those people that the preservation of the Square will save the town." She locked eyes with Brent. "Will you help me prevent the widening of the road?"

"I will," he said. Brent believed in his position more than he believed in Kennedy, and at the end of the day he was staunchly democratic. Besides, working with her might just fit into his plan.

Kennedy pecked Brent's cheek with her freshly re-touched lips. Nate grinned and politely averted his eyes. But I don't need a glob of her lipstick, Brent thought. He forced a smile in return and reached for their check.

"No, silly, Nathan's got it." She laid her hand on Brent's forearm and turned the full wattage of her smile on the older man. The farmer blushed and reached for his wallet.

Brent couldn't avoid her scent as he walked the two to the door of the coffee shop. He couldn't identify it, but the cloud hovered around him after she was gone. More abrasive than Maggie's.

"Sit down, son," Teddi ordered after the door shut behind the two.

He shook his head as if awakening and sat where his co-owner and unofficial grandmother indicated.

"What is the matter with you?"

"What? Nothing."

"That girl is trouble." Teddi's nod left no room for disagreement, and neither did the stern look on her face.

Brent reacted as if he didn't comprehend. This was part of the plan he knew he wouldn't like. "Kay Kay? She's harmless, I've known her for years."

"I know her, too." Teddi re-arranged the sweetener packets in the pumpkin shaped sugar bowl. "Brent, you have a girl."

"Do I?" Brent tried not to look at her but failed. "That's not what I've heard around town. Came right from that table there in fact." He jerked his thumb at the oval table in the window. "I left Maggie, she left me, and our lovechild is an alien. Come on."

"Oh, we ladies do like our little chats, I have to admit." Teddi sighed and dropped her hands into her lap. "But you know that talk is all it is. You're the only one who knows what's truly going on between you two."

Brent managed a grin. His stopover in Chicago had proved that he and Maggie were on the same page. Teddi's reaction meant the plan was working. "Maybe one of two."

"All I'm saying is--"

"--don't fly too close to the sun," he finished for her. As he had the million other times she'd said that to him.

"Just because you've heard it before, doesn't mean it's not true." Teddi aimed her index finger at his cheek. "And wipe that off."

Brent did so as the bell tinkled, and she returned to the counter. He smiled as the two women continued the conversation they had probably started last week. He was still smiling as he pulled aside the plastic sheeting and entered the back room.

He and Irv had no idea who'd first thought of using the extra space as a nighttime attraction to pair with the daytime coffee shop. Brent had seen the coffee business diminishing and the need to expand, and they somehow figured out a solution. Now other businesses on the Square were re-habbing their buildings and re-thinking their futures. It was not the time to overwhelm Benton Center with a flood of new traffic. Maybe after the renovations were complete, but not now.

"When's the sign gonna be ready?"

"Not for a couple weeks." Irv nodded. "I like the graphics." They'd decided to hang an actual coffee pot and a wine bottle instead of using words on the sign that would extend out over the sidewalk. The words themselves would be in gold script on the front window. "Window painter can't make it for a week after that. Gilt shortage or something. The paperwork with the state liquor people will be done by then."

"Always something." Irv pulled two bottles of beer from his cooler. "You look like you could use one." They clinked and sat down.

Brent took a swig. "You noticed?"

"Kinda hard to miss."

"Jet lag?" Brent swallowed more beer.

Irving shook his head. "That fades in a couple days. You still look like you been drug in by the cat."

"Never felt like this." Brent frowned. "I am still catching up on my sleep, but Irv, I gotta tell you. I could not do the things over there that I can do here."

His friend shrugged. "The heat, the altitude, the geography."

"No, I mean yes, those are factors, but walking, carrying stuff. It was so draining."

"Never saw you like that." Irv tapped his fingernail on the longneck bottle. "You couldn't be the team captain, huh?"

"You know me well. But not only that, I could barely follow." Brent opened his face in amazement.
"How do those people do it? I mean I got a little stronger after a couple weeks, but still. I couldn't keep up. That's why they sent me home early."

"You did your best." Irv's eyebrows arched.

"I don't know." Brent clenched his jaw. "You got an idea to rev up my fund raising? It's all I can do for them."

"Well gone dry?" Irv laughed at his own joke.

Brent didn't take the bait. "Yeah, plenty of them."

"Just joshing with you. I do have an idea."

Brent's face brightened. He was hitting up all the people he knew in town, and soon his donation boxes would be in practically every store around the Square. "What do you have?"

"Well, I need to clear it with Sammi first, but she's head honcho of the Fest this year, so it shouldn't be a problem."

"Hey, that's great." Brent beamed as it hit him. "A booth at the PumpkinFest?"

"Lots of folks will be in town for the weekend, might as well separate them from some of their pocket cash."

"Amen, brother."

After drinking to his idea, Irv balanced his empty bottle on a sawhorse beside him. "Speaking of Sammi."

When his friend stopped before mentioning Kennedy's kiss, Brent said, "You heard?"

"I saw."

"Kennedy's a whack job, I know, but she's right about not widening the road." He and Maggie hadn't explained the plan to their friends, so he didn't say anything more about that.

Irv nodded. "Uh-huh."

"You and I have talked about this before. I like the traditional feel of the town."

"I know, but we need more traffic to keep us afloat." Irv took a drink of beer.
Brent arched his eyebrows. "Then what?"

"Should I tell Sammi?"

Brent shook his head. "She probably already knows."

"Probably already out there. In video." Irv tapped the bottom of the beer bottle on the wooden horse a couple times. "Wait a sec. Are we talking politics here or are we talking girlfriends?"

Brent made a line in the sawdust with his toe. "I think we know where each of us stands with the politics."

Irv nodded. "Opposite sides."

"Yeah," Brent nodded. "And you've got to trust me with the females."

"Hoping you'd say that." The strain left Irv's face and he whooshed out a breath. "I was afraid we'd have to discuss our feelings and all that stuff." He reached into the cooler for two more beers.

Brent knew his friend didn't want to talk about his relationship with Sammi. "Yeah, we're good. When you see Ms. Patel, be sure to tell her, I didn't kiss Kay Kay, she kissed me."

Irv snorted. "As if that makes a difference around

here."

"It doesn't, but hey." Brent waited for his friend to look up. "This will make for an interesting campaign, won't it? Friendly competition."

"It will that." Irv agreed, then pointed at the bottle on the thin edge of the sawhorse. "This bottle could fall either way, depending on what happens the next couple of months."

"The master of the metaphor." Brent saluted him. "The issue passes or it fails."

"Yeah, the election, too." He shook his long thin face. "I was talking about our relationships."

Chapter 23

I am still jet-lagged, Brent thought as he yawned again, or in the worst shape of my life. He had landed five days earlier and been in Benton Center for three days but continued to feel drawn out and logy. He was bothered by Teddi's warning and Irv's advice, and didn't want to admit it was more than a physical condition. It was great that his friends cared about him, but equally disconcerting. He hoped he was simply tired from a full day of helping Teddi in the Coffee Pot and renovating the back room with Irv.

The drive from Benton Center to the McGrath house was relaxing in any case, and he had always enjoyed it. He could speed in and out of the descending curves and enjoy the scenery. It was not as brilliant as it would be in the fall when the leaves changed, but the gray green foliage on the late summer trees was comforting and familiar.

He'd mended the political fence with Maggie before he went to sleep last night, fearing the gossip hose would have made a bigger deal out of it than it was. She hadn't

been happy about it, Kennedy had always been her nemesis, but Maggie knew it was part of their plan, the uncom-
fortable part. She'd suggested he check in on her father before she ended the call. Brent wondered again if she could
read his mind, for he had been planning to speak to him
anyway.

He pulled into the McGrath's winding gravel drive
and parked in back under a huge maple. He peeked through
the open barn door and marveled at the stage Terry and Irv
had created. Walking back into the sunshine, he heard a
12-string guitar and quietly rounded the side of the large
log house. From the seat of a front porch rocking chair,
Terry McGrath was playing the final chorus of 'Butterfly
Pond.' Brent felt the words in his chest as he thought of
Maggie; he smiled in understanding as Terry wiped a tear
from his cheek. He waited to climb the steps until Maggie's
father rose.

"For whatever my opinion's worth, Mr. McGrath,
that's the best song you've ever written."

"What? Oh, hey Brent. Good to see you." He strode
quickly across the wide boards and held out his hand. "But
you have to start calling me Terry."

Brent clasped his hand warmly. "Yes, sir, I'll try."

"I know, it's not how you were brought up, but remember." The love pirate winked. "I used to be a hippy."

"Yes, sir, but you're Maggie's father."

"That I am. Butterfly's dad. Come on, sit down here
and I'll get you some lemonade."

The screen door banged shut before Brent could
argue. He picked up the 12-string and strummed it. The
guitar throbbed in his hands as if alive. He tried a couple of
chords.

"That old thing still has a tone, doesn't it?" Terry

appeared with two glasses and a large sweating pitcher.

"Oh, I'm sorry, I--"

"It's a guitar, it's meant to be played." Terry filled Brent's glass and sat down in one of the rockers. "You still play? I thought you did when you were a kid."

Brent tried the refrain from 'Butterfly Pond.' "Never had enough time with all the sports."

"Not bad. Move your finger a little bit on the A-chord."

Brent strummed. "Yeah."

"It'd come right back to you, I bet. You ought to take some lessons."

"In all my free time?" Brent handed back the instrument and sat down.

"Well, that big sponge of a time-stealer, my daughter, is out of state at the moment."

Kennedy flashed through Brent's mind, and he kept from wincing. "She is, but she'll be back."

"Someday, I guess." Terry looked across the pond for a couple seconds. "I just so happen to be giving lessons at your place of employment, so it couldn't be more convenient."

"I thought you were teaching little kids."

"Son, it's music. There isn't any age. Besides, there's a bunch of them and I could use the help. Teddi's nephew, Mary Jane's kid, six or eight others. They're a handful."

Brent changed chords, flinched and tried again. "They're not better than me, are they?"

"Some are, but it's not a competition. It's about everybody learning together. Give it a shot." Terry inspected the younger man. "Tomorrow, at ten, if you've got the time."

Brent handed him the guitar. "I like the idea of

learning together. And I am sure I will have the time."

Terry looked up. "Now, you're sure?"

"I'm sure of a lot of things, sir."

"Terry."

"Yes sir, Terry."

McGrath set the 12-string next to his chair. "What are you trying to say, Brent?"

Brent swallowed. Suddenly his throat was dry. "I know I'll have time to take lessons from you. Because Maggie and I will be living in town."

"Butterfly is coming home?" The musician's eyes unfocused. "You're finally going to marry her?"

"Finally, yes, sir, I want to ask you for her hand."

Terry leapt to his feet, tugged Brent to his, and enveloped him in a hug. "Wait, I--"

"Stop talking, son. Now you're family."

"Yes? I have your permission?"

Terry held him at arm's length and looked up. "I don't know what century you're from, Brent, but it's her decision, not mine."

"Yes, but--"

"Can you imagine what she'd say if I tried to tell her what to do? Have you met my daughter?"

They both laughed. Terry told Brent to take a seat and disappeared into the house. He returned seconds later holding a bottle of scotch. "This deserves a toast." He poured three fingers of the golden whiskey into their glasses, and said, "Yes, young man, you have my permission, for whatever that's worth, to marry my daughter."

"To Magnolia!"

"To Butterfly!"

They set the glasses down and settled into their rockers. "Maggie's coming home." Terry sighed. "And you said you'll probably be living in town. What about her job?"

"If the Chicago thing pans out, or even if it doesn't, she can work in Cleveland. Or Akron. Maybe even Columbus."

"Never thought she would settle down here." Terry tipped his glass at the younger man. "Thank you, Brent."

"As you said, sir, Terry, have you *met* her?"

They shared another laugh and Terry slapped his knee in delight. Brent said, "Now I have another question."

"That deserves another shot. "Terry splashed more scotch into their glasses.

"This is Maggie's question, maybe a little easier."

Terry's eyes furrowed. "That would make it the easiest question she ever asked."

Brent wondered how to phrase it. "So 'Butterfly Pond,' how did you go about writing it? I mean how do you start a song?"

McGrath laughed. "Hell, I've been asked that so many times I can't remember, and I still have no idea. None. Sometimes the words, a poem, or something you hear. Sometimes an image. Paul Simon starts with the rhythm. I've tried that. Sometimes three or four notes form a pattern." He shrugged and opened his palms. "To answer your question, I just don't know."

"OK, I'll put down your answer as artistic license."

Terry laughed. "That should cover it."

They talked about many things as the sun began to set, from sports, to politics, to their favorite person. Brent was in a much better frame of mind as he shook Terry's hand and opened his car door. They instinctively ducked as a flock of geese honked their way through the trees above and splashed down into the pond. "How about an image?" Brent laughed. "Could you write a song about a flock of geese?"

Terry didn't laugh in return. "Come on." He ran back onto the porch and snatched a notebook from the small table between the rockers. Brent closed the car door and followed.

"What do you know about geese?" Terry aimed the pen at him.

"Uh, I dunno, they mate for life. The honking is communication."

"Go on." Terry scribbled in the notebook.

"They fly in a V. It's something to do with wind re-sistance and makes it easier to fly. Like race car drivers do when they draft the car in front of them."

"Boring. Not writing a song about race cars."

Brent cleared his head with a shake. "OK, how about monogamy. Geese mate for life."

Terry grunted something and continued writing. As fast as his hand could, flipping pages in the notebook.

"Well, they migrate. Sometimes 500 miles or more."

"Go on." Terry's eyes flashed into his.

"But they return home every season. To the same place. They winter in one place and return home when the seasons change."

"Yes!"

"I don't know how they actually navigate--"

Terry held up his palm. "No, not navigating. Home. This is about returning home. Flying home."

"Yeah, like I did. Like Maggie's going to."

"Stop." The lead singer and founder of Terry and the Love Pirates flipped pages in the notebook on his lap. He looked up at the geese paddling and honking in the pond, then read the words his hand had written: "She knows her way home."

He slapped the notebook against his knee. He picked up the 12-string and strummed three chords several times, then nodded. He ran down the porch stairs to his recording studio in the barn. "Gotta try this on the keyboard," he shouted over his shoulder. "See you tomorrow!"

Brent watched him vanish and descended the porch steps to his car. He smiled, for now he had answers to both of his questions.

Chapter 24

Maggie had a feeling that she shouldn't take Sammi's call, but she was frustrated. She and Brenda had hit a wall with their proposal, Brent had called last night, and she needed to vent. Or at least hear someone else vent. She nodded to her project partner and pinched her friend's number. Viaggio's was empty this time of the afternoon, so she wandered around the empty tables to a window seat overlooking Madison.

As the FaceTime app loaded, Sammi blurted, "Did he tell you he kissed her? Did he tell you that?"

Maggie took a breath. "That's not what he told me, no. He told me that Kennedy kissed him."

"That's not a difference." Sammi's sharp voice matched the look on her face.

"You've kissed Irving, haven't you? Is that the--"

"You know what I mean, Margaret. It's, it's different with Irv and me. Somehow different. And we're not talking about us."

"Yeah, it is. It's different because you're under the

radar. You and farmer Yoder can kiss however you want. Besides." Maggie let the word hang.

"Besides," Sammi continued, "I wasn't there. But I know what I heard."

"What did Teddi say about it? She saw it, didn't she?"

"She said he was acting like a typical dumb male. Too dumb to even wipe the lipstick off his face." Sammi grinned. "Said she had to smack him upside the head."

"I can count on Mrs. Burns to keep him in line. Probably Irving, too."

"No, yeah, you're right, I guess." Sammi squinted into her phone. "But aren't you jealous? A little bit?"

"No, he explained it all, and I trust him. He didn't call me from Ethiopia, did he?" Maggie eyed her defiantly. She and Brent would have to decide when it was time to tell their friends about their engagement.

Samantha forced a smile. "But the politics? Did he say anything about that?"

"Yes, he did, and I'm a little concerned about that."

Sammi's brows tightened above her bright chocolate eyes. "You're with me and the Mayor, aren't you? For expanding the road?"

"Sure, and that puts me squarely against Brent and our favorite floozy." Maggie grinned mischievously.

"Which means?" Sammi matched her grin.

"Which means we need to think a little bit more about all this." Except for having to mislead their friends, ever so slightly, Maggie grinned. The plan was coming together nicely.

*   *   *

Brent stood in the doorway to the back room of the coffee shop as Terry strolled to the counter. He smiled to himself as two old friends chatted.

"I've been telling you to call me Teddi for what, a hunnert years?" She stuffed some curly gray tendrils under her paisley turban. "What is the matter with you, child?"

Terry set his guitar case and music folder onto an empty table. "Well for one thing, we are pretty much the same age, and for the other, you are the auntie of one of my clients."

"Petey, a client? Why yes, I guess he is." She handed him a cinnamon scone. "To me he's a little guy with a drum set."

"A drum set and a dream," McGrath said. "The boy really wants to play."

Teddi leaned forward and Brett wondered what the secret message was. He took a few steps into the room to hear. "Truth now, Mr. Terry. How's he doing?"

"Better than I was at that age." The musician took another bite of the scone. "Too early to tell, but he's got the itch, for sure."

Teddi's eyes narrowed. "My sister tells me he's been behaving himself better since he started the lessons. Me, I just don't know."

"One of the many benefits of music." Terry smiled and rapped his knuckles on the counter. "It's good for him. Gotta run, class is starting."

The coffee shop wasn't crowded in the middle of the afternoon, but McGrath nodded to several people on his way into the back room that Irv and Brent were renovating. Six kids were seated at music stands, some strumming, one fingering the fretboard, one tuning the G-string, and Peter riffing on his drum kit.

As Terry opened his case, Brent approached, his guitar strapped over his shoulder and his fingers darting over the strings. "How do you want to do this, Boss? Whose side am I on?"

Terry strummed a chord and tightened a string. "Teacher or student? You're both I guess."

"That means I can walk around like I'm a big guy?"

"Yeah, a big guy who hasn't been practicing." Terry adjusted another string.

"Well, I was spending time with your daughter."

Terry returned the grin. "Hey, I really don't know how to teach music. I know how to play and I love it. The one thing I do know is if they never learn the fundamentals, they'll get frustrated and give up."

"Video games are a lot easier." Brent copied Terry's fingering and tried the phrase.

"Not bad. Yeah, so I'm doing it the way I was taught." He stepped in front of the kids and announced cheerfully, "Get out your homework!"

"This isn't school," Petey said. "It's music class."

Allison adjusted her music book on the stand, and her hands on the guitar. "It's like school, Petey."

"OK, it's not really homework." McGrath grinned while playing three chords on his twelve-string. "Get out the parts you practiced for today." He waited as the kids got themselves organized. When they settled, he played the piece himself. "That's what it should sound like, OK?"

The five guitarists played the exercise piece in turn. Peter played along and the others listened respectfully; the adults and the class clapped in appreciation after each piece. As the last girl, Meredith, finished, Brent gestured with his guitar. "Can I try it?"

"It's hard," Hooper said. He was proudly repeating his fingering. "Bet you can't."

"Sit on down and give her a shot," McGrath said.

Brent fumbled through the piece, stopping in the middle and re-starting. "See, Mr. Brent, try it like this." Hooper played the difficult section and Brent copied him. "Hey, that is better." Brent high-fived the youngster and the others clapped.

"See you guys? We can help each other out." McGrath smiled." OK, let's put it all together. Ready, all of us, 1, 2, ready play…"

They played the piece twice, the first haltingly, the second better. When they finished the kids cheered. McGrath nodded at Brent. "That sounded great."

"Boring," Meredith said. "Tedious and slow."

"Basic," McGrath said. "You have to learn the fundamentals before the heavy metal."
Brent looked at him. "What?"

"Meredith, you probably know her mom, Mary Jane. Anyway, she wants to be known as *Meredeath*." He pointed to her black nails and jagged metal chains as he spelled out her moniker.

Brent pumped his fist to the girl. She let a smile escape and returned the sign. He smiled and sat down next to her. As they practiced the assignment for tomorrow, he smiled to himself. She reminded him of a younger, more goth-like Maggie.

Chapter 25

The scenery across Indiana and Ohio was featureless and brown in the late summer heat, matching Brent's mood. He was physically tired from flying to Chicago, loading up the car and battling the big city traffic. He was mentally tired from re-discussing The Plan. Not the marriage plan, that was settled, the Gossip Plan. Maggie snorted and jerked awake. "We need to talk," she said.

He flinched and eased the Jeep back into the right lane. "I'm right here, Magnolia."

Maggie stretched and checked herself in the mirror. As she reached into her make-up pouch, he said. "You look fine."

"Fine for having screwed up my opportunity, packed all my earthly possessions, and driven all night, or just fine?"

"The last one, the normal fine." He passed an orange 18-wheeler. If she was this concerned with how she looked, she must be more worried than he thought. "You know, the fine you looked when you wrestled me to the floor and made me say yes."

"Oh, that one." She grinned but continued to examine her face in the mirror.

Brent tried again. "Drool, lower right side by the big freckle."

She punched his arm. "Brent!"

"Don't hit the driver, it's dangerous." He jiggled the wheel as she wiped a tissue across her cheek and smeared her fresh lipstick.

He held out his hand to keep her from sliding across the seat. "We'll all die in a flaming car wreck."

"Oooohh, Brent!" Her foot beat a staccato on the floor mat.

"Let's talk, shall we?" He stifled his grin and kept his eyes on the Ohio Turnpike.

Maggie re-did her belt and settled into her seat. "Maybe dying in a flaming car wreck would be easier."
He reached over and took her hand. "Easier than the plan?"

"No, it's a good idea. We can't stop them from gossiping, and we have to let them know how annoying it really is. No, the plan itself is sound."

Brent pulled into the left lane to avoid a car speeding down the entrance ramp. "But?"

"But having to actually do it is hard. I'm worried about it."

"That's why we're starting slowly, and we can drop the whole thing if we have to." She nodded but didn't meet his eye. "You just have to put on a show for the gossip club this morning when we get to town. Five minutes, no big deal."

"But being mean to Teddi." Auburn curls jounced as she shook her head. "I don't want to do that."

"You don't have to, Mags. She'll be mean to you. She's the mama bear defending her boy, from the mean girl broke his heart." He smiled sweetly. "All you need to do is act hurt."

Maggie stared into the endless farms blurring past on her right. "That won't be hard."

"Teddi said pretty much the same thing when we went over it. Almost word for word." Brent squeezed her hand. "But she's on board. She knows the gossip girls are a little out of line."

"A little?" Maggie snorted. "They think you're in relationship therapy because of me."

"Yeah, they don't want to hear that *you* are my therapy." Brent checked the traffic, then darted over to land a peck on her cheek. "They want conflict. Otherwise, why would they gossip?"

"So we'll give them conflict," Maggie said while folding her arms across her chest.

"Especially when we take opposite sides on Issue Two."

*   *   *

Drinking her latte several hours later in the sunny Town Square both calmed Maggie's body and infuriated her heart. The day was glorious, and she truly loved this spot in Ben Cen's living room, but playing her scene with Teddi in the Pot & Flagon before the audience of gossipers was different than she'd expected. On one level it hurt that Teddi had played her part so well. The older woman had barely acknowledged her presence, let alone shared her trademark hug. Her frosty demeanor revealed Maggie's abandonment of her beloved Brent. The Gossip Club paid rapt attention.

What surprised her was how easy it had been to get through it. She was probably a little over the top as she'd let her anger bubble over, but the gossipers had gasped appropriately. She realized she could follow the plan.

Maggie finished the coffee and stood up from the park bench. Taking the blame hurt more than she'd expected, but that meant their plan was working. And she had to admit, she kinda liked playing the part of the mean girl.

Chapter 26

Maggie didn't like being the mean girl several hours later in Town Hall before her meeting with the mayor and his committee. As she reached the top stair, Gena, the mayor's secretary, said sharply, "I don't know why you were invited to this meeting at all. I thought you'd never dare show your face in Benton Center again."

Maggie stopped. "Excuse me?"

"You left that poor boy at the altar. You broke his heart. He was just trying to help the unfortunate people of Africa."

"At the PumpkinFest last year?" Maggie smiled to herself. "Brent and I weren't engaged."

"Practically. You'd been together since high school."

"And I should have married him then because it was about time?"

"Yes, yes you should have."

Maggie stepped past the woman toward the conference room. "Any other parts of my life you'd like to comment on?"

Gena spoke as Maggie walked. "Yes, the way you treated Teddi this morning at the coffee shop--"

"Am I late?" Mayor Grieselhuber reached the top of the stairs. Looking at the women's faces, he amended his question to, "Did I miss something?"

"Ms. Cobb was giving me some valuable insights into my life."

"I have no idea what that means. I'm just glad you're here. Those of us supporting Issue 2 can use the help."

The mayor held the door for Maggie and shut it behind her. Gena took a step to follow but slumped instead into her chair. "I believe you know Miss McGrath," Grieselhuber said inside. Samantha smiled, and Nate stood and extended his hand.

"Glad to see you again, Miss. I'm a big fan of your father."

"Thank you, Mr. Richardson. I am, too." The mayor helped her into the chair, and she set her portmanteaux onto the table. "Thanks for inviting me. I want to help."

Maggie smiled across the table at Sammi's upwards nod. She had let her hair grow out while in Chicago and was happy her friend had noticed it. The natural reddish highlights were a perfect contrast to her emerald-green pantsuit and crème blouse.

Grieselhuber summarized the traffic situation around the Square and ended with the ballot issue. He glanced around the table and folded his hands. "Tell us how you would bring more business to our Square without disrupting the 'ambience,' I guess you call it, Miss McGrath. What do you have for us?"

"I have a range of ideas," Maggie said and pulled several packets of papers from the leather bag. "The PumpkinFest is the biggest event in Benton Center." Nods around the table. "With the election early this year, it's the last big event before people will vote. My plan is to state our case enthusiastically and ride the wave to the polls the following Tuesday."

"There already is organized opposition rumbling through our community, right Mr. Richardson?" The farmer nodded. "Strong opposition."

As if on cue, the door burst open. Kennedy Phillips took a step in and posed arms akimbo. Gena peered over her shoulder into the room. "This can't be a partisan meeting, Mayor Tom. Not in the Council Conference Room in the Town Hall." She slowly spread her fixed smile to the others at the table, ending with Maggie. "That would be illegal."

The mayor sat stunned. Nate shook his head as if watching a snake charmer. Sammi's eyes burned across the shiny tabletop. Maggie smiled sweetly. "Nice to see you, Kay Kay."

"I'm surprised to see you here. I thought you'd be working at your big, fancy job in Chicago." Kennedy turned abruptly to the mayor. "In the spirit of bi-partisanship and to keep us free from controversy, I believe I will join your meeting." She settled herself next to Grieselhuber and painstakingly extracted a yellow pad, her iPhone, a pen, her compact, and a roll of Mentos from her bag. "Proceed."

Grieselhuber coughed and collected himself. "As we were saying to Miss McGrath, there will be opposition to Issue 2." He carefully refrained from looking at Kennedy as he spoke.

"Of course there is opposition, and we will counter it along the way." Maggie covered her dislike for the woman with a confident voice and a genuine smile. "Controversy brings enthusiasm, and that's not bad. It gets more people involved. Because of the Pumpkin Peace all campaigning will stop during the Fest. We'll make a big splash at the end, Saturday night, and the opposition won't have enough time to react to it before the vote two days later."

"This is a small town, Miss McGrath, you know that. We don't have much of a budget."

"Maybe not, Mayor, but we do have passion. Everybody in Ben Cen will be talking about the Issue, and they will vote."

"You can't be suggesting we crown you queen, Maggie. We tried that last year." Kennedy pushed a hank of thick blonde hair over her shoulder and arranged her skirt over her slender legs. "Maybe this year you have some magic beans."

Samantha gasped; crowning Kennedy in her friend's place had been her idea. Nate looked confused. The mayor grimaced. Maggie smiled coyly. "Better than magic. How about a Saturday night concert at the PumpkinFest featuring my dad and the Love Pirates? Right out there on the Square." She pointed to the office window.

"It'll be the start of a reunion tour, with cameras, video, the whole deal." She bore her eyes into her nemesis. "What do you think about that?"

"That would pass the issue for sure!" Sammi beamed at Maggie and dared a peek at Kennedy.

"Might just do 'er." Nathan's eyebrows bunched as if drawn by a cord. "Assuming the music's not too loud. Might put some folks off."

"That won't be a problem, Mr. Richardson. Dad's not so young anymore."

The mayor laughed. "A Terry and the Love Pirates

reunion tour starting in Benton Center? With Mick and Jocko? That would be something."

Kennedy let the wave of positivity dissipate before saying, "You're assuming he will support the issue."

"My dad loves this town, Councilor." Maggie re-directed Kennedy's glare back at her. "Like I do."

"Maybe he does." She squared her pen on her legal pad. "But he is also known to be a supporter of historic preservation."

After several seconds of quiet, Mayor Grieselhuber rose. "Thank you all for attending. Especially Ms. Phillips and our special guest Ms. McGrath. This election is going to be interesting, to say the least."

Maggie watched the mayor and Kennedy leave the conference room. She should have expected Kennedy to appear, but her nemesis hadn't said anything unexpected. But she had planted a small seed of doubt. Her dad would surely play at the Fest, wouldn't he?

Chapter 27

Maggie held the door for Sammi at the bottom of the town hall steps. "Is it me, or did the room warm up after Kennedy left?"

"It was about as cold as the reception I got from Teddi."

Sammi stopped and grabbed her friend's arm. "She was amazing, wasn't she? From the look on their faces, Gena and the others were totally convinced she was mad at you."

"It was too good. I felt awful." Maggie spoke slowly. "But it was effective."

"Totally." Sammi's face bunched together. "That's what you wanted, right? Wasn't that the plan?"

"Yeah, but she blamed me for not communicating, not getting crowned queen, running out on Brent." She pulled Sammi down the sidewalk. "Hearing a list of your sins is not pleasant, especially from a person you admire, even if it is part of the strategy."

"You got into the role, Maggie, didn't you? And seeing Kennedy? It looked like you enjoyed that part of it."

"I did." Maggie smiled widely. "She even had the grace to take a shot at me first for losing the job. It's always easy to confront her."

"And fun." Sammi punched the light at the crosswalk. "What about Brent? Will you be able to work against him? He's co-chair against Issue 2."

"No problem. We're solid." Now was not the time to show her friend her engagement ring. Somehow Brent had found an opal set in a delicate filigree of old gold that resembled her mother's. She was dying to wear it, but didn't dare until their plan was complete. "We worked it out on the drive back from Chicago," she said.

"Can't wait to get started. You and me versus Brent and Kay Kay." The light changed and the girls crossed the street. Maggie stopped on the opposite curb and admired the façade of the Dress Shop. "I love what you've done to your place. The color is fabulous."

"Colors," Sammi said. "Orchid, Apple Blossom and Porcelain."

"It's even better close up." Maggie stepped nearer to the Victorian building and admired how the three oddly named colors worked so well together. "Design school was worth it, Sammi. I would've called them shades of purple. I wonder who you got to do the painting."

Sammi was saved from answering as the door burst open and Riya Patel grabbed Maggie in a huge hug. Sammi's mother was an older, slightly larger version of her daughter, the same bouncy smile, shiny black hair, and take-charge demeanor. She stood back and examined Maggie. "You look tired. Come in, sit, I will make tea." Riya pulled her into the shop so quickly, Sammi had to hurry to keep up.

Inside, Mrs. Patel nearly tossed the two into a deep, thickly cushioned davenport, and disappeared through the beaded doorway into the back room. Soon her husband, Arjun, was setting placemats on the low table in front of the sofa and squeezing Maggie's hand.

"We have missed you so much, dear girl. Are you back in Benton Center to stay?"

"For the time being, yes. I have a consulting job with the town." As she explained, he sat next to his daughter and listened carefully. "You will be a great asset to our community," he said. "Please don't leave us again."

"We'll see, Mr. Patel. I'd like to stay."

Arjun stood as his wife appeared and helped her lay the cups, teapot and plateful of butter cookies on the table. As he reached for one, his wife slapped his hand softly. "These are for our guests, Arjun."

Maggie sipped the tea. "Heavenly, Mrs. P. It's good to be home again."

Riya arranged herself on a chair and smoothed the tunic over her flowing trousers. "I think you should stay away from him, Margaret."

"*Mom.*" Sammi's eyes widened.

"Who, Brent?" Maggie steadied her hand as she set the cup onto its saucer. This was another part of the plan she hadn't been looking forward to. "We're fine."

"He hurt you, dear. I know you've been hurt."

Maggie could feel the love from Riya's warm chocolate eyes. She smiled. "I'm over it."

"Are you over him?"

Arjun used the conversation as cover and darted his hand to the plate. With a grin he winked to his wife and popped one into his mouth.

Riya let out an exasperated sigh. "Come, you, we

will leave the girls in peace." She led him into the back room by the hand.

Sammi poured the tea, and they burrowed themselves into the welcome softness of the squishy pink sofa. "This is nice." Maggie took a sip of the herbal brew and sighed. Quite a different feeling than she'd received in the coffee shop. She felt the questioning look on Sammi's face and spoke before her friend could.

"I hate to lie to your parents, Sammi. I love them."

"Not really a lie. Besides, they both love you. They'll understand when it's all over."

Maggie finished the tea. "This is the hard part."

Sammi's eyes twinkled. "Parts of it will be fun, too."

"If I can stay a step or two ahead of the lynch mob." A laugh escaped from Maggie, then bubbled out of Sammi, then they were ensconced together in a hug in the overstuffed sofa.

When the giggling slowed down, Maggie wiped a tear from her cheek. "Your turn, girlfriend. Spill it."

Sammi pulled away and whooshed a breath. "Wait. What? Me?"

"Yes, you." Maggie tried to reassemble her face into a stern expression. "All this talk about me and Brent. I got your parents all worried. What about you and Mr. Yoder?"

"Irving?"

"No, one of his five *brothers*. Come on, spill it."

Sammi's face glowed. "He is such a sweetie. He's so quiet, I kind of overlooked him. He's very sincere and kind and…" Her voice eased into a sigh.

"You're *smitten*, Samantha!" Maggie's squeal brought both parents to the doorway where they could hear better. "Yea!"

"A handyman who appreciates purples." Samantha

sighed again. "Wants a big family, loves kids."

Maggie wished it were that simple for her and Brent. She filed away a small bit of jealousy with the rest of the plan and enjoyed the look on her friend's face. She squeezed Sammi's hand. "I am so happy for you."

Sammi sat up as if shocked. "No, I need to thank you. It's all because of you."

"Samantha, get a grip. He loves you because of you."

"No, that's not what I mean." Sammi managed to get her hands to stop fluttering and lie peacefully in her lap. "You and Brent are all anybody talks about."

Maggie shook her head. "Yeah, so let's talk about you guys."

"I am, I am. Since all the talk is about you, Irv and I got to know each other in peace. Nobody hassles us." Sammi's face beamed. "Nobody even knows about us."

Maggie slowly relaxed. "I get it. You two can fly under the radar."

Sammi giggled. "Irving says we're having a stealth love affair."

"Gossip has a good side. Who knew?" Maggie had never considered a good side. Her life had been scrutinized and judged in proportion to her father's fame since she'd been a kid. She snorted a breath. "However you look at it, you two deserve to be happy." Sammi beamed, and Maggie let her friend's happiness wash away her own doubts.

Riya returned with more tea and cookies, then retreated to the back room. This time she made sure to leave the curtain parted. Arjun followed along, mournfully keeping his eyes on the pastry.

"You going to be OK when you *accidentally* bump into Brent?" Sammi asked when her mother had left.

"Yeah, I'll be fine. It's not exactly my favorite part of the plan." Maggie popped another cookie into her mouth. "But at the moment that's not even my biggest worry."

"What's bigger than exposing your broken slash repaired heart to the Benton Center Gossip Club?"

Maggie smiled to ease the concern in Sammi's eyes. "I may have oversold the concert."

"That's the most important part! You promised the mayor." Samantha's eyes grew even larger. "That's why he hired you."

"I had to do something to wipe that smile off Kennedy's face. No one else could pitch that idea."

"Well, it worked. She shut up." Sammi paused. "Besides, he's your dad."

"Sure, but he's stubborn about one thing: he doesn't want to perform their old music."

"That's the music that made him famous." Sammi's dark eyes narrowed into a frown. "That's what people want to hear."

Maggie pursed her lips, then voiced her real worry. "Maybe he doesn't want to perform at all."

Chapter 28

It was easier for Irving, Brent thought as he turned off the state road onto the Yoder's farm road. It was paved, but bumpy and he slowed down. In the fields to his right three men in three different sizes followed a gray and red Ford tractor. The largest drove the machine, the other two followed behind, one on either side of the harrow. Two of the three were dressed alike: denim overalls, blue work shirt with sleeves rolled up, and straw hats with black bands. The third wore a ball cap. The larger man had a beard, the other two were clean-shaven. As Irv had explained, the Yoders were transitioning from their traditional Amish customs. Brent tooted his horn and the driver waved. Probably Mal, Irv's oldest brother.

Irving was bent over his workbench as Brent entered the white monstrosity of a barn. The WWI bi-plane Irv was constructing from a kit was nearly complete.

"Hold this." Irv neither looked up nor stopped adjusting the drill bit.

Brent leaned onto the bench and pinned down the piece of metal with his hands. Irv stepped between the hands and in an instant bored three holes into the aluminum. "Teamwork."

"Makes the dream work," Brent replied. "Using metal, not fabric?"

"Aluminum frame, too." Irv unplugged the drill and wiped his hands on a rag. "Actually a little lighter than the wood."

The two sets of wings and the tail were attached, the propeller jutted into the air, and the Sopwith Camel looked ready to leap into the air. Irv screwed one of the few remaining pieces of sheathing. Brent ran his hand along the edge of the box-like fuselage. "Pretty small."

"Fits two."

"Looks more like a coffin than an airplane."

Irv grinned. "Never say that to a guy who's taking skywriting lessons."

"Saw Mal and the boys on the way in. With that tractor you renovated."

"Winter wheat. Uh-huh."

"How's it going?"

"Good time to plant, Brent."

"Not what I meant."

Irving set his lanky frame on the workbench. Brent had to crane his neck to see his face. "With the farm and your new job."

"Mal is really excited. He gets to be in charge. The little fellas, they don't care much either way."

"Your Paw?"

Irv's face clouded. "He's OK with how Mal's doing."

Brent knew better than pressing his friend. He

looked at the partially completed biplane. Sheets of aluminum covered about a third of it.

"Paw's just not happy with the whole idea." Brent raised his eyes. "The eldest son is supposed to stay on the farm. Not leave the farm."

"You're not really leaving."

Irv raised a long arm and pointed. "My name's up there on the roof. I won't be under it."

"It's not the Middle Ages: the first son inherits the land."

"Kinda is. That's the expectation." Brent started to speak, but Irv continued. "Stay on the land and marry someone from our culture."

"Samantha?"

"Yup. Bigger issue than the farm. Paw's more OK with it than Maw."

"You'll be fine. Nobody doesn't love Sammi." Brent shook his head. "I wish it was that easy with Maggie."

Irv arranged some tools on the bench before turning back to his friend. "Have you seen her since she got back to town?"

Brent looked away. He knew why they were doing this, but he just wanted to be with her, and show the world she was his. "No. It's not part of her plan. *Our* plan."

"Good. I thought maybe you were hiding out here."

"Not hiding, but not seeing her either. I thought being thousands of miles away was hard, but being in the same town and not being with her is harder."

"At least you have Kay Kay," Irv said with a smirk.

"Not funny." Brent looked away. "I've never met anyone more self-centered, and I have to spend the whole campaign with her."

"Part of the plan." Irv dropped the snarky tone.

"It is. And I have to admit, parts of it will be fun."

When he didn't say anything more, Irv said, "It must be hard to be in love with the whole town watching. Going through all these machinations."

Brent grinned at the word, then saw his friend's serious expression.

Irv toed a piece of scrap aluminum on the scarred wooden floor. "It's hard enough for Sammi and me with just our two families."

"I have no idea which of us is facing the most expectations." Brent waited till Irv met his eyes. "But we're all going to find out, brother."

Chapter 29

Terry whispered into his daughter's ear. "You're not crying, are you?" They were standing in the driveway of their family home.

"No." She took a step back and managed a grin. "Maybe a little."

"So good to see you." He swiped a hand across his own eyes.

"Good to be home." She noticed the tear, and the quaver in his voice. "I would have been here sooner, but I had to do a couple things in town."

"Thought I'd lost you to the big city." He screwed up his eyes. "Sorry about the Cleveland gig. It's their loss."

"Yeah, but it was a good experience, and there are plenty of other jobs. I have important work to do in Benton Center." She playfully slapped his arm. "I told you all about it on the phone, remember?"

"Yeah, yeah you did." He looked closely at her. "Now tell me the good stuff, the more important stuff."

Happiness replaced the seriousness on her face. "Brent. He was wonderful, it was wonderful, and the ring."

"He showed it to me, looks like your mother's."

"How did he know that?"

"The boy's more perceptive than he looks," Terry said. "More heart to him. Must have noticed her ring."

"Way back then? Before we were even dating?"

"I think maybe he's had his eye on you for a while."

She felt her whole body glow as she smiled. "I just wish we didn't have to hide our happiness."

He nodded. "But you made a plan--"

"--and we're going to follow it." Maggie grabbed his hand. "Let's take a walk and see Mom."

*　　*　　*

As they followed the path up the hillside behind their house, Maggie explained how Issue Two was worded, and what the passage or the failure would mean to Benton Center. Terry nodded several times and asked for details.   When she finished, he said, "That's great, Maggie, but I thought you didn't want to work in Ben Cen. When you left, you said it was too small for you."

Maggie bounded along the curving rocky path like she had as a young girl. "I need job experience to prove myself. Working for the town is like an internship. Otherwise, a big city won't even give me a look. Besides, it gives us time to work our plan."

They stopped as two squirrels wound their way up a massive oak. "Playing tag," Maggie said. "You taught me that."

"You remember? Must have been fifteen years ago."

"At least fifteen. Probably more." She kicked a softball sized rock off the edge of the path. "I never forget the stuff you tell me."

He gave her a lopsided grin. "But you don't always follow my advice."

They trudged up the path toward her mother's grave. Sunlight pooled on the stones in the alcove cut into the side of the forested slope. "Not always, Dad. You wanted me to learn how to make my own decisions." She stopped in front of him. "That's why I'm strong enough to come back to Benton Center."

Terry said, "Butterfly, I'm sorry I wasn't around for you when you were little."

She held his hand but kept her gaze on the gently rising path. "You gave me your time and your love," she said. "When you could."

He pulled her to a stop and put his arm around her shoulder. "That was the hardest part about being on the road. Not being with you and Mom."

Maggie looked closely at her father. "When Mom died, you gave up your music, you gave up your life. For me. To raise me."

"You were always more important than my music. You still are." He handed her a cloth for her runny nose. "Besides, I'm writing again, a little bit, and even better, I'm teaching music. I love it. And I love working with your young man."

They sat down on the sun-warmed stones arranged in a half circle around her mother's grave. Although her father blamed himself for their lack of communication, and today was better than usual, she knew they had both relied on her mother to be the communicator and mediator; she and her father were too much alike.

"You were, you are, a great dad."

He reached across the stone and took her hand.

"No, I really wasn't. I traded time with you and your mother for fame and money. It's time I can never get back."

"No, Dad--"

"Let me finish." Terry took a deep breath. "On the one hand I dodged many a bullet on the road. Not like Jocko and Mick, three divorces and a handful of drug busts." He shook his head. "No, I wasn't bad, I just wasn't present. I missed you growing up, and Lindsay..." His voice fell off as he gazed at Lindsay's headstone.

She saw the jagged shadow slanting across Mom's grave and swallowed the lump in her throat. "I miss her, Dad."

He kicked a pebble down the slope. "I do, too."

"It'll never be the way it was, will it."

"No, Butterfly, it won't." He waited a beat looking at her green eyes, auburn hair and heart-shaped freckly face, and felt like she was his little girl again. "But it can be good. You can do good things. Great things. I am so proud of you flying out of the nest and taking a shot at that opportunity. Very proud." His brow furrowed. "Tears? Again?" He handed her the damp handkerchief.

"Daddy, I need your help."

Terry's heart flipped and his breath caught. "Wait, you're Wonder Woman, right? You can do anything. Why do you need help from your father?"

She dabbed her nose and her face lit up in a smile. "More of a favor, a small favor, just this one time."

"Anything for you." He stretched out his legs and they watched the shadows edge further across the valley toward their home.

"I pretty much guaranteed the Mayor that Issue Two will pass. It got me a seat on his committee." She brought her hands together as if praying. Her words sped up. "It's gonna be close, this election, really close, but I know the one thing that will put it over the top."

Terry's head moved slowly side to side.

"Daddy, if you played a concert, just a little set, on the Square, Saturday night, three days before the vote. You're the most famous man in Benton Center and it would mean a lot. It would pass the issue. Please."

Terry's head jerked back as if shocked. Maggie knew her father felt his playing had ruined his relationship with his family. Now she was asking him to play in public again, and it was the one thing he promised he'd never do. She saw the agonized look on her father's face and her heart ached. "I don't want to hurt you, Dad, I don't."

"Butterfly, I--" His voice caught.

"I know Dad, you stopped your career for me, because you love me. I love you for that, but, look at me!" She brightened her smile and opened her palms. "I'm a grown-up now, you don't need to stay at home and protect me anymore."

"I missed so much of your life. I wasn't here for you."

"That's old news." She leapt to her feet and put her hand over her heart. "I, Margaret Mary, aka Butterfly Mc-Grath, do solemnly release you from your vow of being my stay-at-home daddy. Amen."

This time Terry feigned shock. "Wait. What? You don't need me anymore?"

"Of course I need you." She pulled him to his feet. "But I'm not a little girl anymore."

"So then, you do need my help."

"I do, Daddy, and Benton Center needs your help, too."

"It's getting dark." He took her hand, and they

began walking back down the hill. "I know it's for a good cause and it'll help your career, but it's been ten years since I played in public."

Maggie noticed the worry lines around his eyes, and the way the skin bunched together between them. "Did you forget how to play?" she asked mischievously.

He answered seriously. "I'm different now and so is the music. The audience won't know me. I don't know if I can perform without the Pirates."

She took his hand in hers and guided him down the slope toward home. "Details, my dear father, that's what you used to tell me. Let *me* handle the details."

Chapter 30

Maggie had been summoned to the mayor's office for an update. Grieselhuber was fussing with a sheaf of papers when there was a soft knock at the conference room door. Eugenia Cobb stepped inside. "Councilperson Patel is here, your Honor."

Maggie smiled across the table. "I think she's here for me."

The mayor looked up. "Five minutes, Gena." He waited for her to leave, then said, "It sounds like you've made some progress with your father."

"At least we're talking about how a concert would work. He hasn't ruled it out."

"He better not."

Maggie looked at him closely, wondering if he was threatening her.

"Sorry, that came out a little harsh." The mayor jabbed a thumb over his shoulder at the Square. "That demonstration or rally, whatever you call it, yesterday. The marching, the commotion, the stupid signs." He shook his head. "Come on, 'Foot Traffic = Good, Truck Traffic = Bad'?"

"That's democracy though, isn't it?" Maggie offered. "We'll have our own demonstrations, don't worry."

"Sure we will." Grieselhuber waved his hand dismissively. "But way too many people are against the Issue. My phone's been ringing off the hook."

Maggie saw the frustration in the man's face. "It doesn't help that Committeeperson Phillips was up there fomenting the crowd."

Grieselhuber nodded. "Your boyfriend wasn't much help either."

"I don't see how--"

"He was up there in the gazebo holding Kennedy's hand!" The mayor stopped her with a hard look.

"Brent's been teaching with your father. Everybody knows it. They're connected to the music."

"That doesn't mean he and my father are both against the Issue." Maggie held her temper. This was a dangerous part of the plan. Only a few people were in on it. "They're also connected to me."

"Yes, they are." Grieselhuber ran a tired hand across his tired face. "And, no, it doesn't, but that's how it looks." He gestured to the land line on his desk. "That's what they're saying."

Maggie had to ask. "Who are we talking about?"

"Voters." He gestured vaguely with his arm.

Maggie didn't know how to respond. She was sure it was gossip he'd heard himself or been told by Gena.

"You know," he continued, "it's critical we pass Issue Two and attract the business we need to keep the town vibrant." He stared across his desk at her. "As you so clearly stated when we took you on, your dad is the key."

Maggie had steeled herself for this. "He hasn't toured or even played in public for years. At least he's considering it."

"We need him to do more than that."

"He loves this town, sir. I'll keep working on him."

"You'd better," the mayor said. "If this doesn't work the way you planned it, I'll be out of office. We don't have a plan 'B'." He clenched his jaw and raised his eyebrows. "And your resume will still lack work experience."

Maggie saw the set of his jaw and decided against arguing any further. The man's mind was made up: she needed her dad to decide to play right now. She excused herself and left the room. Samantha had been waiting in the outer office and followed her down the stairs. On the sidewalk Maggie whirled to her friend. "He thinks I can tell my father what to do!"

Samantha nodded encouragingly.

"Does he think I just snap my fingers and dad jumps to obey?"

Samantha's face opened into a broad smile. "That it? Got it all out now?"

Maggie's jaw dropped open before noticing her friend's smile. "OK, OK, I'm a little bit wired here."

"It's politics, Mags."

"Not that, I can deal with politics. This is personal. My father, my family." She stopped the rant with a wry grin. "I need a coffee, a large very strong coffee."

Samantha glanced at the Pot & Flagon and pulled Maggie into the crosswalk instead. "What you need is a walk in the fresh air to clear your head."

"OK, maybe," Maggie said, and they crossed the street into the Square. City workers on ladders were attaching sheaves of cornstalks to lamp posts and posting parking restrictions for the week of the Festival. Political campaign signs on the light fixtures ringed the green space but were not allowed in the park itself.

Maggie stopped on the path and stared from one corner of the Square to another. "Isn't the trebuchet always set up next to the howitzer? Did you move it?" The high school Latin Club used the device as a fund raiser.

"My first official act as Chairperson this year." Sammi pointed. "Someone chucked a pumpkin across the square and into the street last year. Darn near onto the courthouse steps."

"That's a long way." Maggie laughed. "Hit anybody?"

"No, but I had to shut it down. Magistra Richardson and those kids in the togas were not happy."

"So you compromised this year and moved it." Maggie took her arm and continued down the path. "Good leadership, Madam Chairperson."

"There's an additional benefit," Sammi grinned. "Given Connie Richardson's political position, I was afraid she'd shoot the pumpkins at one of us."

"I'm surprised," Maggie said. "Nate's very open minded. I don't think he's decided yet."

"Not his wife. She's as anti-Issue 2 as there is." The two friends completed their circle of the gazebo. "Anyway, I hope it works. We're running out of space for all the booths and games."

"I'm sure it will," Maggie said. "I love the fresh fall air, but I really need coffee." She took the path toward the coffee shop.

"Don't do that, Mags."

"What? Why not."

"It's, erm, not good for you. Too much caffeine."

"OK then, a decaf latte. But Samantha, you are neither my parent, my doctor, nor... She waggled a warning finger. "The mayor."

Sammi caught up to her in the crosswalk. "No, really, you can't go in there."

Maggie's face crunched up. "You talked me out of coffee when we were shopping yesterday, too. What's going on?"

Samantha shook her head. "Are you sure?"

"You were at the rally yesterday, right? You saw what he and Kennedy were doing."

"But you're going into their headquarters and starting a fight?"

"*He* started it, Sammi."

"I know it's part of the plan, but I didn't think--"

"There might be a minor confrontation, no big deal. But after what the mayor just told me, I have to move this along. Besides, I've barely said hello to Teddi. I love her." She walked quickly across the sidewalk and jerked open the door of the Pot & Flagon. Her friend hurried after her.

Inside the coffee shop, Samantha placed herself between Maggie at the counter and the rest of the customers. She joined the conversation with Mrs. Burns who seemed equally happy to see Maggie. "The last iced lattes of the season, honey. Pumpkin spice coming soon." The older woman glanced furtively at the seated customers behind the two women, then snapped plastic lids on the paper cups. "These are on the house."

"To go?" Maggie protested but turned away from the counter and handed one to Samantha. "I'd rather sit inside."

Sammi blocked her view of the seated customers.

"Fresh air is good for you."

"We did the fresh air, remember?" Maggie laughed and wove her way through the tables to an empty one, set down her coffee and took off her coat. "What is going on with you?" she said as Samantha caught up with her.

Her friend gestured to the brick wall. Green 'Vote No On Two' posters covered most of the available space. She dropped her voice to a whisper. "I didn't want to depress you about the vote, and you know, confrontation scares me."

Maggie looked from wall to wall, before turning to the bay window facing the street. There the posters were hung above the glass. Her eyes followed down the window into the shocked face of Brent Wellover.

At her side, Sammi whispered, "I didn't want to depress you about *them* either."

Brent caught her eye and started to rise. Kennedy Phillips put her hand on his forearm and kissed his cheek. "Are you leaving the dark side and joining us?"

Maggie didn't reply. She stood up slowly and put her coat back on. Facing Sammi with her back to the window, she noticed her father peering out of the music room in the back. She calmly re-arranged her scarf and removed the lid from her latte. She took several sips while walking slowly to the door, and behind her Sammi relaxed.

Maggie then veered abruptly to Brent's table. Focusing her eyes on Kennedy, she said, "Hello, Brent," and poured the icy drink into his lap.

The Pot & Flagon erupted in noise. Brent's face flickered from shock to pain to embarrassment. He swiped at the napkin in Kennedy's hand and struggled to get to his feet. Sammi gaped at the scene, covered a smile, and hustled Maggie out the door.

Chapter 31

The Pot & Flagon's door slammed behind them as Sammi shepherded Maggie across the length of the Square and down the slope into RiverPark. At the foot of the bridge, the two plopped down on a wrought-iron bench. "Safe at last," Sammi said and let out a breath. "I think we've escaped the posse." She hoped her friend's face had the glimpse of a smile, or at least had lost the indignation.

Maggie spun on her heel. "Criminals? Like we're escaping justice? For what? I didn't do anything wrong."

Sammi offered a weak smile. "There may be freezer burn involved."

"No, I'm sure Kennedy dried him off in plenty of time."

Sammi flinched. "Noticed her, huh?"

"How could I miss? She was all over him."

"They're, she and Brent--"

Maggie held up one hand to Sammi while scrolling her phone with the other. "No, it's fine, she's fine."

"It's fine that she kissed him?"

Maggie jammed her phone at her friend. "Look at this. We got the whole thing."

Sammi couldn't believe what she was seeing: the entire scene in the coffee shop was playing on Facebook, from the kiss to the latte to their escape. "You had it recorded?"

"Oh, stop it here." Maggie grabbed the phone. "The look on your face is *priceless*."

Sammi craned her neck to see. "Wait. That's from a different angle."

"And here, watch Brent's face. Look, look at that."

Sammi snatched the phone back from Maggie. "This was part of the plan you two hatched? You had two people videoing it? It was all *staged*?"

"You can't know all the details." Maggie's face contorted. "You'd freak out and ruin the reactions. And it worked. We gave the gossipers something to yak about." She took her phone back and hit re-play.

Sammi looked at her friend hunched over the device. "You could have told me."

"No, I needed the authenticity." Maggie tapped the screen. "That's the problem with staging things. You have to make it look real."

"You succeeded. I thought my two best friends were having a fight." Sammi clenched her jaw. "I really did."

"Look at that. 180 likes, no, 205. I gotta check Twitter."

"Don't tell me. #coffeebath? No, #ColdCoffee-Bath?"

"We're *trending!*" Maggie lifted her arms and danced in a circle.

Sammi slumped onto the bench. "Yeah, that's much better, #LatteInTheLappie."

Maggie stopped dancing and sat beside her. "Are you OK?"

Sammi shook her head side to side. "Is this how the campaign is going to be? I don't think I can take the emotional roller coaster."

"I *hope* it's this effective. Look at these num--"

"--that's not what I mean, *Margaret*." Sammi waited till her friend finally looked at her. "I mean personal. The campaign has to be professional. This was personal. This was you and Kennedy and Brent. And you gave me a minor role that I didn't ask for. I didn't like it."

Maggie hugged her quickly. "I'm sorry, Sammi, I was going after the gossipers. I gave them a great big heap of what they want."

Sammi tried to see behind Maggie's green eyes. "As much as I believe in Issue 2, I won't work with you if this is the kind of stuff we're going to do."

"What? No, this was just the first skirmish in a longer battle. To focus the issue, you know." Maggie took her friend's hand. "Again, I'm sorry if you got hurt. I didn't mean to do that."

Sammi watched the stream burble around the rocks and disappear under the stone bridge. "Brent was in on it. He must have been."

"He knew I'd do something the first time we were in public, but he didn't know what."

"More authenticity." Sammi smiled wryly. "Kennedy?"

"No, absolutely not."

"Well, I'll say this. You gave me a heart attack, but you did manage to get everyone's attention."

"That's what a political campaign is all about. You got to lay everything out there." Maggie's face was overly enthusiastic, fervent. "She and Brent want to stop Issue Two. Keep little old Benton Center, little and old. We can't let that happen."

"No, what we can't do is make this political issue into a lover's spat."

"I agree. That was for show, now we get into the professional campaign." Maggie peered into Sammi's face. "Now are you OK?"

"You mean that?"

Maggie nodded. She would be sure not to hurt her friend again. If she could avoid it.

"And you'll keep me in the loop?" Sammi looked directly into Maggie's eyes.

"Absolutely." Maggie bounded to her feet and marched quickly up the winding path from the river to the Square. She didn't want to hurt her bestie, but it was crucial to teach the Gossip Club and Benton Center itself a lesson. Otherwise, she glanced over her shoulder at Sammi hurrying to catch up, she and Brent would never be free.

*　　*　　*

"That's going to stain," Kennedy said. Brent pushed her hand away and accepted the towel from the waitress. Teddi remained behind the counter, her lips tightly shut and her expression hard. He sopped the latte from his khakis and grimaced as his embarrassment waned and the damp cold waxed. "What was that girl thinking? She could have hurt you. Are you OK?"

Brent patted Kennedy's arm. "I'm fine. The pants aren't, but I'll survive." The waitress refilled their cups and retrieved the wet towel. "I have no idea why." He raised his eyebrows to mask his lie.

"Out of control temper. She hasn't changed since

high school." Kennedy checked herself in a small mirror and reapplied her lipstick. "I have *no idea* why the Mayor wants her on his side. She must have pulled strings. I hate misusing personal connections."

It wasn't too much temper, Brent thought. Maggie's impulsive, intuitive and, he had to admit, maybe a little crazy, but she'd never really hurt him. She had surprised him. He nearly jumped out of his skin, but that was just part of the plan, the fun part. He felt his lips turning up in a smile. He'd return the favor.

"Hello, McFly, are you there?" Kennedy yanked his sleeve again. "Where'd you go?"

Brent shrugged and grinned sheepishly. "Sorry, zoned out there for a minute."

"Well?"

"Kennedy, sorry, I didn't hear the question."

She made pouty lips and sighed as if wounded. "Well, what I said was, the only way to deal with a person like that is professionally."

"I hear you, but I still don't get it."

She humpfed and gathered her handbag. "What I mean is, you and I are going to bring down Issue Two and her along with it."

"What? Yeah, the campaign. We'll definitely win. 'Keep this small town a small town'," he said as if by rote.

"Wait, I got a better one." She smiled and squeezed his arm. "How about, 'Ben Cen Like It's Always Been'. How much do you love it? See, it's Ben and been."

"Abundantly." He pecked her outstretched cheek and gestured to the back room. "I got music lessons now." He had been warned not to kiss her freshly glossed lips which was fine with him. They weren't Maggie's.

He watched her spin and stride out the door. He

felt kinda bad about playing Kennedy. But that's how she strung people along, and besides, it was a crucial part of the plan. As he passed the bakery counter on the way to his music lessons, Teddi said to him, "Sometimes two is not better than one. That's what my mama said."

Brent stepped closer and dropped his voice to a whisper. "You know it's part of the plan."

Teddi wagged a finger in his face. "Don't play your part so well."

Chapter 32

The first battle of the very professional and not at all personal Issue Two campaign began in a typical small-town way. Everyone reads *The Benton Center Bugle,* and no one believes the internet, so both sides placed their messages in the local weekly newspaper. In print advertising size and color matter; over the course of the campaign, the Yes and No sides increased their ads from 1/8 to ¼ to ½ to full page, from black and white, to one-color, and finally to four-color.

"I don't understand why we need the extra copies of the *Bugle,*" Sammi asked. Maggie's back was to her as she struggled to cut the twine on a bundle of the weeklies. "I mean everyone has their own subscription."

The last bit of twine snapped, and Maggie straightened up. "Two reasons, my dear." She opened the first section to page three and pointed. "First, our ad is bigger than theirs."

Sammi peered at the quarter page ad. "Move Ahead With Issue Two," she read aloud. "Looks nice. Clean. Good picture of Mayor Tom."

"And?" Maggie prodded.

"And I don't see the Vote No ad anywhere." She paged through section one. "Wait. You're right. It's nearly too small to see."

"Inside bottom of page seven. Smaller and harder to find."

"*No Bueno*, Kennedy," Sammi smiled. "We were bigger than they were last week as well."

"Two more editions until election day. We have to keep it up. Especially since the *Bugle* editors are refusing to endorse either side."

"Let democracy reign!" Sammi shook her head as she repeated the *Bugle*'s headline. "Maggie, I get the bigger ad sizes but why the extra copies? What are we going to do with them?"

A sly smile grew across Maggie's face. "Look at section three."

Sammi paged past 'Sports' and gasped. The top half of the first page of the 'Local' section was a Vote Yes ad, complete with pictures, copy and gold highlights. "This must have cost a fortune. The color alone!"

"Mayor Tom thinks this is really important."

"I'll say, but, still, what are we going to do with the forty copies?"

"You know most people have home delivery, but…" She made a circular gesture through the Town Hall window at the Square below.

"The *shops*." Sammi's face lit up. "We leave them all around the Square so nobody misses it." They marched down the steps minutes later, each armed with a stack of *Bugles*. "Meet you at the Pot & Flagon." Maggie grinned. "We'd better do that one together." She turned one way, her friend the other.

Most of the storefronts in Benton had a seating area for guests, and the owners were glad to receive a free copy of the paper. It was a gift with a message inside, Maggie figured. A timed-release info bomb, first the small ad, then the half-page feature. Twenty minutes later she let the door of The Book Store close behind her and waved to Sammi.

"How'd it go?"

"Great idea, Mags. Everyone likes a freebie. It was fun to chat with everybody." Sammi furrowed her brow at the Pot & Flagon. "But the belly of the beast?"

"This is a competition. We can't be afraid." Maggie re-arranged the Bugle so the Local section was in front. "A special delivery!"

Sammi hurried to follow her friend through the door.

Teddi gave them a suspicious look as the door tinkled shut. "We don't want another controversy in here, ladies," she said.

"Free *Bugles!*" Maggie stood among the tables waving a paper over her head. "Vote yes on Two!" Several customers laughed, one applauded, and Teddi, safely behind the counter, tried to look away. Maggie and Sammi circulated through the coffee shop handing out papers until they reached the table in the front window.

Kennedy put her hand on Brent's and rose. Maggie plopped a Bugle onto their table. "Check out section three."

"What, no iced coffee this time?" Kennedy ignored the paper and glared at Maggie. "Not going to drench him again?"

Sammi edged closer to her friend. Brent stifled a grin.

"Nope, this is a present, a make-up gift." Maggie

smiled sweetly first at Kennedy, then at Brent. "My apologies, sir. I hope you weren't too badly injured."

By this time there was no other sound in the coffee shop. Teddi and the waitress huddled by the counter hoping to avoid trouble. All eyes were focused on the scene at the window, especially those eyes obscured by cell phone cameras.

Kennedy took a protective step between Maggie and Brent. He looked closely at her and answered, "Thank you, no. I have managed to retain most of my normal bodily functions."

Teddi covered her mouth. Sammi's eyes widened in surprise. Brent's eyes approached sincerity. Maggie's eyes twinkled in merriment, and Kennedy's burned in anger. "Get out of here," she hissed. "Now!"

Sammi tried to pull Maggie away, but she kept her glare on Kennedy and didn't move.

Behind the counter Teddi held her breath. No one in the coffee shop spoke.

Kennedy spun over to Brent, her hands on her hips. "You could say something." He opened his palms and nodded sheepishly.

Maggie blew a kiss to Brent and let herself be led away. Behind them Teddi let out a worried breath. When the door tinkled shut, everyone began talking at once.

*   *   *

Maggie pulled out of Sammi's grasp after they were out of view from the coffee shop's window. "I'll meet you later. I gotta talk to my dad. He's teaching his music class today."

Her friend's face exploded in shock. "You can't go back in there. Brent and Kennedy just chased you out!"

"What, are they going to kidnap me or something?"

Maggie's smile faded as she saw the concern in her friend's eyes. "No, I'll go around the back way. Don't worry." She handed her the remaining *Bugles*.

"Me worry? You go from starting one fight to provoking another one." Sammi watched her disappear around the corner of the Benton Center Five Cent Savings Bank.

Maggie turned at the first alley and carefully walked past the rear of the bank, then the lawyer's office that was the original home of the *Bugle*. She pulled a battered green metal door open a crack and listened. Satisfied when she heard guitar music, not high-pitched female voices, she slid through the opening and tiptoed her way up the cluttered hallway. She stopped again and peeked into the music room of the wine bar.

Her dad was showing the small group huddled around him where to put their fingers on the guitar strings. She stuck her head around the corner to get a better look, but Brent was standing to the side strapping his guitar around his neck. She retracted her head like a turtle into its shell. That was too close.

Her dad played the section of music, then called Brent over to try it. Maggie's political opponent and fiancé slowly fingered the notes and smiled to Terry and the kids. "Not bad, Mr. Brent. Now if he can play it, so can you all." Terry nodded a smile toward the other man and the kids joined in.

They played the phrase and Maggie found herself humming along. It sounded like a section of one of her dad's songs, and she wondered if the children realized what they were playing. "Well done, everybody. Now take that home and practice it for next time."

The kids started putting away their guitars and music books. "Mr. Terry," black-haired Meredith said. "When are we ever gonna play something hard, something that moves my soul? When are we, huh?"

Terry took her guitar and slammed the opening chords of "In A Gadda Da Vida."

"Yeah, like that!"

"Awesome, dude." Petey held up his fingers in devil's horns.

Terry stopped abruptly. "Never! We're here to learn the basics, kids."

"I know, maybe when we get older." Meredith took back her guitar and pouted. "That's what they always say."

"Now, Mere*death*." Terry's eyes twinkled. "It'd sound better on an electric ax, wouldn't it?"

Brent beside him said, "I've heard that if you've been good this year, maybe Santa?"

Terry nodded. "Yup, I heard that too."

Meredith's eyes grew to the size of salad plates. "Really?"

"If you work on your fingering, the basics, you know. An electric guitar's no good if you can't play it."

The ten-year-old grabbed her case and her music book, and raced from the wine bar into the coffee shop to tell her aunt. "I will, I'll practice. Promise!"

The rest of the kids and Brent left shortly after, and soon Terry was playing by himself. Maggie clapped softly and he stopped. "Always loved that one, Daddy."

"Wrote it for you, kiddo." He played the last few bars again as hard as he could. "That was the Meredith aka Meredeath version!"

"She is something, that girl." Maggie grinned.

Terry returned to the original song, and they finished the chorus singing together. "So how goes the big fight?"

"You noticed I had to sneak in the back way, didn't you?"

"And wait for your enemy to leave."

"My enemy and fiancé, your music teacher and future son in law."

"He's all that and, my, he is so good with the little guys."

"I'm sure he is." Maggie's eyes narrowed. "But you're admitting he's my political enemy?"

Terry snapped open the lid on his guitar case. "Not me. I'm admitting nothing."

She gave him the look she had learned from her mother.

He lifted his hands in mock surrender. "I know you have his ring and you're not wearing it. I know you love him but you're acting like you hate him. I know there's a plan or something, Hey, I'm just your father."

"But if you had a comment, you'd keep it to yourself, and let me make my own life decisions, right?"

"Absolutely," he said. He flinched at the term 'life decisions' before, but kept his mouth shut.

Maggie checked his face and smiled. "To answer your original question, the campaign fight is going well, but it is going to be close. Awfully close."

He collected forgotten music books and stacked them on a shelf. She helped him move the music stands into the corner of the room. "So you need me to play, do you?"

"I really do Daddy. If you play, I think we can pull it off."

"Well, I have good news and bad news."

"Daddy, it's my only job at the moment. It's progress and good for the community, and--"

"Butterfly. I've heard it." He held up his palm. "You

know how I told you the audience wouldn't like me and all that? Yeah, well, I've re-thought that, and you know, I really miss playing for people, a live audience. So yes, I'll play a set Saturday night. Maybe two."

She bounded to him and grabbed him in a hug. "I'm so happy, thank you, thank you." She pulled herself away and her face fell. "What's the bad news?"

Terry stepped back and took her hands in his. "I'm an old-timer here in Benton Center. I like it the way it's always been. Besides, Brent has done an awful lot for this town. It wouldn't look like this if he hadn't convinced the other business to agree to a restoration plan."

She pulled her hands away. "No. You can't be saying that you'll play, but you're going to vote against Issue Two."

"Well, I guess I like Ben Cen how it is." Terry bent to snap his guitar case shut. Maggie ran out the back door and let it clang shut behind her. A couple of her dad's songs would not be enough to satisfy the mayor.

Chapter 33

As effective as advertising in the local newspaper was and especially because the No side seemed to be losing that battle, Kennedy, Brent and their supporters launched a lit drop campaign. 'Lit' was short for literature and in this case stood for a flyer on green paper that listed the reasons for voting No on Issue Two. 'Drop' simply meant going door-to-door and dropping the papers at individual houses.

The two of them sat at a table on the sidewalk under the Pot & Flagon sign, Brent with a pile of street maps and Kennedy peering at the screen of her laptop. She looked up at the two volunteers and said, "OK, you guys have section 18. Brent?"

He selected that map, rotated it, and gestured with a pen. "Start here, corner of Elmwood, go down Dogwood on one side, come back the other and you're done. Forty-two houses."

The volunteer nodded and took a stack of green flyers from the table and handed a copy of the map to his wife. "Should take about an hour, huh? That doesn't seem enough."

"Don't worry, we'll be meeting every couple of days. There'll be plenty more work if you want it." Kennedy smiled. "We've been lucky the weather is holding."

"Thanks, you guys," Brent said and turned to Kennedy. "That's the last of this group of volunteers."

"That means it's our turn." She gave a stack of flyers to Brent and took the last one for herself. He did the same with the maps, and they walked down the block to his car.

"I got an idea," he said. "You still have the stapler in your bag?"

They stopped in front of The Book Store as she rummaged through her enormous leather bag. "Should be here," she mumbled. "Somewhere. Hah!" She held up the heavy-duty staple gun like an angler with her catch.

"Watch this." Brent held a green flyer on the telephone pole and fired two staples into it. "Whadya think?"

"May be the last time we can use these old poles." She smiled and her eyes widened. "Let's take a stroll around the Square, shall we?"

A half hour later, Brent and Kennedy found their drop-off point in a neighborhood several blocks from the Square. They took the same side of the street in opposite directions, planning on meeting back up at the car. "Remember, Brent, we can't use the mailboxes, only the porches and doors."

"Yes, mam," Brent said. "You've only mentioned it 17 times today."

She flashed one of her patented eye rolls. "We don't want to get in trouble with the Board of Elections, do we?"

There were parts of the plan that Brent especially

disliked. "See you soon," he said with a forced smile. He strode down the short cul de sac; five houses, no one home. He slid the flyers into storm doors or under welcome mats and one under a large flowerpot. Probably where they keep their spare key, he thought, but didn't look for it. He turned the corner on the other end and started up the driveway to the next house.

A yellow piece of paper peeked out from the edge of the storm door. He ignored it and put his green flyer under the mat. The second house had a yellow flyer, too. He looked around, saw no one, and snatched it out. "Vote Yes On Two!" it screamed at him. No, the scream came from farther up the block. High pitched and angry: Kennedy. He trotted down the steps and spotted her racing down the sidewalk toward him.

"They got here *first*," she panted. "They did the whole *street*."

Brent waited until she caught her breath. "At least they missed the cul de sac."

"But the whole street!" She glared at him. "What are we going to do?"

"Simple." He smiled and looked to see if anyone was listening. "If their flyers are still outside, it means nobody's seen them, right?"

Kennedy's face brightened. "We take theirs and leave ours!"

Brent erased the smile on his face. "Actually, I was thinking we'd put ours with theirs so they could see both sides of the issue and make a logical choice."

Kennedy's laugh was as piercing as her scream. "Sure you did. No, we'll replace the yellow ones with green. Great idea, dear." Before he could react, she pecked his cheek and turned back to her part of the street.

Brent watched her blonde ponytail swing like a metronome above her slim waist and long legs, then shrugged. He went to the next house, and carefully covered the yellow flyer with a green one.

They met at the car 45 minutes later, and Kennedy showed him a pile of crumpled yellows. "They did all this work, and we left our message," she crowed. "They got nothing." Her good mood lasted till Brent parked and they walked back to the Pot & Flagon. Every available telephone pole around the Square revealed an Issue Two poster, but now a yellow 'Yes' was carefully stapled over their green 'No'. Kennedy elbowed him in the side with a hiss. Brent assumed it was somehow his fault, and smiled to himself.

*   *   *

To anyone seeing Sammi and Irv sitting together on a bench in the Square a half hour later, the two young people could not be more different; she was petite, quick and dark, he lanky, unhurried and sun reddened. She exotic and urbane, he home-grown and as obvious as the Oshkosh overalls he was wearing.

To Kennedy carrying a box lunch and leading Brent, neither their differences nor their similarities registered at all. To Brent trailing behind, he steered Kennedy to a picnic table close behind the two, where he faced them, and she didn't.

Sammi slid closer to Irv and curled under his arm. Brent smiled to himself and unwrapped his sandwich. It might be eavesdropping, but the two of them looked so happy.

"As content as a cat on the back stoop." Irv's enormous hand embraced her shoulder. "Only thing missing is the purr."

She held up her fingers like claws. "I can hiss, but not today. I'm so happy."

Brent stifled a giggle. Kennedy looked up. "Love this macaroni salad." Brent dropped his eyes to the forkful of noodles. "Mmm."

"Me, too." Irv squeezed her shoulder. "The Dress Shop really looks nice."

"It wouldn't if you hadn't helped."

"I didn't know about your color choices, I thought to myself, I thought--"

"Shut up, Irving. That's not why I'm happy."

"What?"

Sammi reached her face up to his and kissed it. "I wasn't sure they would all get along."

"Hey, what are you looking at?" Kennedy turned her head and looked behind her. "That's Sammi and Irv. Why didn't you tell me?"

Brent shook his head as Kennedy rotated herself completely around. "They're my friends." he began. She shushed him. "Quiet, this might be good."

His arm around Sammi, Irv stammered, "Oh, yeah, our families. They're way different for sure, but I, uh, never had a doubt."

Sammi's eyes opened in surprise as Irv deliberately kept his face turned away. She jabbed him in the ribs, and he exploded a laugh. "Maybe I was worried. A little bit."

"What are they talking about?" Kennedy whispered. Now Brent shushed her.

"Irving, you were terrified. I was, too." Sammi clasped her hands together and her voice raced. "What if they had hated one other? What if they had forbidden us to see each other? What if your Maw hated me?"

Irv settled his hand softly on her leg and she slowed

to a stop. "What if your folks hadn't been so nice to my sisters? What if your dad hadn't told so many corny jokes? What if we hadn't hugged each other so often?"

She sighed so deeply it was nearly a purr. "But we did all those things, didn't we?"

"We did. It could have gone wrong, but it went right."

"Your Maw invited us to dinner. I can't wait."

"That will be a test, Sammi. Now you get to meet my brothers. All four of them."

"It'll be fine. I know it will." She snuggled closer and laid her arm across his chest. "I'm not going to worry about us anymore."

"You're right. Me neither." He kissed her cheek and grinned in spite of his public show of affection.

"Racy," Kennedy said. "In public." Brent thought, this was not part of any plan he knew. "We should leave them alone," he said. Kennedy shook her head and stared.

Sammi sighed happily. "I was always jealous of Maggie. Now I kinda feel sorry for her."

Irv closed his eyes to focus. "Jealous?"

"She always had Brent, they've been in love forever, you know, and now all the controversy."

"It's tough being Benton Center's favorite couple."

Kennedy grabbed Brent's arm. "See?"

Sammi looked into Irv's eyes. "Were you ever jealous of Brent?"

"Jealous, why would I be jealous of my friend?"

"He was the star of all the sports teams. His picture was in the *Bugle* every week. You were kind of ignored, weren't you?"

"Maybe, not so much in basketball, but he was good. I wanted him to be good so our team would win."

Kennedy stood and gathered the remains of their lunch. "You're right, this is boring."

"You go ahead."

She stared at Brent in disbelief. "Small town, small people," she huffed. "I am out of here."

"Class president, Mr. Popular," Sammi was saying. "Homecoming King. Come on, not even a little jealous?"

Irv looked at the lilac trim on the Dress Shop across the street as he considered. "Brent never once acted like he was better than me."

Sammi screwed up her face in disbelief. She was Maggie's friend too, but sometimes a little competitive.

"Besides," Irv said. "Do I look like a guy who wants to be Mr. Popular?"

"You're popular with me."

"That's enough for me. It truly is." Irv stretched his legs out and waggled his feet. "Samantha and Irving, happily flying under the radar."

She sat up straight and crossed her arms. "Do you think he really likes Kay Kay?"

At the bench behind them, Brent nearly bit his tongue.

"Nope. He's just playing that part," Irv said.

"But you've seen them together."

"I have." Irv spit into the grass. "It's part of their stupid plan."

"But they spend so much time together, and everybody says--"

"Stop it." Irv slowly turned and waited for her eyes to find his. "I love them both."

Sammi nodded and started to speak. He held her hands to stop her. "We know they're meant to be together. They'll figure out how to make it work."

"Like we did," she said and laid her head on his chest.

"Like we did." Irv brushed a strand of shiny black hair off Sami's forehead and kissed it.

Several minutes later Brent watched them stroll from the Square hand in hand. They're walking around together, and I'm pretending to be Maggie's enemy. Maybe our plan is working, I hope so, but at times like these... His face bunched in frustration as he slowly crossed the grass. I really miss Maggie.

Chapter 34

It was quiet down in RiverPark where the water gurgled happily among the stones before disappearing under the bridge. Maggie sighed and glanced at her cell. Brent was several minutes late. Birds chattered in the trees overhead and a glorious breeze ruffled the shrubbery that shielded the cinder path. She scrolled through her email and waited.

Brent appeared suddenly from the other side of the bridge where the arch had hidden him. She was surprised, but jumped to her feet and held him in a long hug. "I expected you from the other direction."

Brent stepped back but held her arms in his. "It's the expectations that will kill you," he said somberly before releasing a large grin. "No, I got here way early and couldn't sit still. I'm so happy to see you."

They kissed and sat down on the bench. "I miss you," Maggie said. "A lot."

He kissed her again, then held her eyes in his. "Are you happy with how our plan is going?"

"Not the missing you part, but the plan itself. Yes, I am."

Brent settled himself shoulder to shoulder and held her hand. "What does Sammi think?"

She pulled her hand free and said sharply, "What does Irv think?"

"He says we should back off."

Maggie's eyes widened. "Sammi *supports* me."

Brent watched the water eddying in the stream. "Irv supports me, too. Let's not get into what others think."

"You brought it up."

"I'm sorry I did, Magnolia." He faced her again. "That's the whole idea, isn't it? Worrying about others?"

Maggie furrowed her brow. "Even our best friends?"

"When you get right down to it, yeah. Even Sammi and Irv."

She kissed his cheek. "OK, then, to answer your question, yes, the plan is working for those two now, and later it will for us."

Brent tried not to be distracted by her eyes and those darn freckles. "Go on."

"Part of our plan is keeping the pressure off them. They fell in love without being hassled by the gossip crowd."

"Yeah, but?"

Maggie frowned up at him. "Isn't that what *we* want? To be left alone, like we are right now, right here?"

Brent leaned away. "Ah, yes, on the infamous bench. This is where they said I dumped you."

"But they're not talking about that anymore, are they?"

"No, but they--"

Maggie's tone rose and she spoke rapidly. "Because *we're* controlling the narrative. It's all about the election, because we are all about the election."

"24/7." It was always hard for him to disagree with that heart-shaped face. He put a smile on his own.

"Since it's going so well, we can scale back our feud a little. Can't we? Tone it down?"

"No way!" She straightened up and extended her arms. "We got it going, people are following us. Let's bring it *up* a notch."

"I have to keep pretending I like Kay Kay?" He shook his head. "I can barely fend her off."

"Try harder, Brent." Maggie dropped her arms and her smile. "Sammi says--"

"Nope." Brent held up his palm. "Not hearing it from anybody else."

"Check," Maggie said and kissed him.

After a few seconds, Brent said, "So what do you say?"

"I trust you, Brent," she smiled warmly. "It's good for our friends and it'll be good for us. Let's escalate our plan!"

They'd agreed to arrive and leave RiverPark separately. Brent watched Maggie disappear around the curve into the tunnel of greenery. He longed for days with her, not merely a random hour like this. He loved her enthusiasm and was captivated by it as usual. But maybe she was a little too caught up in the whole thing. Sammi and Irv survived, prospered actually, by living their lives without caring what others thought.

Meanwhile he and Maggie were totally consumed by what others thought. Brent shook his head. He wasn't bothered as much by it as she was, but that was probably because so much gossip about her dad had been heaped upon her when she was a kid. He knew she'd been hurt by that. But as he rose and followed the path back up to the Square, he wondered again if maybe she was too absorbed in the plan.

Chapter 35

The next afternoon, Maggie stood on the sidewalk in front of the Pot & Flagon impatiently tapping her foot while waiting for Sammi to return. The door swung open, and Maggie released her arms and relaxed her leg. A little bit. "Well, are they inside?"

"Nope. The coast is clear," she whispered.

Maggie burst past her into the coffee shop. "If they're not here, you don't have to whisper, do you?"
Sammi sighed and followed behind. Maggie felt bad for sassing her friend who had only been scouting the area for her.

"It's always safe in here." Teddi raised her eyes above a wide grin. "Except when you two get up to your hijinks." She snapped lids on two to-go cups and slid them across the counter. "Try these out for me, would you?" She nodded her turbaned head. "If you can behave yourselves."

Sammi tasted the drink. "Hey, this must be your new recipe. It's fantastic. Taste it, Mags."

"It's this year's Pumpkin Spice. I wasn't sure you'd like it." Teddi dropped her voice to make sure she wasn't being overheard. "You're my guinea pigs."

Maggie swallowed the dark, sweet-smelling liquid. "There must be something special in here. It tastes the same, but different. Better."

The barista wagged a finger at them. "Now don't you two ask me what my secret ingredient is."

The girls reverted to their ten-year-old selves and obediently shook their heads 'no' in tandem.

"Because I'm so proud of it I'd probably tell you." The three laughed until Teddi excused herself and went back to work.

Sammi would have preferred staying in the coffee shop, but Maggie was worried either Kennedy or Brent would appear. No reason to push their luck. Sammi saw her glance worriedly around the coffee shop and into the wine bar, and said, "Well, we still have more work to do outside."

"Another glorious Indian Summer day. Way better than staying indoors." Maggie quickly exited the Pot & Flagon and strode down the sidewalk. She hoped her breezy tone wouldn't betray her feelings. "Wait, look at this one." She pointed at the nearest wooden telephone pole. The stack of alternating 'Vote Yes' and 'Vote No' posters with a green one on top. She covered it with a yellow and beckoned Sammi to staple it in place. "Hey."

Sammi dropped her gaze from her face to the stapler in her hand, "Oh, sorry I was thinking of somebody, uh, someplace else." She snapped several staples through the posters.

"Someplace with a beach where we're winning this election?" Maggie asked.

"Yeah, and drinks with little umbrellas." Sammi

managed a small grin.

"Are we losing? You think Issue Two will fail?"

"No, I don't think we're losing, but we're just not winning."

They stopped by a free-standing municipal message board, one of several around the Square. Sammi took out her key. "My committee has the only key. Kennedy can't open it, so they taped their poster on the glass so you can't see ours posted inside."

"I know what you mean. We can't seem to get ahead of them." Maggie stuffed the stapler in her bag and ripped the green 'Vote No' flyer from the glass. "We keep removing their flyers, and they keep covering up ours."

Sammi stopped her from stomping away by running ahead. "That's how campaigns work, Mags. You know that. What's the matter really?"

"Nothing, I'm fine."

Sammi moved around to face Maggie directly. "No, you're not."

Maggie couldn't help from smiling at Sammi's persistence. "Like you said, it's more of the same. We're not quite winning or losing. Now my dad is playing, but he's not voting either way."

"But he's not voting No. That's good."

Maggie shrugged. "It's better, but not as good as supporting Issue 2."

"No reunion tour for the Love Pirates. That's bad."

"For now. At least the kids he's teaching are playing and that will be fun. He'll probably be on stage with his guitar, but not with the old band."

"If the kids are playing, that means Brent will be playing, too. That's like an ad for the No voters."

Maggie nodded doubtfully. "Can you see why I'm a

little *meh?*"

"You're a little grumpy, too, but I still love you." Sammi took her friend by the hand and led her across the street into the Square.

They finished re-postering the Square at the far end. As they walked back down the path toward Town Hall, they noticed Connie Richardson and a troop of her Latin Club members, some wearing togas, others dressed in Roman battle armor and helmets. The Club sponsored the Punkin Chuckin game every year for their fund-raiser, but with new students in the group, the trebuchet needed to be re-calibrated before it could be used at the PumpkinFest. For a small donation, people could load a pumpkin into the hopper and try to hit a straw-filled dummy thirty yards away. Richardson and her students used the money to support field trips and participate in the state Latin exams.

As the two women approached, the group of students was clapping. "That's it," Connie said excitedly. "Now all we have to do is fire a test shot to make sure it works."

"Then we have to take it apart and put it back together again," a squat kid with an overbite grumbled.

"That's why you get extra credit for Latin Club, Gaius," Connie said.

"Sorry, Magistra."

Connie spotted Maggie and Sammi. "And here come our volunteers now!"

"What?"

Connie pulled the two women in front of the kids. "We need someone to try out the trebuchet. See if it works." She looked at Gaius. "Tell your squad to load it up, Centurion. Let's go." The Clubbers ran to their stations, some hauling the ropes, others carrying pumpkin ammo to the basket.

Maggie shook her head. "We got a lot of work to do."

"We'll do it!" Sammi grabbed her arm. "Come on Mags, it'll cheer us up. I got an idea!" Sammi grabbed a black marker and one of the green 'Vote No' posters they had ripped down, and ushered her friend toward the target dummy at the far end of the Square.

"Whatever," Maggie said.

When the two women reached the stack of hay bales holding the target scarecrow, Sammi told Maggie to cover her eyes. "You dragged me over here and I can't look?"

"Give me a second." Sammi got her giggle under control and began drawing on the green paper. "There!" She pulled her friend's hands from her face, turned her around and pointed at the green paper covering the dummy's head. "Look like anybody you know?"

Maggie's face lit up. "It's Brent! With his ponytail, yes! He never should have cut it."

"Race you back!"

"Cohort! Cohort, are you ready?" Connie's voice called her troop to order. "Centurion Gaius, are you?"

"Sic, Magistra," the boy said and handed the lanyard to Maggie. "The pumpkin is loaded, so all you do is give it a yank, ma'am. It's pretty hard. I can help you."

Maggie looked suspiciously at him, then Sammi, then Connie. They all nodded, and she jerked the cord. The rope unspooled, the long arm sprang forward, and the orange orb flew high into the sky. The Latin Clubbers raced beneath it toward the target.

Connie clapped her hands. "I think you hit it!" The kids stuffed the pumpkin remains into trash bags and hauled them and the dummy back to the adults.

"That *was* fun," Maggie said.

"Direct hit!" Gaius said and dropped the straw man. "Got him in the head."

Sammi collapsed in Maggie's arms. "You smashed Brent in the kisser. Right in the kisser!"

Connie and her troop re-wound the catapult, then assembled in the gazebo to discuss how the test shot had gone. Meanwhile, the two women were high-fiving strangers and giggling as if they were kids themselves.

*   *   *

A few minutes earlier in the middle of the Square, on the deck of the Gazebo in fact, Brent was helping the kids pack up their instruments when he noticed Maggie and Sammi running across the grass. Because the weather was so nice, Terry had suggested taking the young musicians outside to practice. He also knew that it would be good for them to play in different conditions. Brent straightened up and took a closer look. Actually, it was more like Sammi running while towing Maggie behind her. He picked up Peter's snare drum case in one hand and his own guitar in the other. "Meet you guys back at the shop." Meredeath and the others blew past him down the path toward the coffee shop, and Terry stopped at the bottom of the gazebo steps.

"Looks like my daughter. What are she and Sammi doing?"

"I'll check it out." Brent set the instruments on the Gazebo steps and loped down the path.

Terry watched him approach the group of high schoolers wondering if his interest was professional or personal. He took a step to follow before remembering his promise to stay out of Maggie's personal life. He shrugged and tried to catch up to his students before they ran across the street without him.

As Maggie and Sammi skipped around the square in celebration, Brent picked up the scarecrow. Under the yellow strings of pumpkin goo was a sketch of his own face on the green poster. With his former ponytail.

He pulled from his pocket a yellow 'Vote Yes' poster that he'd confiscated earlier in the day. He quickly scribbled rows of Maggie's curls around what he hoped she'd recognize as her face. The women were now sauntering down the path toward Town Hall, and the Latin kids were de-briefing the launch in the gazebo with Magistra Richardson. Brent carried the scarecrow with Maggie's face to the hopper and replaced the pumpkin. He picked up the lanyard and yelled, "Hey, ladies!"

Maggie and Sammi turned at the sound of his voice. "This one's for you!" he shouted and pulled the lanyard. The scarecrow arced high into the blue October sky, arms and legs flailing as if reaching for a parachute. Brent was half-way to the Pot & Flagon when he heard Maggie and Sammi scream; he smiled and kept on walking.

Chapter 36

Kennedy lifted the latte, skinny-decaf-oat milk, to her lips, blew across the surface and set the mug back down on the table in the front window of the Pot & Flagon. Brent watched her sigh and finally pull her gaze from the Square and look at him. "You OK?" he asked her, but he knew the answer.

"Even. We're even with them, if that. Working our asses off, and still it's too close to call." He was hoping to hear anger or determination in her voice, but an air of desperation bordering on despair crossed the space between them.

"It's like they're one step ahead of us."

"That's it, right?" She bobbed her head. "What I don't get is, they're just not that smart."

"Ouch."

"I mean it, Brent."

He heard the anger return to her voice. "It's a complicated issue, Kennedy, and they got a lot of people on their side."

"But who's leading them? Mayor Tom? Sammi Patel? Come on, they're lightweights."

Brent half-expected her to include Maggie in that indictment, but she didn't. He watched her rap her spoon on the mug, then said, "Maybe it's time to deploy our secret weapon."

She looked up. "Don't even mention stealing ballots or miscounting them. That's fraud, that's, um, uh, illegal. We shouldn't do that. We might get caught."

"I didn't mean anything like that."

"Besides it's not worth it. This is just a municipal issue, not a national or even a state election."

Brent held up his palms for her to stop. "Kennedy, un-lax, please. I'm not suggesting anything remotely illegal."

She sipped some latte. "Secret weapon?"

"Something different, something nobody's seen around here."

"I can't imagine what. We've tried everything, canvassing, rallies, and marches. Even that silly trebuchet." She squeezed his hand. "Launching her into the air was great."

"It was kinda fun, I have to admit."

Kennedy's smile turned into her trademark pout. But what can we do to defeat Issue Two?"

"Airpower." He stood up and held out his hand. "Come on, we're going to see a man about an airplane."

The airplane was a Sopwith Camel, the WWI biplane Snoopy flew in battles with the Red Baron in *Peanuts*. The man was Brent's friend, Irving. On the way to the small airfield where the craft was stored, Brent explained to Kennedy how Irv's hobby was turning into a business. How Irv had taken his love of all things WWI, purchased a kit and built a replica bi-plane in his barn.

"And then he taught himself to skywrite? Isn't that dangerous?"

"He found some old codger at the airfield to teach him. The hard part for Irv won't be the flying, it'll be the spelling." Brent grinned as he turned into the driveway of the Benton Center SkyPark. Twenty minutes later. Several Quonset huts stood in a semicircle around a small cinderblock building with a tower on its roof that looked like a Widow's Walk. An American flag and a limp windsock drooped from poles flanking the door.

"I didn't even know we had an airport." Kennedy scrunched her nose as if smelling something bad. "It looks dangerous."

"Not any more dangerous than taking off and landing on a grass runway like he can from the farm." Brent ran around and opened her door. "Here comes the pilot now."

Irv was wearing a one-piece set of worn blue overalls, a wool-lined leather jacket and what probably had begun life as a football helmet. In 1917, like the plane itself. "Got her all gassed up and ready to go."

"You're flying a plane that you built yourself?" Kennedy screwed up her blue eyes into a squint.

"Do it all the time, Kay Kay."

She twirled to Brent. "How come I never knew about this?"

"Man's gotta have some secrets, I suppose." Irv winked and began a loose-gaited stroll toward the plane sitting outside one of the hangers.

Kennedy looked to Brent. "Got it all done by himself, started while I was in Africa," he said. "With a wrench in his hand, the man's a genius. The skywriting? He's just learning."

"But--"

Brent didn't answer. She shrugged and followed the two men.

"--yeah, right, this is the British night model, the Comic," Irv was saying as she caught up. "It had the guns mounted on the top wing. The US version had the twin Vickers on the cowling. I thought the guns on top were cooler, so I stuck them up there."

"Machine guns?" Kennedy sputtered.

"They're not real," Irv said. "Just for show." He pointed to the tail. "That pipe there, that's where the smoke comes out." To Brent he said, "I put the tank behind the seat. Had a heckuva time fitting it in. With my legs, there wasn't much room."

Kennedy extracted a paper from her bag. "Can you really skywrite?"

The pilot grinned. "I'll admit I'm a work in progress, Kay Kay. That's why you're getting a bargain rate."

He looked at Brent. "Rate?"

The two men laughed. "Free, hon, Irv's donating it to the campaign."

Kennedy smiled to cover her uncertainty. "Well, OK, here's the message."

Irv glanced at the note. "Seems straight forward enough. 'Vote No On Two'."

"Thanks, man."

Irv adjusted his goggles. "Don't you guys worry. With a clear sky like this and hardly any wind, I can't miss. You're gonna love it."

Brent hoped his idea would work and that a giant campaign message above Benton Center would improve Kennedy's mood. He glanced at her as they drove through the brilliantly colored woods east of town. He couldn't tell what she was thinking.

"Well?" He poked her shoulder.

"Was this a good idea?"

"We'll see."

She saw the disappointment on his face. "Well, it's free, so it really can't be too bad."

"Irv's the only guy in this part of the state who does skywriting. The guy who taught him retired, so there's no way Sammi and the Mayor can top it."

"But Maggie. Don't forget her." Kennedy bit her tongue too late. "How do you know so much about skywriting?" she added hurriedly.

Brent focused on the blacktop flickering in and out of the afternoon shadows. "His business plan. I helped him write it. He wanted to research the competition."

"You found out there wasn't any." She clasped her hands in her lap. "That's good then."

The rest of the drive into town was passed in silence, each alone with their own thoughts. They parked in Brent's space behind the P&F, grabbed sandwiches from Teddi, and took them across the street into the Square. Brent flipped the back of the bench forward and set their food on the flat space.

"Just like a picnic table," Kennedy said and sat down next to him.

"Listen." He craned his neck around and back. "I can't see him, but that's his engine all right."

The rotary engine of the Camel made a distinctive puttering sound, not unlike that of an old VW Beetle, but stronger. Brent thought Irv told him it was a Bentley, but the technical jargon was beyond him. "There, over the library."

Kennedy turned her head. "Look at it. It's beautiful."

Brent saw her smile and grinned himself. "It is."

The glossy yellow paint stood out sharply against the cloudless azure sky.

They watched Irv descend over the gazebo and waved to him as he waggled his wings. The biplane rose and circled the town slowly several times.

"He's got to use the wind to spread the smoke so we can read it." Brent kept his eyes on the plane. "So the smoke doesn't blur when it blows."

"Now you're mansplaining, Mr. Wellover. Really?"

"Just saying. Look!"

They watched the plane dive then rise. Puffs of smoke followed and formed a V. People had stopped at the sound, now more had gathered, and many were pointing their faces and cell phones at the sky.

"Here comes the voting public, Ms. Phillips. If we're lucky, it'll stay up there all afternoon, and everyone can see it."

"There's the photographer for *The Bugle*." She nodded. "Your idea might just work."

"Yep, I called him this morning. Look at all the cellies."

While they were watching the people in the Square, they failed to hear another sound in the sky behind them to the south. Not the drone of a motor, a subtler, softer sound, audible only when the traffic ceased and the plane was downwind. It was the hiss of propane gas igniting and expanding into an enormous bag. A wicker basket hung from ropes below a brightly colored sphere, several people waving from it. When Brent and Kennedy finally heard the voices and looked up, they saw a single word covering the near side of the hot air balloon: YES.

Kennedy gasped. Brent cursed. The balloon coasted to a stop above the gazebo. The photographer and the cell phone users now had two great pictures, the skywriting bi-plane and the hot air balloon.

"Brent! Hey, Kennedy!" Maggie and Sammi waved from the slightly swaying basket. They both took pictures of the crowd below, then posed for selfies at the railing of the basket.

Meanwhile above and behind the balloon, Irv continued writing 'Vote No On Two'. From where Brent and Kennedy sat, the balloon hovered in front of the 'No.' He scowled. The words in the sky now read 'Vote Yes On Two.'

The Bugle photographer raced near their picnic bench. "Great picture, huh?"

"No, it's not." Kennedy got up from the table and marched off. Brent shook his head, but he couldn't prevent a slight grin forming at the corners of his mouth. Why did all the women in his life stomp like that?

Chapter 37

The next morning Maggie followed Gena through the office door and found the mayor brooding at his desk. "Ms. McGrath is here."

Grieselhuber raised a dispirited hand as Maggie entered. "You wanted to see me, sir?"

"I do." He sighed then lifted his eyes.

Maggie sat down. "I thought I had some good news and maybe I do, but then there is some bad news too, and I don't want to tell you about it, I should and--"

"Stop. Your dad just spoke to me."

"Yes, he said he'd play with--"

"He's not playing, Maggie. He won't play. He says he doesn't want to take sides." The mayor rubbed his eyes. "You told me he'd play. That was part of why we reached out to--"

"But I--"

"--No." Grieselhuber directed his index finger at her face. "Do you know who I got off the phone with five minutes ago?"

Maggie didn't risk speaking and kept her mouth closed.

"Grantham Phillips. Kennedy's father and CFO of BiggInsCo." The mayor's face clenched around his nose like fingers in a fist. "Do you know what he said?"

Maggie shook her head dumbly.

"Well, I'll tell you what he said." Grieselhuber papered a thin smile over his thin lips, but to Maggie his tone grew harder not softer. "He said if Issue Two fails, they're backing out of the agreement to fund the removal of the telephone poles around the Square."

"But that's--"

The mayor's voice overpowered hers, and he emphasized his words by slamming his hand on the desktop. Maggie's face burned as his rant continued. Much of it was lost in the volume and bitterness, but words stood out like "ruined," "loser," "legacy," "higher taxes," and finally "your job, too." She bit her lip and stared at the space between his eyes to keep herself from crying.

The last thing the mayor said was the worst. He lowered his voice, let out a breath, and said softly, sadly, "Maggie, I trusted you."

Maggie couldn't speak. She burst from the office, bolted past the horrified secretary, and nearly stumbled down the long flight of stairs to the street. The last straw was crashing between Brent and Kennedy as they were opening the door. Brent called her name, but she kept running toward the dress shop.

Kennedy was smiling. "Well, that couldn't have gone better, could it?" Brent watched Maggie dodge traffic and disappear into Patel's. "What do you mean?"

Kennedy cocked a leg forward and jammed her fist

onto her hip. "She must have been in a meeting with the mayor. He probably ripped her a new one for blowing her daddy's big concert."

Brent's eyebrows knit together. "You think?"

"I know. What else could they have been talking about?"

"It could have had something to do with your daddy. Did it?"

"It's not about the daddies Brent, it means the mayor's giving *up*. He realizes Issue Two is *done* and *she's* done. We win!" When he didn't smile, she took his hand and led him to the crosswalk.

He pulled his hand from hers and stopped. "You think it's good that Maggie might lose her job?"

The concerned look on Brent's face caught her attention. "You still care for her."

"Kennedy, no one should lose a job over an election. Our campaign is looking good, I agree. I want to defeat the issue. But all I really want is to make Benton Center a better place."

"That is why you are so adorable." She put her arms around his waist and her face where he couldn't miss it. "You don't ever have a mean thought about anybody."

"That's not true."

"That is so true. You are the original Mr. Nice Guy. Come on." She marched toward the Pot & Flagon.

"No. We have to talk."

She stopped and turned around. "We have to tell the ladies."

"You do that later. We have to talk now." Brent led her to a bench in the Square away from the volunteers setting up decorations.

After a few seconds he said, "Why are you here,

Kennedy?"

"You made me, you wanted to--"

"I don't mean here on the bench. Here, in Benton Center. Why did you come back?"

"Whatever do you mean?" She opened her face to him and slid a little closer.

"Stop it, Kay Kay."

She replaced her honest look with a pout. "Not that either." Brent kept his hands in his lap and stared at her. "You went away to school, you don't need an internship with the town, and you certainly don't need an entry level job at your dad's company. Tell me what's going on."

Kennedy sighed. "It turns out, I really do need these little jobs." She sighed again and her face relaxed. "I was never meant to work, Daddy always said. I didn't need to get a job. That's how I was raised."

"You never had a part time job, did you." Brent nodded as he recalled.

"I wasn't allowed. I wanted to, but I was Grantham's little girl."

"I thought, we all--"

"I was too good to work." Kennedy smirked bitterly. "Yeah, that's how you treated me."

"And you went along with it."

She turned to him. "That was the role I was given. That's what I was *allowed* to do."

"Wait, so all that 'too cool for school' was an act?"

"If you're playing a role, you play it to the hilt." She waved a royal hand. "I was the Queen of Sheba."

"That you were. An excellent queen." Brent smiled thinly. "Why didn't you say anything?"

Her blue eyes narrowed. "Would you have believed me if I had?"

"No way."

She elbowed him in the side. "See?"

"OK, maybe I believe that now, but why in world would you come back to Ben Cen? You must have hated it here."

"I told you. Because I have no work experience, my resume sucks."

"You need jobs, any kind of jobs to spice it up." Brent finished for her. "Your grades are good, right?"

"Sure." She batted her eyes. "No problems there."

"Queenie, you are a piece of work." He shook his head. "I gather you're not planning on staying here for long?"

"No, it's great here, relaxing and all, but no, I'm off to bigger places."

Brent watched volunteers decorating for the Pump-kinFest before asking her, "What do you really want to do?"

She moved her face close to his and ran her tongue slowly across her lips. "Work with you, my dear." She moved her lips nearer and deepened her voice. "I want to spend every day of my life with you."

Brent blanched. Kennedy laughed and leaned away. "No, I don't. You're great, but you're staying here, and I've got some feelers out for a job in Columbus."

"But all the snuggling and the hand holding?" Brent slapped himself on the forehead. "Acting, right?"

Kennedy's eyes clouded. "At first, years ago, maybe not. And it looked like the SS Margaret Mary had sailed away."

"I liked you, too, Kay Kay. You're kinda cute." He saw the corners of her lips edge upward. "But that's not the whole story, is it?"

"Damn it, Brent. No." She slapped her knees with

her palms. "Look, irritating Maggie is about the most fun I've ever had. It is so easy to get her goat, then she goes off stomping like a crazy person."

Brent had to laugh. "I love her, but she does have rabbit ears."

"So true."

Brent's eyebrows furrowed as he scanned the activity in the Square. "Now that we've established your credibility as an actress, maybe you could help me with my own little plan."

"Sure." Kennedy turned to face him. "Just like your girlfriend, I'm all ears."

"And you have a cute little bunny nose, too." They both laughed, then Brent dropped his grin and said,

"First, you need to inform the Ladies across the street what just happened."

"Issue Two is DOA, Mayor G. is losing his job and Maggie's losing hers." Kennedy nodded. "Got it."

"Keep up your usual string of lies about me deserting Maggie, et cetera."

"Lies?" Kennedy's eyes twinkled. "I prefer half-truths."

"Cute," Brent said. "Please don't refer to them as alternate facts."

"Promise." She held her fingers up in the Boy Scout salute. "But none of this is new."

"No, it's not," Brent replied. "I want things to keep to the course we've set up. You and I are the winners, the issue fails, and the mayor and Maggie take the fall."

"But that's what I've been doing."

"Now, Kay Kay, we get to the part about acting."

Several minutes later, Brent jogged over to where Irving was unloading pieces of a PumpkinFest booth. Kennedy watched the two men laugh. Brent waved, she laughed herself, and rose from the bench. It was time for her to talk to the Ladies of the Gossip Club. Brent hoped she'd play her part well.

Chapter 38

"Can I give you a lift?"

Brent looked up into the smiling face of Irving barely contained in the cramped front seat of the four-wheel
ATV. "Plenty of room."

"No, there really isn't." Brent wedged himself in
and lurched back as his friend mashed the pedal. "No head
restraints in this thing either."

"Your neck is fine," Irv said and went on to explain
he needed help transporting the booths from the Quonset
hut behind the church to their assigned spots around the
Square. He jabbed a thumb at the small trailer bouncing
along the sidewalk behind them and explained how important it was to tie down the flimsy booths so they wouldn't fall
off.

All of which Brent knew, as they'd had the same volunteer assignment several years in a row. He braced himself
as the ATV raced around the corner. "Hold on Fittipaldi,
you're really wound up today. Talking, speeding." He let his

voice drop as his friend didn't return his grin.

They jounced across the street into the Congregational Church's driveway, but instead of following it into the barn, Irv parked on the left side of the driveway and turned off the key. "What the hell is the matter with you?"

Brent's mouth gaped open. Irv rarely spoke, and never used that tone of voice nor an expletive. "I got whiplash, what's the matter with you?"

Irv turned his long, horsey face to his friend. "Every time I see you, you got your hands all over her. Kennedy." He said her name like he was spitting. He must have seen their embrace at the crosswalk.

"It doesn't mean anything."

"Doesn't mean anything? Then why are the two of you all over town, holding hands, giggling like you were kids?" Irv focused on Brent. "You two are all anybody talks about."

"The Ladies Gossip Club is not everybody."

Irv raised an eyebrow and kept his lips pressed shut.

Brent raised his hands in surrender. "You know it's part of the plan, Irv. Maggie's plan to give the gossipers something to gossip about."

"Never liked it. Samantha neither."

"It is what it is." When tall handyman didn't respond, Brent added, "Of course we spend a lot of time together. We're working on the campaign."

"Working." Irv nodded. "Is it hard to work with her hanging all over you?"

Brent thought about snapping back. Instead, he took a slow breath. "What's this really about?"

"You're playing your part too well." Irv kept his eyes on the barn. "Is this great plan of yours more important than losing Maggie?"

"Irving, we've been friends how long?"

"Long enough to say Kennedy Phillips is bad news."

"Come on, it's just--"

Irv finally turned to face him. "You know you can do better, Brent, you know Maggie is better. You two have been in love for years."

The ATV and its trailer were in the wide, open space beside the church, but Brent felt trapped. "If you're talking about relationships, how about you and Sammi?"

Irv stared at him several more long seconds. "If you don't want to tell me what's really going on, don't." He switched the motor back on. "We've been friends too long for me not to say something is wrong between you and Mags. When's the last time you even talked to her? But don't tell me it's nothing, and don't tell me it's the damn Issue Two."

Brent was quiet as they drove into the barn, loaded the Pumpkin Sweep ticket counter onto the trailer and strapped it in. As the ATV paused before turning into the Square, he reached over and switched off the ignition.

Irv picked at the cuticle on his right thumb with his index finger and didn't look up.

"I don't want to lie to you," Brent said.

"Any more." Irv bit the corner of his thumbnail.

"Any more." Brent nodded. "It was more like leaving stuff out."

"Well?"

"Don't worry, Irv, nothing is going on between me and Kennedy." Brent said. "We're just playing our parts of the plan."

"Maggie's plan?" Irv's eyes narrowed as he stared at his friend. "Or yours?"

"That's the problem with plans. Everybody's got one, and they all contradict each other. I even have another plan myself."

Irv held up a stop sign hand. "I don't want to hear about it."

Brent waved as Teddi and her sub-committee passed their vehicle, carrying bundles of corn stalks and singing "Bringing In the Sheaves." Irv nodded to the ladies. "I suppose Ms. Burns has a plan as well."

"She has the best plan. Nobody loses in hers."

"That's how Teddi is, all right."

Brent turned to his gangly friend. "Sammi have a plan, too?"

"Yup, we're both on the same page, and I hope you and Mags are, too." Irving expelled a whooshing breath and re-started the four-wheeler. "I thought I'd lost you there, but I believe you." He spun the wheel and the two pulled out of the church driveway into the Square. "Whew. I've unloaded enough of my feelings to last a month. Let's get to work and unload this booth."

Brent grinned at the side of Irv's earnest face. He was tired of playing a part, he hated keeping things from his friend, and he really, really missed being with Maggie. Brent was happy to jump out and do physical labor. Anything to keep his mind off the other stuff.

Chapter 39

Maggie sat alone in the living room staring at the fire. The cozy, timbered room was her favorite place in the house, and normally would make her happy or at least help her to calm down. But not tonight. Tonight she was thinking about the Issue Two campaign, her tenuous grip on her position with the town, and the strained relationship with her father. She had left Brent, gotten her advanced training in Chicago and come back for this?

The doorbell tinkled and she ignored it. It rang again, then the bell turned into knuckles pounding on the heavy oaken door. "OK, OK, I'm coming," she muttered and dragged herself from her nest of blankets on the sofa.

"Deaf much?" Samantha gestured at the sofa with a wine bottle. "Or sleeping?"

"Sammi, this is not a good time."

Her friend burst past her. "I remember the wine glasses being right over here." She snatched open the door of the Hoosier sideboard. "Hah."

"No, really, I'm beat, very tired and really, truly crabby."

"No better time for a friend. Take this." She thrust a goblet at her and began pouring.

"Come on, Sammi--"

"Come on yourself." She flopped onto the sofa and patted the cushion beside her. "Sit."

"I'm not a dog," Maggie muttered.

"No, dogs obey. You don't." She smacked the sofa again. "Now. Get over here. Sit."

Maggie couldn't stop the grin. "Woof-woof."

"No, that's a Cleveland Browns Dawg Pound accent. Try arf-arf."

Maggie elbowed her friend, then clinked her glass.

"I know you're worried about your job and the vote, and you can't boss your dad around, but come on, that's not the real problem, is it?"

"Probably. Maybe." Maggie hid her confusion behind the wine glass.

"I'm your bestie, you can tell me."

"OK, I'll play along." Maggie sipped the wine. "Kennedy. You think Brent's really in love with Kennedy Phillips."

"He is. Everybody says so." Samantha snorted.

"Whatever." Maggie watched the colors in the flames. She knew it was a charade but Brent was playing his part well. Maybe too well.

Samantha slapped her friend's knee. "Hey, come back here. Focus."

"You know it's all part of the plan." Maggie set the glass on the table. "Maybe *she* loves *him*, but not the other way around."

"I am your bestie, but face it, they're together all

the time. Not just when they're working." When her friend didn't respond, Samantha continued, "It's a small town. You can't hide anything."

Maggie hoped that wasn't true. Their happiness depended on it. She trusted Brent, but hated the tiny, nagging doubt. "Benton Center is small and there aren't that many good-looking guys around here," she said. "So Kay Kay latched onto him. Simple."

"The latching was mutual." Samantha rolled her eyes. "Besides, why wouldn't he? She's gorgeous."

"She's vacuous, Sammi. The lights are on but nobody's home." The fire popped and Maggie looked at the sound. "He does *not* love her. Why are you bringing this up anyway?"

"That's what it looks like to me. Especially since they're winning the campaign."

"That's the gossip club consensus?"

"Yup. You two are toast. Kennedy's the winner in more ways than one."

"That's not what Teddi thinks."

"She's sad about you and Brent. Won't talk much about it, but I can tell."

Maggie now looked at her friend. "That's good."

"How can that be good? Have you lost your mind?"

"Samantha, Samantha. It means the plan is working. We're fooling the whole town. Even you and Teddi, and you guys knew about the whole thing."

"But it looks so *bad* losing Brent to your worst enemy." Sammi face tightened as she thought about it. "I guess it does kinda fit your goal, but what if it backfires?"

"No, it won't. You worry too much." Maggie grabbed Sammi's hand and led her to the lower shelf of the hutch. Several framed pictures were displayed there. The

McGrath family in various groupings; all three, husband and wife, dad playing his guitar, mom on a front porch rocker, Maggie at various ages. After several seconds, she pointed to pictures on the upper shelf.

Maggie and Brent had many posed professional pictures taken at prom and homecoming, the others more like snaps than portraits. In one they were tossing water balloons at each other, in the next they were in the middle of a food-fight. Sammi picked up the third: Brent and Maggie rolling around in a mud pit. "What were you doing here? Did you guys ever go on a normal date? Wait, I do remember this one."

"You were there. That was a fund-raiser for something, drama club, wasn't it? The mud bath was really a car wash." Maggie grinned as she recalled. "Always doing something fun."

"Together." Maggie looked at her. "Connect the dots."

Sammi spoke her thoughts. "Doing things together. Having fun. Having an argument. Smiling a lot. Running away mad. Duh."

"I thought of these pics when you two were yelling at each other last week at a rally on the Square. You had a bullhorn; he had an air horn."

"He started it."

"Just like he started the food fight." Sammi grinned. "And the mud fight and the water balloons and all the other ones."

"And all that means?" Maggie prompted her by lifting her eyebrows.

"You two bickering is nothing new. I feel like a dope. That's how you've always been."

"Ta da!" Maggie led them back to the sofa. "That's

why it'll all work out in the end."

"Here I was thinking you were upset about it." Sammi poured herself some wine and offered the bottle to Maggie. "But then if it's all going according to plan, why aren't you happy?"

"I miss him. Part of it was to have no communication between us. I haven't done much more than text him in weeks."

"It'll be over soon. PumpkinFest is in a couple days."

"Yeah, I can manage that. But then what? I thought running this would shake things up. The gossipers would realize how their words can hurt people, and keep their noses out of other people's business. I hoped things would change, but everything is going on like it always has."

"Yup, it looks that way." Sammi smiled broadly.

"Some friend *you* are. What are you grinning about?"

"Well, as your best friend, it is my duty to tell you that whatever happens, you should follow your heart."

"*Samantha!*" Maggie swung a cushion at her.

When the two stopped laughing and caught their breath, Maggie said, "It's not really about my heart or Brent's."

"But--"

"No, it is about love, of course it is." Maggie stared into the crackling flames. "But at this moment, in this town, it's about what people think."

Sammi's eyes widened. "You have a plan. Another plan."

Maggie turned to her. "I do, but the funny thing is, it's my dad's idea."

Sammi took her friend's hand. "I didn't think you two were getting along."

"We weren't, I mean we were, but politics and the

mayor." Maggie paused, then her voice brightened. " B u t then Brent called, and we met down in the park, you know by the bridge, and we had a great talk."

Sammi squeezed Maggie's hand. "I'm so happy for you."

"It's the best, I love him, and now we're communicating." Maggie brushed a tear with her free hand. "And then he came up with this weird, lame plan."

"Wait. What?" Sammi's smile disappeared in doubt. "*Another* plan?"

"You're going to love it," Maggie smiled and dropped her voice. "Or hate it."

Chapter 40

The kids in the music group finished their song and looked at their teachers, first Brent then Terry. Meredith slung her guitar around her back and jammed her fists onto her hips. "Well, how great was that?"

Terry turned to Brent. The younger man nodded, and Terry said, "Not bad, not bad at all."

Petey beat a snappy tattoo on his snare drum. "Not bad? That's as good as I can play."

"That's as good as you can play *now*."

Brent grinned. "Mr. Terry's right. It was good, but we'll get better."

"If we *practice*." Meredith slumped onto her chair. She looked up as the two teachers clapped, then brightened as she realized what the applause meant.

"See, even Meredeath thinks practice is a good thing." Terry gave Brent a high five, then said, "That's it for today, kids. See you all next time."

Terry followed the children out, while Brent set up

the furniture for the wine bar. When he finished storing the music stands, he dropped into a booth in the coffee shop. Teddi whooshed the steam into a latte and took it across the room. "Thought you could use this."

"You're a mind reader, Ms. Burns." He took a drink. "Hey, new recipe?"

Teddi sat down in the booth beside him. "Not here to talk about pumpkin spice."

"What, it's great."

"Stop the nonsense, Mr. Brent."

"No nonsense, Ma'am." He made to get up; she laid her hand on his arm.

"Don't tell me you're working too hard, don't tell me you're tired, and don't tell me you're stressed about the election campaign. Uh-huh."

"All of the above?" He tried a smile. She didn't return it.

She arranged the pumpkin salt and pepper shakers and matching sugar bowl into a symmetrical pattern. "You been dragging yourself around here for a month now. Grumpy, distracted, and a first-class pain in the butt."

"I know, I know." Brent shrugged. "I don't know what's wrong with me."

"Yes, you do." Teddi nodded, holding his gaze.

"No, I don't. All those things you said are true."

"You really don't get it?" Her forehead furrowed beneath her gray curls. "Let's see, when did the symptoms start?"

"I don't know, like you said, a couple weeks ago. A month."

"And who returned to Benton Center about that time?"

"What? Maggie? You think I'm upset about Maggie?"

"No, son, you're in love with Maggie and you're pretending not to be."

"Of course I am. That's not it." Brent looked from her face to the coffee mug.

"But look at you. Look how it's affecting you."

"You know it's part of the plan. We explained it to you."

"You did, and I went along with it because you asked me to." Teddi's frown filled her face, and Brent had to turn his head. "But it was stupid when I first heard about it, and it's even stupider now. All because you care about what others think."

Brent's face spun around, his eyes flashing. "You know how it is around here. They really gave Maggie a hard time when she was a kid. You know that."

"I remember." Teddi reached for his hand. "You think you can change the whole town."

Brent slumped into his chair. "Not everyone, maybe a few, they need to see--"

"Maybe they do, maybe they don't, but it's not your job to teach them. You can teach the kids to play, but not the gossipers." Teddi squeezed his hand. "Brent, it's hurting you and she's upset--"

"No, Maggie's fine." Brent spoke softly, keeping his head turned toward the window.

"The girl is not fine. I can see that, and besides I spoke to her father." When he continued to stare through the window at the gazebo, she slapped her hand lightly on the table and his eyes returned to hers. She waited for him to speak, then said, "I hope it's worth it, Brent. I hope it's worth it."

"We need to be free." Brent took his virtual gramma's hand in his. It was not the time to tell her what else he had in mind. With a small and determined smile he said, "We need to be who we are, not who they say we are."

*   *   *

Maggie pulled a yellow gown from Sammi's costume closet in the Dress Shop and held it in front of her. "This will fit, I think."

Her friend reached past her. "I like this one better. Green's a better color for you. Your eyes and your hair."

Maggie floated around the room as if dancing with the dress and didn't answer.

"Except that's not part of your plan, right?"

"Exactly, my dear Ms. Patel. I need to wear *this* costume because it's the same as the one she'll be wearing."

"And you know that how?" Sammi helped her step out of the green gown and into the flowing pale-yellow gown.

"Kay Kay and I have a lot in common, you know. We share lots of personal stuff." Maggie bit her tongue to suppress her urge to laugh.

Sammi tried to finish the last button at the top of the gown while snorting a laugh. "What you two share is a deep and mutual mistrust. How can you say that?"

Maggie adjusted the shoulders of the dress. She would have to wear a different bra.

"Yet you know which costume she'll be wearing Saturday at the Fest?" Sammi's forehead crinkled in doubt.

"Our Ms. Phillips does like to talk about herself." Maggie spun one way, then the other and examined herself in the mirror.

"Hmmm."

"Hmmm what? Is it OK?"

"Take a look." Sammi stood behind her in the full-length mirror.

"Not bad, but my hair is wrong."

"What do you mean? Belle has chestnut hair. Brownish anyway, yours is fine."

"We're not only trying to look like Belle." Maggie focused on her friend's image in the glass. "We're trying to confuse Brent, remember?"

"Yes, but--"

"So darling Kennedy has to wear a wig to cover up her blonde hair."

Sammi's face brightened, and her words quickened as she figured it out. "We'll get you a wig, too. A chestnut one, just like she'll be wearing. I'm sure we have one around here someplace."

"Great, and I have to hold this."

"It's so little." Sammi took the mask on a stick from her. "Won't Brent know it's you behind the mask?"

"Oh, Samantha. What am I going to do with you?"

Maggie patted the dressing room sofa and they both sat down. "First of all, men are dumb."

Sammi nodded.

"Second, men see what they want to see. Brent is expecting to see Kennedy in a chestnut brown wig and a yellow dress, so that's what he'll see."

"He'll see Belle. He's the Beast, you two are the Beauties. Got that part." Samantha shook her head. "But up close? Your plan can't work up close."

"Well, we'll get the same color lipstick and fix my make-up."

"Your eyes are close enough and it'll be dark." Sammi looked doubtfully at her friend.

Maggie held the mask in front of her face and said,

"Clark Kent." She removed the mask. "Superman." Mask back on. "Clark." Mask off. "Man of Steel."

Sammi's face brightened. "It fooled Lois Lane, didn't it!"

"She never figured it out." Maggie laughed remembering how Clark Kent's glasses had protected his secret identity. "Besides, Brent won't be able to see much from inside the Beast head, and I won't be having long conversations with him. I'll flirt with him. Keep him off balance until the big moment."

Sammi grinned. "Sounds like a ninja guerilla love thing."

Maggie laughed. "It may not work, but it should be entertaining. If nothing else, the ladies of the Gossip Club will have a topic for the next month. That's a much bigger deal around here."

Sammi heard the humor in her friend's words, but also the hurt in her eyes. "Your whole plan is that you know he's in love with you, not Kennedy. Deep down in his heart of hearts, he *wants* to see you, not her. Maggie, he wants it to be you."

Maggie's eyes narrowed above her smile. "But for the Midnight Kiss to work, it has to be a *true* kiss, right? If he thinks he's kissing her when he's kissing me, it won't work."

"I'll be sure to distract Kennedy. Keep her out of the way." Sammi's eyes drifted off into the future. "When the moon is full and the countdown gets to zero, take off the wig, drop the mask and boom!"

"The town doubters will have their proof, and the rest of the Gossip Club will believe what we already know to be true." Maggie shook her head slowly. "It's all kind of a waste of time."

Sammi looked closely at her friend. "You know, you don't have to do any of this. You don't have to play their game."

"I've tried that, we've tried that. You know we have." Maggie's shoulders slumped as if deflated. "Ignoring them, hoping they'll go away. No, it doesn't work. They just keep yapping about us."

"But you have Brent." Sammi took Maggie's hand. "That's way more important than them or any plan."

Maggie's eyes brightened at the sound of his name. "I never would have made it without him. I'd have left town and never come back."

"OK, you know I'll support you if that's how you want to do it." Sammi's voice was cheerful as she squeezed her friend's hand. "OK, so the Midnight Kiss is lame, and you're putting on a show, but if it finally, truly, gets the town off your back, you can get married in peace."

"Married in Peace." Maggie sighed deeply. "That sounds nice. Very, very nice."

Chapter 41

Why do I always have to be the servant?" Irv squirmed as he tried to adjust his brown Cogsworth costume while wearing thick brown gloves.

"Tall, skinny guys got to be the servants. Everybody knows that." Brent stopped at the entrance to Pumpkin-Fest and tipped his fiberglass costume head at his friend. "At least you have feet. You could be a mantel clock."

Irv gestured to Brent's blue dress coat and stockings. "But I never get a chance to be the Beast and find my Beauty?"

"Sure. All you got to do is find a skinnier friend."

Irv grumbled and followed Brent across the street and into the Square.

Saturday night of the PumpkinFest was costume night. Orange lights bathed an enormous pumpkin in the center of the gazebo. Ben Centers and tourists jostled each other as they visited the booths lining the paths of the Square in the center of the town. Foods of all kinds, from cotton candy to kettle corn, to apple cider, to pumpkin burgers tempted the throngs of happy costumed and masked people.

Brent raised his arm to stop his friend. "This is amazing. Look."

"What? It's like this every year."

Brent removed the Beast head and held it under his arm. "Sure, but think about it. The last three weeks the Square hasn't been filled with happy people in costumes, but wound up people waving political signs and yelling at each other."

Irv removed his own mask and swiveled to take in the view. "That's Benton Center. We argue, but we respect each other in the end. You know, the *Pax Cucurbita*."

"One of the reasons I love this place." Brent put the Beast head over his own as they began to walk. Irv helped him not to stumble over the curb. "Everyone getting into the costume thing is good, but controlling the angry rhetoric is even better."

"Wait a second, there's somebody not in a costume." The Grandfather Clock gestured to a pack of kids dodging through the crowd.

Brent laughed. "That's Meredith. Yeah, and it's not a costume. She always looks like an escapee from Kiss. Another thing I love about this place."

"Hey, Mister Brent, where's Belle?" Meredeath voice shouted through the skull mask. "Where's Belle?" The kids with her laughed and followed her down the path.

"See, Irv, the plan is working. Everyone is getting into it."

"They surely are." Irv stopped at the coffee shop tent. "If you're really that happy, you could buy your servant a coffee."

"Line's too long, let's try the new game." Brent crossed the path and into the Punkin Guts tent.

Long wooden tables stood in two lines facing a pile of large pumpkins. Volunteers dressed as dogs and cats circulated between them handing out tickets and stuffing money into orange fanny packs. Others were distributing large bibs and setting pumpkins in front of people who had paid. Men were seated along one row of tables, women along the opposite.

Brent rotated his massive head to his butler. "I never heard of this game before."

"It's new this year, The Kiwanis Club discovered it somewhere. Should be fun, and the money goes to a good cause." He paid the volunteer and handed Brent a bib. "Put this on."

"Why do I need it?"

"Look at the sign."

Rising from the mound of orange gourds was a slate with 'Punkin Guts, Battle of the Sexes' written in chalk. "You're kidding."

"Look who's here." Cogsworth pointed to Raggedy Ann and Belle sitting down across from them.

"See, the plan isn't so dumb." Brent nudged his friend as a volunteer cat plopped a small tin pail on their table. A large puppy set a giant pumpkin with the lid cut off next to it. He peered into the round opening of the pumpkin. "Oh, man."

"Yeah, we take out all the pulp and seeds--"

"--that yucky, gooey stuff! Yes!"

Irv's eyes lit up. "Yeah, and we slop it into our pail. When it's full we race over to those big scales over there. We dump it into the big bucket that says 'Warlocks.' Then we come back and get another pumpkin load until the bucket's full. The women use the 'Witches', see? First team to push the arrow to *full* wins."

Irv was interrupted by a large cheer. Several people stood and applauded as another Belle, this one accompanied by Daisy Duck, entered the tent and posed. "Belle, Belle, Belle!" Several others chanted "Maggie Belle, Maggie Belle!"

"I thought my plan was secret," Brent said.

"Sure you did, Beast. Great. Both of them are in here with you. "Look at that."

Brent squinted to peer out of his spherical head to see one of the volunteers erasing Witches and Warlocks and writing in Kennedy and Maggie. The new Belle, Kennedy, took her seat across from Maggie. "We help Mags win. How bad can it be?"

"Yeah, what could possibly go wrong?" A bell clanged, voices raised, the volunteers backed against the walls, and hands reached into the gooey gourd guts. "Look for yourself," Irv said. "Shrieking, panicking, flailing."

From all sides, people scraped their pumpkins and filled their pails with wet and slimy seeds. Brent bobbed his giant head and slapped a handful of guts into their pail. They each put in several more, then sauntered toward the scale. "This might be fun."

A large piece of cheese jostled them as they made their way to the Maggie's bucket.

"I bet her name is Brie."

Irv elbowed him in the ribs and grabbed a handful of goo from the girl's pail and dropped it into theirs.

"Isn't that cheating?" Brent said. "I'm shocked."

Irv couldn't answer as he disappeared suddenly under a crowd of Kennedy supporters who had formed a wall around their favorite Belle. In front of the other bucket,

Maggie's supporters were forming as well. Brent tried to locate Maggie as a handful of pumpkin splattered through his eye hole. Then another, and another.

"Kiss Kennedy!" the crowd pelting him chanted. "Kiss Kennedy!"

Brent pulled Irv to his feet under a barrage of pumpkin guts from the other horde. "Midnight Kiss Maggie," they yelled.

In the old west it would have been a shoot-out in a saloon, here it was a riot of wet, orange, seedy fun.
Or a mob voicing their opinions of Maggie and Brent's personal life. Blobs of pumpkin guts flew through the air, people screamed, others laughed. Tables and chairs were kicked to the side. "Kiss Kennedy! Kiss Maggie!"

The two men managed to get behind a table. "Democracy, huh?" Irv snatched a handful of orange goo from the top of his Grandfather Clock head. Brent watched a blob of seeds strike the back of Belle's head. The lines in front of the buckets had crumbled and he couldn't tell which, but she rose up and tossed the remains of her bucket at the person in the Brie costume. Both disappeared into the melee.

When too many pumpkins flew and too many people began falling, the judge finally blew a whistle and the brawl slowly wound down. "Our chance to get out of here." Brent lifted the canvas and pulled his friend out of the chaos into the cool, dark night.

Chapter 42

Maggie's honor guard of supporters bustled her and Sammi out of the Pumpkin Guts tent and deposited them in the middle of the path, then continued toward the Gazebo chanting "Midnight Kiss Maggie" at the top of their lungs. While costumed revelers surged around the two as if they were an island in a stream, Sammi searched her Raggedy Ann costume for more clumps of pumpkin goo. Maggie was doing the same to her yellow gown, then they cleaned off each other.

"We may have found a hole in your plan, Margaret." Sammi tossed a handful of seeds into the grass. "That was way too violent."

"You can't say the people of Benton Center aren't involved in their community." Maggie pulled her friend out of the human traffic flow, and adjusted the off the shoulder Belle gown. "It's the only plan we have. Come on, you agreed."

Her friend ran her eyes over Belle's yellow dress and

flicked away another seed. "Well, the costume works, and when you're holding the mask, even I can't tell who you are."

Maggie adjusted the chestnut wig again. "This thing itches."

"You'll get used to it." Sammi flinched as a pack of small kids burst past them yelling 'Kiss Kennedy.' "I did agree on the *plan*, but not the *violence*. I know how much you've been hurt by gossip, but violence is not the answer."

You only know the half of it, Maggie thought and took her friend's hand. "I have no idea how it got this far. How does everybody know about the Midnight Kiss?"

"There are no secrets in Ben Cen. You know that." Sammi started down the path. "We better tell the mayor what's happening."

As the two women worked their way through the crowd, they passed groups supporting Kennedy and others Maggie. The costume must have worked, for no one could tell which Belle she was, and didn't seem to particularly care. The competition was fun.

"I do declare this to be a mighty fine festival, my friend." Tom Grieselhuber was gesturing at Nate Richardson with a dueling pistol when Maggie and Sammi entered the comparative safety of the Town Tent and plopped down on camp chairs. The mayor was dressed as Aaron Burr, complete with a long maroon jacket, white jodhpurs and tall black boots.

"The best part is, there's no malice, sir," Nate looked like a taller, paler version of Alexander Hamilton. "Participation, but no confrontation."

"Mayor, have you seen what's going on in the Punkin Guts tent?" Sammi said.

The mayor ignored her and grabbed the councilman's forearm. "Really, Nate, this is what I want for our town: involved citizens who respect one another."

Maggie shrugged a question to Sammi and said, "But they aren't respecting--"

"I do too, Mr. Vice-President." Nate turned his back to the two women and grinned as the mayor's upraised arm took in the crowd. "It is great to see all these people enjoying themselves together."

"But they're throwing stuff and flipping tables and--"

"The women are missing the big pic*ture*, *sir*." Nate grinned.

"What these good folks are doing is supporting the local economy, Councilman. With the new road we can have the Square full all year long."

The faux Hamilton shook his head slowly. "I don't know for *sure, Burr*. It's tough to get enough volunteers to run this event. We couldn't do it every week for *certain, sir*."

Sammi winced at the forced rhymes. "They have no idea what's going on and they're trying to *rap*?" She arched her painted eyebrows at the two politicians in disgust.

"See?" the fake Burr replied after a moment of thought. "Two reasonable positions expressed reasonably. I love this town."

Sammi slapped her hands on her knees, then burst out the back of the tent. Maggie followed. "Hey, wait."

"Those two aren't going to do anything. They think it's all peaceful. Do they have a clue?"

"Well, they are having fun trying to do *Hamilton*." Maggie hoped her friend would smile, but she didn't. Instead Sammi said, "Maggie, I'm out."

"What do you mean?" Maggie pulled some orange pumpkin goo from Raggedy Ann's red orange wig.

"I mean I gave it a shot, but it's gotten out of control. It's too much." Sammi waved at the tent. "And as long as it's good for business, those two are OK with it."

"Sammi, come on." Maggie found Sammi's eyes hidden in the red triangles of face paint. "I need your help to beat the gossipers."

"No, Maggie, you don't. You love Brent, he loves you. Quit playing this lame media game and marry him. If you think otherwise, you're as loony as Hamilton and Burr in there." Sammi jabbed a finger at the tent and disappeared into the crowd.

Chapter 43

Maggie raised her eyes at the last instant and jumped off the cinder path to avoid being knocked down by a small pack of kids in costumes. There were seven or eight of them, led by a skeleton brandishing an electric guitar and an orange-haired Muppet waving drumsticks. She managed a small smile as she recognized Terry and Brent's music class, and carefully made her way into the Pot & Flagon tent.

It was a long canvas-sided affair with heavy ropes and several thick wooden beams supporting the peaks. Clusters of lanterns cast a warm yellow glow on the round tables and folding wooden chairs on the grass below. She stepped out of the way of a mouse cleaning pumpkin seeds and orange glop from a large piece of cheese, and strode to the makeshift counter.

"Latte, coming right up." Yoda turned to place a cup under the steam faucet of the espresso machine. Her pale green ears waggled and her beige robe spun as she did so. A short, hooked walking stick lay on the counter.

"Belle, oh, I didn't see you come into the tent." Inside the Yoda costume, Teddi's brows furrowed. "Wait, you were just in here."

"No, just walked in." Maggie looked to Sammi for confirmation before realizing she was alone.

"No, you were here a few minutes ago. Lord, I am so confused." Teddi looked into the flickering glow of the pumpkin on the counter beside her, then focused her eyes on Maggie. "Unless there are two Belle's running around here tonight."

Belle held her mask in place and leaned toward the Grandmaster Jedi. "Which one am I?"

"You're Miss Maggie, Miss Belle." She bobbed her head and the large green ears wiggled. "I can tell by the way you carry yourself." Teddi lowered her voice. "And I bet I can guess who the *other* Miss Belle is."

"It's kind of a competition for the Beast. The Midnight Kiss."

"That lame old thing? Well, at least it's more grist for the gossip mill." Teddi handed a Pumpkin Spice latte to her, and led her to a table. "I have to get off my feet."

"I don't know how you do it." Maggie sat down beside her. "You work all day and volunteer at night."

"Don't know how *not* to do it." She took a sip of the hot sweet liquid and bobbed her head. "But it's good sometimes to sit back and watch the world pass by."

"A world of crazy costumes." Maggie pointed her mask at the two-person horse trotting down the path outside. "How do they decide who's in front?"

Teddi snorted. "Front's not the problem. Who has to be the other end?"

When Maggie barely smiled, Yoda said, "Your daddy was in here a little while ago."

Belle looked over the rim of the paper cup. "Terry, the Love Pirate?"

"Yeah, him and that parrot on his shoulder." Her robe shook as a laugh rumbled through. "He's looking forward to playing but he misses his pirate crew."

"He really does." Maggie nodded, then reached for her buzzing cell. "I gotta go." She stood up quickly.

"Where? What's the rush?"

Maggie explained that Mick and Jocko were landing an hour earlier than planned, ending with "And Sammi was going to pick them up, but can't." She slumped back down to her chair.

"The Love Pirates are playing?" Yoda's ears flopped wildly as she bobbed her head. "Then get going!"

"But if I go to the airport, I'll miss the Midnight Kiss."

Teddi's calm, kind voice came through Yoda's mouth. "What's the problem with that?"

"It's what we've been planning, I should be there. With Brent. It's--"

"Your *own* stupid plan. You don't have to follow it, Maggie."

Maggie looked up as if scalded. "Stupid?"

Teddi removed her green headpiece. "I want you to hear this, OK?"

The flush spread up Maggie's neck.

"The only question you need to answer is this: What. Is. More. Important. To. You?"

The girl in the Belle costume didn't respond.

"Well?" Teddi's voice was soft yet firm. "Brent and your dad, or your plan and the gossipers?"

Maggie leapt to her feet, took two strides, stopped, and nearly spat, "Brent, of course. And dad."

"Then the right thing you go and do." Teddi bobbed

her head like Yoda.

Maggie laughed at her Yoda voice in spite of herself and let out a long sigh. How could she ever have doubted this woman? "Thank you, Teddi. I'm going to the airport. Please keep the concert a secret."

"A secret I promise." Teddi's face beamed in the glow of the pumpkin on the tabletop, and in her normal voice she said, "You're a good daughter, Margaret Mary, a very good daughter."

Chapter 44

The Beast and his trusty butler Cogsworth had had a difficult time extricating themselves from the chaos in the Punkin Guts, and a worse time along the congested paths of the Square. Every way they turned, crowds chanted, screamed and yelled for him to either 'Kiss Kennedy' or 'Marry Maggie'. His enormous costume head made him easy to spot and follow. Finally, Irv thought of the storage area beneath the Gazebo, and had managed to lock the door behind them.

"Tough crowd." Irv grinned.

"Why don't they mind their own business?" Brent had removed the head and slumped down onto the seat of a riding mower. Music stands and chairs had been set up as a practice space for his music class.

Irv moved a stand out of the way. "Why? Because you practically begged them to get into your business."

"What? You think I wanted to be pelted with pumpkins? Yelled at by every yahoo in the county? I didn't want all this. Neither did Maggie."

"Actually, I think you did."

"It's the plan, Irv, you know that."

"If that's all it was, you could have stopped with the election. That was plenty of competition, plenty of contro-versy."

"Look, all I want is to kiss the right Belle at mid-night, let everybody see it, and we'll be done with the whole thing."

Irv examined the cuticles of his thumb. "You can't be serious about going on with this."

"At this point I have to. We have to." Brent looked at his cell. "In fact, I better get over to the Pumpkin Sweep field."

"Good luck, Beast."

Brent adjusted the giant costume orb on his shoul-ders. "You're not coming?"

Irv shook his grandfather clock face, no. "If winning the Midnight Kiss is that important, you're on your own, my friend."

"It's the plan." Brent stood up. Maggie would kill him if he didn't show up, and he'd deserve it. "What are you going to do?"

"I'll head over to Patel's booth and get some cook-ies. Maybe Sammi will be there."

Inside the orb, Brent furrowed his brows. "See you at the concert?"

"Wouldn't miss it." Irv opened the storeroom door a crack and peeked out. "Coast is clear."

Chapter 45

Maggie raised the key fob above her head in the municipal lot behind the firehouse and bleeped twice. Her car winked its lights in response, she jumped in, and tried to settle her breath. After reading the text from the airline, she had run all the way through the crowd from Teddi's coffee tent. She adjusted the itchy chestnut wig so she could see and punched the start button. She tried to speed through the traffic between the Square and the Interstate, and experienced first-hand the necessity of widening the road. She glanced at the flight information on her phone as she waited at what seemed like the fifteenth traffic light, then sped up the ramp to I-71 when it finally changed to green.

She was expecting Terry's former band mates to look like Cheech Marin and Tommy Chong, and when they strolled through the door from baggage claim a half hour later, she was not very disappointed. Mick's full, gray beard, headband and wireframes resembled Cheech, and Jocko's handlebar stache and stocking cap reminded her of Chong.

She tapped her horn and they ambled toward her.

"Dude, you're not Raggedy Ann. We were expecting the girl with the triangle eyes."

"Yeah, she don't have flaming red hair." Jocko squinted at Maggie. "Maybe it's the girl with kaleidoscope eyes?"

Maggie removed her wig. "Hey, it's me."

"Butterfly!" The three of them hugged joyously; it had been a long time. As they loaded their equipment in the car, Maggie explained the change in plans, ending with, "And it's a surprise. Terry has no idea you're coming."

*   *   *

Maggie parked behind town hall when she returned to Benton Center, and used Sammi's key to open the back door. She stowed Mick, Jocko, their guitars and luggage inside; her original plan was to use the storeroom beneath the gazebo, but realized Terry would see them as Brent and the kids warmed up.

Mayor Grieselhuber's voice flew through the night air as she hurried across the street to the PumpkinFest. "We'll be starting the Midnight Kiss countdown shortly, folks. Remember everyone, the person you kiss at midnight is your forever love. Find your partner and get ready to pucker."

There was some background discussion over the PA system and Maggie couldn't make it out. Grieselhuber's voice returned, saying, "I have been informed that Benton Center and its employees, elected or otherwise, are not liable for any relationships resulting from the Midnight Kiss."

Maggie heard a group of people chanting "Maggie, Maggie," and cut through the line of game booths to avoid them. Off to her right, by the old howitzer, others were yelling for Kennedy. The mayor started counting down, "25, 24..." She began to run, or there was no chance of reaching the Pumpkin Sweep field in time.

Chapter 46

Pumpkin Sweeps was another festival game that Ben Centers believed to be a substitute for civic discord. Over the years, candidates and issues battled each other vigorously in the weeks preceding Election Day, but paused during the PumpkinFest. Mayor Grieselhuber and many former office holders believed that this Pumpkin Peace, translated *Pax Cucurbita* by Connie Richardson's Latin students, was founded on the respect the townspeople had for democracy and for each other. To some extent this was true, but many a cagey citizen knew that the political conflicts were simply covered by the thin veneer of competition played out on the Festival grounds. A psychologist might say the town's competitive passions were transferred to the games, not eliminated.

On the surface, Pumpkin Sweeps was a race. The object was to be the first to propel a pumpkin across the finish line using a broom. As good citizens expect the best from their competitors, Ben Centers didn't believe that lanes were needed. Each group of 8 or 10 contestants could roam across the grass from the starting line to the finish line in whatever route they chose. Often they chose not the straightest path to the goal line, but a path where instead of winning themselves, they could hinder their opponents' chances to win. This was one of the games that had caused the town to make sure the EMT unit was on site.

Brent hefted several brooms to find one with some whip in it. He looked down the line of competitors in his heat and saw one of the Belles. If only one were there, he hoped it was Maggie, so the whole mess would end. He checked again: Brie the cheese, a mouse, a two-person horse but only one Belle. A large crowd had gathered around the playing field exchanging chants and insults.

The bell clanged and pumpkins started rolling across the Square. Brent's first two mighty swings moved his gourd only a few feet, and he found himself at the rear of the pack. As usual, he forgot the brooms had long bristles and the pumpkins were small so he couldn't simply use his strength to whack them. That's why they call the game 'Sweeps,' he thought, and his third swing made better contact and rolled the orb farther. Feeling better about himself for a full three seconds, he crashed face-first to the turf. He looked up to a swish of yellow gauzy fabric and a trill of laughter.

"Come on, Beastie," Belle called with a grin.

"That's how you want to play it, huh." Brent sprang to his feet and chased her flying chestnut locks. He wove around the mouse and Brie, and somehow bowled his gourd through the four running legs of the two-person horse. He sped up his pace and closed in on Belle.

She spun and faced him, her broom held like a hockey stick, her own pumpkin forgotten. He moved left, she sprang in front of him. He faked, hesitated, then darted right. She calmly poked his pumpkin aside. He peered at her through the holes in his headpiece, and she stared back, tapping her broom on the green grass.

"Hey, come on, I won you a--"

She was a lightening blur of soft yellow. Sweeping his pumpkin away from him, she raced back toward the starting line. He took a step to follow, tripped over her pumpkin and crashed to the turf again.

Beast got to all fours and shook off the cobwebs. When he adjusted the headpiece and his eyes focused, he managed to see Belle running back toward him. She held her broom in front of her face and dropped Brent's pumpkin at his feet. "I think this might be yours."

"I don't get it. First you hit it the wrong way, now you're helping me? Who are you?"

"We're a mysterious gender," she said and swept her gourd toward the goal line. Brent stood dumbfounded.

At the microphone on the Gazebo stage, Mayor Grieselhuber was beginning the Midnight Kiss ritual. "Remember everyone, the person you kiss at midnight is your forever love. Are you ready? OK, here we go 25, 24...!"

Belle turned and waved to him. "Come on, we can still win!" She gave his pumpkin a sweep, then hip-checked Brie the cheese to the ground.

He grabbed his broom and chased after her billowing yellow gown.

*   *   *

Maggie had managed to work her way close enough to watch the Sweeps, but the crowd of Kiss Kennedy supporters wouldn't let her on the field itself. They were demanding that the Beast quit playing with pumpkins and get on with the kissing. As the countdown progressed, she struggled harder, but couldn't fight her way to Brent.

Maggie took a long breath, removed her wig, and dropped her mask. "10, 9, 8," the mayor continued. She realized it was too late for her Midnight Kiss, and told herself she wasn't that upset at losing. She swallowed and straightened her costume. Maybe Sammi and Teddi had been right.

She turned around and walked away from the crowd and the field where Brent was chasing Kennedy. The throng decided she was no longer needed and let her pass, continuing to chant "Kiss Kennedy." She would retrieve Mick and Jocko from town hall and re-unite the Love Pirates.

*   *   *

Brent scanned the field as he raced to catch up to Belle. The rest of the competition was spread out, with only a few actually attacking the finish line. Most were impeding others and having a grand time doing it.

As Grieselhuber counted down, the crowd and several of the competitors paired off. Brie hugged her big-eared mouse, and the front of the horse embraced the rear. The four of them cheered along with the mayor, "6, 5..."

Not Belle. She was making a beeline to the finish, bobbing through and around anyone in her way. Brent poked a pumpkin away from a pink-helmeted fire person and caught up with Belle only a few yards from the goal line.

"4, 3..."

Belle turned to smack him with her broom, then saw who it was and smiled. "Hey, there." She passed the gourd to him and he swept it over the line.

"2, 1, Midnight Kiss!" Mayor Grieselhuber's voice boomed over the PumpkinFest. Scores of couples followed his advice, kids, teenagers, adults of all ages. The Square was suddenly quiet, the trebuchet still, gourds and brooms and piles of pumpkin guts abandoned. Meredeath and her posse stood gaping, both fascinated and repulsed by the sight of people kissing in public.

Brent tossed away the Beast headpiece and embraced Belle. "We won!" Kennedy leaned back her head and parted her glossy lips.

Chapter 47

Maggie beat most of the crowd flowing from the Pumpkin Sweeps field to the gazebo, and managed to descend the steps beneath the stage before being spotted. She rapped her knuckles on the door. It opened and she darted into the storage space. The youngsters in her father's music class were putting on their costumes and warming up their instruments. She only had a few minutes before Brent would be joining them.

"Maggie, what's the matter?" Terry reached for her hand and pulled her to a quiet spot in the corner of the low-ceilinged room.

She swiped at a tear rolling down her face. "Nothing."

Terry rotated his daughter's chin toward him. "Butterfly."

"Oh, daddy." She fell into his arms and sobbed. "I screwed it all up, and now they think he loves somebody else."

Terry pushed away the parrot on his shoulder and hugged her tighter. "Who cares what they think?" He made small circles on her back as his pirate costume sopped up her tears.

With a sigh Maggie pulled back and recounted her evening as Belle, ending with, "We followed the plan, but he kissed her, he kissed Kennedy. I couldn't get there in time to stop them. The crowd wouldn't let me."
Terry stepped closer to be heard amid the clatter and random snatches of music in the storage room. "But I don't think it's a big deal."

"He was supposed to kiss me."

"Sure, but he doesn't love her, he loves you." Terry exchanged her soggy Kleenex for a fresh one. "I been teaching music with Brent since you were in Chicago. I've seen him with her, Butterfly, and well, I don't know for certain, and it's clear they like each other. But love? I don't see it."

"You're just saying that because you're my dad." She grinned at him. "And the Midnight Kiss was kinda your plan in the first place."

"It was, and I am, and I love you." He reached and gave her another hug. "Now what could you have done differently?"

She spoke into his neck and her voice was muffled. "I could have stopped making silly plans. I thought I could teach them a lesson and get back at how they treated me. For all the things they said about you."

Terry stepped back and looked at her teary, puffy face. "I've forgiven them, Butterfly. You can, too."

She nodded and wiped her nose. "But they hurt you."

"Yeah, the gossip hurt me, and it hurt you. That's a

fact. You can't change that."

"No, but I can change the future. Sounds like one of your songs." She managed a smile. "Instead of worrying what others did or what they think, I should believe in what we have."

"Go find him." Terry held her shoulders and waited for her red-rimmed eyes to find his smile. "It's not too late."

Chapter 48

The crowd surrounding the Pumpkin Sweeps field pressed in toward Brent and Kennedy. "Kiss Kennedy, Kiss Kennedy!" they cried.

Brent didn't kiss her. The crowd booed lustily.

She cocked her head and gave him a rueful smile.

He opened his hands. "Thank you for your fine acting job."

She stepped closer and pecked his cheek. "For you anything, for this town, I'm done."

"That's not a real kiss!" someone yelled from the crowd milling around them. "We want a real kiss."

"Remember, everybody," the mayor was saying over the sound system. "The girl you kiss at midnight--" A slap and muffled laughter escaped through the speakers. "Er, um, the *person*, you kissed, I mean the boy, girl, whoever it is you kissed, bring them to the concert on the gazebo stage."

"So that means I'm not taking you to the concert?" He raised his eyebrows in shock.

She smacked his beastly arm. "You've got your own plans, don't you? With your *favorite* Belle?"

"Hopefully it's my last plan. The last time I'll have to worry about all this nonsense."

Kennedy watched his arm encompass the Square, the Fest, the whole of Benton Center. "Don't worry, it'll work out for you guys. She adores you, Brent."

"I know, it's just--"

"The attitude of the town." She finished his thought. "That's why I can't stay here."

"But you're so good at it, Kay Kay. Nobody plays the gossip game like you."

She covered her face with her famous I-got-this smile. "Thank you, kind sir, but I have had my fill of playing up to this crowd."

They worked themselves through the remnants of the disappointed crowd to an open spot on the path. Brent pulled her to a stop. "Wait. What? I thought you wanted to go into politics."

"I am. Senator Rasmussen has offered me a job on his staff in Columbus."

"Your father's fraternity buddy." Brent nodded. "But you said you were done playing the game. Isn't that what politics is?"

She took his free hand and led him down the cinder path. "Do I have to explain everything to you, silly Beast? I said I was done with *this* crowd. I need to work on a larger, more important crowd."

"Sure you do." Brent slapped the headpiece against his leg and didn't try to hide his grin.

"The big PumpkinFest concert is starting in a few minutes, folks, featuring our very own Terry McGrath playing hits from his original band, The Love Pirates." Grieselhuber's voice was tinny coming through the speakers. "Don't miss it. Especially if you kissed somebody tonight. Uh, anybody, a boy or a girl or a man, you know."

Brent faced Kennedy. "I hope it works out for you in Columbus, I really do."

Kennedy applied her wicked smile. "Why Beast, I do believe you're blushing. That must be why you usually wear a mask instead of carrying it."

"Damn it, Kay Kay, I've got two things I really want to say to you."

Her eyes flickered left, then right. Her smile slipped off. "Yes?"

Brent dragged a hairy foot through the cinders. "You really *do* have a career in politics. Working with you was an eye-opener for me."

Kennedy looked away from him. "Speaking of masks." He held up his. "I'm not the only one." He waited for her to look. "Am I?"

She brushed her hand across her eyes and smiled brightly. "Whatever do you mean?"

Brent grinned. "Your secret is safe with me, my friend." Her chin quivered, so he continued.

"Secondly, I want to thank you for helping me."

She shook her head. "I didn't do anything. Just playing my normal bad girl role."

"No, this whole Belle gig. Come on, you did it for me."

"It was my last chance to win you." She flashed her wicked smile and twinkled her eyes. "And by the way, mister, you really thought I was Maggie, didn't you? For a minute anyway."

"No, uh, yes, uh, I was confused." Brent could feel his face flushing. "I'll admit I was confused. A little bit anyway."

Kennedy batted her eyes in full flirt mode. "What confused you the most?"

"You were nice," Brent stammered. "*Too* nice. You let me win."

"That's a bad thing, Beast?" She ran a finger down the edge of his cheek.

"No," Brent said and took her hand in his. "But it's not our way. Maggie and I, well, we don't really fight--"

"--but it looks like that. Darn it, for once in my life I was too nice." Kennedy stepped back and jammed her hands on her hips.

Brent nodded. They were back to more familiar ground. "Anyhow. You didn't have to play along, Thank you, Kennedy. Maggie and I owe you a lot."

"Now you're making me blush, Brent." She put both palms on his hairy chest and pushed him down the path. "Go, Beast. Tell her what we were up to and get on with the second part of your plan. The important part."

Chapter 49

Maggie burst up the storeroom stairs and away from the people now finding spots around the gazebo to hear the concert. Without the chestnut wig and her mask, she passed more easily through them, but wished she had something to cover Belle's yellow gown. She would talk to Brent, she really wanted to talk to him, but first she had to retrieve Mick and Jocko and get them to the gazebo.

An arm grabbed her, and she nearly tumbled to the ground. "We need to talk," Kennedy said.

Maggie straightened up. "If you want to gloat, I've got nothing to say to you." She folded her arms across her chest.

"Gloat?" Kennedy said. "What do I have to gloat about?"

"You won. He kissed you in front of all those people. That's all you're concerned about, isn't it?"

"He *didn't* kiss me."

"Yes, he did, I saw you."

Kennedy slapped the flyers she held against her knee, then stashed them in her bag. "No, Maggie, kissing Brent was never the plan."

"Wait. You two had a *plan?*" Maggie felt her temper rise and yanked the other Belle off the path where it was darker and quieter. "Spill it, Kennedy."

"Relax, Maggie, take a breath."

Maggie did neither; she bored her eyes into her nemesis instead.

"Look, I really don't need to be in the middle of you two. You're exhausting." She dropped her voice. "He said something about you needing a plan, I didn't follow it, but we made it look like we were actually in love during the campaign. But no, there was no Midnight Kiss."

Maggie stood in front of her, arms akimbo. "Why should I believe you?"

"I don't really care, but ask Brent." Kennedy raised her hand. "Wait, I want to be fair. I did kiss him at the Sweeps field, on the cheek. A goodbye kiss. Somebody probably posted it online."

"I'm confused, I really am." Maggie shook her head, but kept her eyes fixed on the other Belle.
Kennedy returned the glare. "Maggie get a grip. I'm not the bad guy here."

"But--"

"I know, I know. I do like playing Mean Girl. Always have." She smiled and stepped toward Maggie, not away. "Look, you have nothing to be confused about. Forget all the other stuff. He loves *you*, not me. He never did."

Maggie watched the crowd squeezing closer to the stage in front of them. "I always thought you liked him. Back in junior high."

"What's not to like? He's kind, sweet and totes gorge.

But I don't love him. Besides, I'm leaving Benton Center. I have a job offer in Columbus."

Maggie said, "I thought you wanted to be here. Defeat Issue Two and work at your dad's company."

"Small town's not for me." Kennedy handed Maggie a flyer from her bag, and her eyes took on a serious tone. "It's ironic isn't it? You left and came back. I stayed and now I'm leaving."

"Columbus." Maggie's brow furrowed above her green eyes as she read the pro Issue Two flyer. "You got a job in politics, didn't you."

"State Senator Rasmussen's office. He's *for* the road, so now I am too. Besides, the state capital is a step up from a small-town council."

Maggie caught herself before reacting to the blond woman's snarky tone. "Congratulations."

Kennedy nodded absently and her smile faded. It looked to Maggie as if she couldn't quite believe what she was about to say. "You know, Margaret, you're kind of my inspiration. You grew so much when you were gone." Kennedy's eyes drifted toward the crowded gazebo. "You came back stronger, more confident. If it worked for you, I hope it might work for me."

Maggie was stunned as Kennedy continued. "You never gave in to what others thought about you. You kept fighting, both of you did, and I want to be independent, too. I need to get out from under my father's shadow to do it."

It was the last thing Maggie expected to hear from her nemesis. She tamped down her urge to cry, gave Kennedy a quick hug, and dashed away to get Mick and Jocko in time for the concert.

Chapter 50

From the stage in the Gazebo, Mayor Tom Grieselhuber again raised his arms high over his head and waved to the crowd. When they were quiet enough, he said, "And now for the act we've all been waiting for, Benton Center's very own four-time Grammy Award winner, Terry McGrath! Arrrggh!"

"Arrrggh," the crowd roared back. Terry hit the opening riff and off they played. He was backed by Brent and a percussionist and a guitar he had hired locally. When the first song ended, Terry walked to center stage and raised his guitar as high as he could. "Benton Center! This is for you!" The Square erupted in noise.

With the crowd focused on her father, Maggie ushered Mick and Jocko down the stairs into the storage room. "With your warm reception, I want to apologize for not playing for you sooner," Terry was saying above them. "Years ago." The crowd applauded for a long minute. Maggie brushed a tear from her face when her father's voice started to break.

"You people are special," Terry continued. "This town is a special place. This is where I married my wife, Lindsay, buried her, and came back to heal." The Square was absolutely still. "A place where I raised my daughter, Maggie, yeah she's out there in the crowd someplace. Looks like some Disney princess, I think." He led a round of applause. "Benton Center's where I practice my art, writing music and teaching music. It's a place where I want to stay.

"Benton Center is so special to me, that I want it to always remain how it is. But things change, you know? And I really, truly, do not want to see our town torn apart by the ballot issue in Tuesday's election. Three days from now." Voices rustled through the crowd like dry corn stalks whispering in a field. "I was against widening the road, then I changed to neutral, and Mayor Tom is not happy with me. My daughter is for Issue Two, and she's not happy with me either.

"What to do?" He scanned his eyes over the audience. "I have a plan where both sides can win, where there are not two sides, but only one, the Benton Center side!

"Well, what do you think?" He encouraged the crowd to applaud.

"You're applauding without hearing my plan?"

"You're one of us, Terry," someone yelled from the crowd.

"I am one of you, so here's the deal. We need the additional traffic to help the businesses around the Square. I get that. But we don't want the extra traffic to tie everybody up. That's the gist of it, right? My idea is, we don't funnel the new road directly into the Square, we route it into town from the south. On the south side we have space for parking, and we can preserve the Square."

"But you can't get here from the south!"

Terry repeated the man's objection into the mic so the others could hear. "He's right. But we can run the by-pass across my land, and I'll donate the right of way." Brent strummed a 'Ta-da' chord. The audience exploded.

"Not all my land, I'm keeping the house and barn and I'm never giving up Butterfly Meadow." Brent played the opening bars of the song. "What do you think about that, Ben Cen?"

The gathering of Festgoers liked it. A lot. Mayor Tom hugged Nate, then Gena, then anybody in arm's reach. Even Kennedy seemed thrilled by the news; she handed her remaining leaflets to those standing nearby.

"Now we've got that settled," Terry repeated again over the enthusiastic roar of the crowd, "the premier of Terry and the Love Pirates with the *Love Pirate Crew!* Come on out here, kids."

The curtain parted and Meredith, Petey, Hooper, Allison and the rest of the Crew took their places on the stage, wearing red and white striped shirts and raggedy denim cut-offs. Most wore pirate hats and eye patches; Meredeath wore her skull mask. Terry said, "I wrote 'Butterfly Pond' for my daughter, you guys probably know all that, but anyway, I want to call her up on stage to help us sing it. "Butterfly, come on up here."

The crowd hummed as Maggie threaded her way to the stage steps trying to avoid the TV cameramen. Friends and people she didn't know patted her back as she passed. "I started writing 'Butterfly Pond' about a week before she was born." Terry drew a tear from the corner of his eye. "But I couldn't finish it until I saw her." Maggie crossed the stage to her father.

She hugged him and they stepped to the mic togeth-er. She glanced around the stage and winked at Brent. Her dad gave her a smile, then counted the rhythm, and they sang her song. When they finished, the crowd stood silently for several seconds. Terry raised Maggie's hand, congratulated the kids, and the people found their voice.

When the crowd settled, Maggie said, "Thank you dad, now I have a surprise for you."

Terry eyed his daughter suspiciously, then turned as the crowd began murmuring. The murmurs turned to shouts, then applause as Mick and Jocko wound through the people and up the stairs. "Arrrgh!" Terry screamed and engulfed his two friends in a hug. Maggie joined them.

The crowd roared, the Mayor and Nate slapped hands and Meredeath jammed the first bars of 'Butterfly Pond' several times.

"Damn, that girl can play," Jocko said as he jacked into an amp. Mick jumped onto the drum kit. The Love Pirates joined the Crew, and everyone in Benton Center sang along. The political crisis was averted, and the band was back together.

Chapter 51

Two thoughts competed inside Brent's brain. The first was how much he was enjoying playing with the professional musicians and his students. The looks on the kids' eyes alone were worth it, but it was obvious that the three old Pirates were loving it every bit as much. He grinned as he felt the electricity extend from the gazebo to the crowd.

The second thought was how glad he was that the plan was over. He winced at all the plans, the myriad of deceptions that had kept him and Maggie apart. The song ended and Terry caught his eye. Brent nodded.

Terry stepped to the mic. "Now we have something special. Extra special I should say after hearing the kids play and seeing the Love Pirates back together." He had to pause as the crowd erupted once again.

"I've written a new song. First one in quite a while." Several people clapped. "Thank you. Brent, here, my co-conspirator in teaching the Crew, was with me when I started it, so I thought it was a good idea to let him premiere it for you. Here is Brent Wellover with 'She Knows Her Way Home.'

Brent checked to see if he was still connected to the amp. Terry patted his shoulder then left him alone in front of the huge mass of people, the video cameras, the cell phones, and his nerves. And Maggie.

He strummed a chord, checked the tone and returned her a wink. "As you may have heard, Terry's daughter and I have been having a heck of a time getting ourselves together. Or just getting together at all." He laughed along with them. "Terry wrote this song about Maggie coming back home, but I have to admit, it could also be about me finding my way back to her."

When he was finished with the song, no one made a sound, and he was afraid he had blown it. He was sure his nervous fingers had missed several phrases. Then the crowd roared as Maggie sprinted across the stage and wrapped her arms around him. "Midnight Kiss! Midnight Kiss!"

"So now I'm supposed to kiss her?"

The crowd roared louder.

"And then get down on my knee, and open the ring box?" Brent grinned at her.

"Marry her! Marry her!"

Maggie grabbed the mic. "And I should put my hands over my mouth and cry and try to say yes? Is that what you want?"

"Yes! Midnight Kiss!"

Brent raised his hands and the noise slowly abated. "Yeah, well, we can't get engaged."

The crowd moaned.

Maggie held up her left hand and waved it around under the lights. "See, we already are."

"Couple of months ago in Chicago." Brent strummed

a ta-da chord. "When I got back from Ethiopia." He played a couple more notes. "Hey, that reminds me. Stop by my booth and make a donation to my NGO, will you? The people need it."

The crowd clapped politely and murmured. On stage behind the two, Jocko elbowed Mick. "Marketing. The kid's a genius."

"So," Brent continued. "If Maggie and I are already engaged…" Beside him Maggie waved her ring some more and showed it to girls leaning onto the stage. "What are we doing up here?"

"Let me try, honey." Maggie grinned as the crowd awed. "See, we're really engaged." She gestured to her father and the other musicians on the stage. "What these guys have been doing up here is *entertainment*." She clapped her hands. "Let's give them a nice round of applause.

"Thank you, everyone. Right, so what they've been doing is entertainment." Maggie stopped center stage. "Our lives are not."

The crowd fell silent, but cells continued flashing, videos continued recording, and texts continued flying through the meta-verse.

Brent looked at Maggie, then the crowd. "OK, you guys don't get it, so maybe we should demonstrate."

Beside him at the mic stand, Maggie said, "I know you've seen it in the movies many times, but when two people pledge their troth--"

"Their what?" Brent looked as dumbfounded as the crowd. Standing with the musicians on his left, Terry stifled a giggle.

"Get engaged, Brent. Duh." Maggie opened her hands. "Ladies, what am I going to do with him?" That got a small laugh. When it settled, she said, "When two people get engaged, it's a private thing. Intimate. It certainly was for us."

Brent nodded. "Not because we're ashamed or anything."

"Not at all," Maggie said. "Brent, play a chord."

He did so. "No, an engagement is *private*. It's nobody's business but the two people in love."

"It's not entertainment?"

"No, dear, it's not. It's not everybody's business."

The crowd was still. Eyes dropped away. Shoes toed the ground. Behind the two, Petey nudged Meredith. "What is going on?" She shushed him. At the edge of the curtain, Gena eyed the mayor, but he didn't return the look.

Brent strummed another chord. "But everybody's business is kinda what we do in Ben Cen, right?"

"What my fiancé is trying to say." Maggie shook her head. "Boy, is it great to say that word out loud." Several people clapped, and she nodded her thanks. "What he's trying to say is that you guys have been up in our business way too much, for way too long."

Brent stepped toward the now silent throng. "But that's how it is around here, and hey, we know there's no malice. We know you like us." He nodded as they began to applaud.

"Right, so we decided to demonstrate for you our engagement scene since you missed it."

"Mags, you have to give me back the ring."

"I don't want to. I can finally wear it." Maggie feigned not being able to get it off her finger.

Brent turned to the crowd. "Now we're all going to have the same pictures, so you don't need to be uploading them all over. And you don't have to make stuff up."

Someone in the crowd yelled, "Too late!" The

crowd laughed.

"See, Brent, I told you."

"Well, I had to try." Brent handed his guitar to Meredith. "This is how our engagement really went."

"Is there going to be a Midnight Kiss?"

"And fireworks?"

The crowd laughed. Brent shook his head at Maggie. "Have they been paying attention at all?"

"Not a bit," she said to him. Then to the crowd, "OK, so here we are in my dorm room in Chicago."

"Where's your roommate, Brenda?"

Maggie shaded her eyes. "Out there in the audience, I think. There she is." She waved at her friend in the crowd.

"But Brenda wasn't at our engagement, Brent. It was private. It wasn't anyone's business but our own."

Brent faced the crowd. "This is how it really went." The crowd, the entire square, probably all of Benton Center fell silent. He dropped to one knee in front of her and pulled the ring from his pocket. Their faces were projected on the big screen and hundreds of cellphones.

Maggie put her hands over her mouth. At the edge of the stage Terry grasped Teddi's hand. Gena Cobb slid herself closer to Mayor Grieselhuber. Meredeath elbowed Petey to be quiet. Jocko and Mick checked to make sure the mic was live.

"Margaret Mary McGrath, will you do me the honor of becoming my wife?"

Several people *awe*d, and were quickly shushed.

Maggie couldn't keep her smile hidden on her lips or her hand from extending her ring finger. "Yes, yes, of course yes!"

Brent slid on the ring and lifted her off her feet.

The crowd cheered and many wiped their eyes. He set her down, kissed her and turned to the crowd. "That's pretty much how it went in Chicago. Now you know."

After the applause faded, he smiled at Maggie. "Just to be clear. No audience? No Likes? No hits? No Follows?"

"None of that stuff." Maggie held his hand and shook her head. "Nope. Just the two of us, pledging our troth."

"What about fireworks?" somebody yelled from the crowd.

"Oh, there were fireworks all right, but none you could see." Maggie peered into the crowd at the speaker. "A lifetime commitment, a ring, a kiss, well several, but no boomy boom booms." Maggie sighed dramatically. "No sparkly showers of lavender falling from the sky."

Brent held her hand and took a step toward the side of the stage. "Hey, Mayor, we got any fireworks around here? The people want to see fireworks."

Mayor Tom and Councilman Nate stepped onto the stage in their costumes and spoke into a mic. Tom said, "We don't have any more *duels*," Nate continued, "but in the sky we got *jewels*."

"For the last time, ladies and gentlemen, the cast of *Hamilton*," Brent said as the rockets fired and the crowd cheered.

"Hopefully," Maggie added.

"I love you," Brent said and kissed her under a spray of lavender sparks and thundering booms. Terry and Teddi, Mick and Jocko, the Crew and many others rushed to their sides.

"Sorry it's not really a Midnight Kiss," Brent said inside the human cocoon of hugs.

"It's better than that." Maggie kissed him again. "It's a lifetime kiss."

Epilogue

One year later...

Brent watched Maggie hold her breath and carefully lay the baby into his bassinet. She held her hands over him until she was sure he was asleep and breathing before letting herself exhale. He reached out his hand and she sat down onto the top step of the gazebo. "You're a natural at this." He kissed her cheek and smiled.

"Beautiful night," she said. "The sun is setting right over town hall. Like a post card."

"What's a post card, Mommy?" Brent said in a squeaky voice. She bumped her shoulder against his and he returned to his normal voice. "The square is peaceful, and the PumpkinFest is nearly all cleaned up."

"And we're sitting here with little Seth, not doing any of the work." She nodded her head. "I admit I kinda like it."

"Not like the last two Fests, huh?" Brent reached his

arm around her, and she snuggled under it. "This year we just enjoyed it like tourists."

"Two years ago there was the coronation, and the conflict, and we split. Last year was the election, and more conflict. and we got engaged. And this year." Maggie let her voice fade away.

"This year no conflict, no drama and barely a word of gossip." Brent kissed the top of her head. "Just bliss."

Maggie pulled out of his embrace to look at him. "Two years ago we were thousands of miles apart. No jobs, no idea of what to do with our lives."

"Well, we did know we loved each other." Brent cocked his head to the side, and she elbowed him. "And the Gossip Club was kind enough to fill in the blanks."

"I'm serious Brent." Maggie paused as if hearing something and checked the baby before saying, "Now I've got a job, you've got a job. Jobs we like."

"Even Kennedy has a job." Brent knew it was a risk bringing up his wife's nemesis. Before she could respond he added, "And to her credit she got her dad to pay for taking down the telephone poles and burying the electric lines."

Maggie narrowed her eyes. "I know you're trying to rile me up, mister, but it won't work. Kay Kay and I are friends now." She let a smile curl the corners of her lips. "As you well know."

He couldn't resist the shot. "Friends or frenemies?"

"Don't push it." She cupped her ear to hear the baby over the noise of a passing semi.

"Is he OK?" Maggie nodded, and Brent continued, "It's about time to get home. Three-day tour early tomorrow."

"Dayton, Cincinnati, and I forget?"

"Columbus," Brent said. "Actually Dublin. At the

zoo."

Maggie sighed. "My dad, my husband, and the Love Pirates playing for the primates."

"No, you're thinking too small. Vertebrates; we're playing to the apes and anybody with a spine. You could come along, you know."

"Can't this week. Gotta take the mayor on a tour of the bypass."

"Making progress?"

"We are." Maggie waved to someone across the street from the square. Brent couldn't tell who it was. "Something about aesthetics," she said. "Council wants to be sure we're adding enough greenery. They're worried about the concrete to leafy tree ratio."

"Come along next time then. I need help with the fund raising. People are donating so much to the NGO at the concerts that I could use another pair of eyes to keep track of it all."

She leaned her face closer and batted her eyelids. "Like these?"

"I adore your eyes." He kissed her then noticed the couple waiting for the light to change in front of the church. "Sammi and Irving on their way."

"I saw them," Maggie said and sat upright. "Speaking of conflict--"

"Which we weren't."

"Which we had been previously." Maggie waited for his attention. "In many ways we blew it."

"We got through the conflict." Brent knotted his brow. "All's well that ends well."

"But we were so focused on our problems, we missed theirs. They had real problems. Her family's from India, his from rural Ohio. Different cultures, different religions.

Wildly different lifestyles."

Brent thought for a second. "Yeah, we did blow it. We didn't help them, because we were so damn busy worrying about what others were saying about us."

"Those two falling in love was not what we expected. What no one expected."

"We should have noticed." Brent shook his head. "We have got to be better friends. Those two deserve it."

"Sammi and I were talking about it the other day when she brought the baby over. Do know what really happened?"

Brent watched little spit balls form and pop on the boy's lips as he inhaled and exhaled. "I don't."

"While we were kissing on stage under the lavender sparks?"

Brent turned around and shrugged.

"They were kissing on the bridge down in the park. At the same time. Under the same fireworks," Maggie said. "The irony."

"The ignorance." Brent snorted in disgust. "We weren't there to support them, and I was even a little angry that they weren't on stage supporting us."

"We're quite the pair, aren't we?" She took his hand. "But we're all happy now, like you said, right? We just took different paths to get there than they did."

"I guess so, but still." He rose and helped her to her feet as Sammi and Irving arrived at the gazebo.

"You guys got it all sorted out?"

Sammi burst past him and dropped down beside the baby.

"I pity those kids in Latin club." Irving reached out his hand and said slowly, "Connie Richardson is quite the stickler. Organized, but man. Every piece had to be put into the exact same spot."

"More organized than her predecessor?" Brent cocked his head at Sammi.

"Do not get me started, my friend."

They both turned at the sound of the baby crying. Sammi picked him up and said to Maggie, "Has he been fussy? Maybe he's hungry."

"He's been a little dear." Maggie beamed. "I hope ours will be so good."

Sammi, Irving and Brent looked at Maggie as if they couldn't quite grasp what she meant.

"Are you?" Brent managed.

"I am." Maggie smiled and placed both her hands on her stomach. "You and I are going to be parents, too."

THE END

About the Author

Unexpected Love is one of two unexpected consequences of the COVID pandemic. My wife, Marie, and I watched hundreds of Hallmark movies during the shutdown. I thought it would be a good idea to try a format different from my "Joe Lehrer Mysteries." From a writing standpoint it was, but I thought it would be easy, which it wasn't. In any case I hope you enjoy it.

What comes next is a puzzle. Maybe I'll finally get around to publishing "The Faculty Lounge Stories." Maybe another Benton Center Romance. As for Joe Lehrer? I've got the next title, *Dangling Participles*, but as of now, no plot. Oh, well, the muse will tell me when she's ready.

Stay in touch with me on Facebook, Twitter, Instagram, LinkedIn or Goodreads, and visit the website www. davidallenedmonds.com.

Reviews are especially important to Indie authors. Please tell me what you think, good/bad/meh, on Amazon at: www.amazon.com/David-Allen-Edmonds/e/B06XQN-6HGQ/

Acknowledgments and Thanks

To those who helped create the book: Julie Bayer, Sue Grimshaw, Barb Kauffman, the staff of Astro Computers

To those who encouraged the book along the way: Connie Raybuck, Paula Lynn, Peter Danszczak, Paul Kubis, Tom Heinen and Bob Stowe

To the writers who inspired me: John Bruening, John A Vanek, Dana McSwain, Marie Vibbert and Robert Allen Stowe

To those who support the Arts in the region: Brandi Larsen and Literary Cleveland, Ken Schneck, the Medina County Arts Council, Main Street Medina and the Medina County Writers Club

To those who carry my books in Medina: JK Gift Shop, Medina County Visitors Bureau, Cool Beans and H2 Wine Merchants.

To those who carry my books in the region: Fireside Books in Chagrin Falls, the Bookshop in Lakewood, The Bibliophile in Dover, Visible Voice Books in Tremont, The Learned Owl in Hudson, and Apple Tree Books in Cleveland Heights

To those who support Indie Authors: Read, Write, Local at the Avon Lake Public Library; the Local Author Fair at the North Canton Public Library; the North Coast Indie Author Book Fair in Elyria; Medina Fest sponsored by Main Street Medina

To my family: Marie, Brian, Anne Marie, Mike, the grandkids, and all who call me Apu.

Book Club Discussion Questions

1. The book is dedicated to the freedom of expression. What does that have to do with the book or its theme? Are people in Benton Center allowed to express their opinions despite the harm they may cause? Are their limits to this freedom?

2. Much of the gossip is alluded to, but not specifically expressed. Why is that so? Are Maggie and Brent too sensitive? Do they have 'rabbit ears' as Kennedy puts it?

3. What do you make of the citizens of Benton Center's interest and participation in local politics? Is it healthy? Is it believable? Would you like to live in such a community?

4. *The Pax Cucurbita*, or Pumpkin Peace, is an agreed upon pause in the middle of a political campaign. Could that happen in today's politically charged society? Does it make you think of Christmas carols sung between the trenches of

WWI?

5. At some point the Gossip Club defines one of the two lovers as the planner and the other as flying by the seat of the pants. Which one is Maggie, which is Brent? Are the gossipers accurate in their assessment? Is an accurate knowledge of facts a prerequisite for gossip?

6. Why is the emphasis on Maggie and Brent while the real work of Sammi and Irv building a relationship and overcoming cultural differences left in the background? Why do you think the focus is on the expected love while the title is Unexpected Love?

7. What is Teddi's role: is she a gossiper, a parental figure, a friend? Why is her choice of Halloween costume, Yoda, appropriate?

8. Do you see any similarities between this novel and Shakespeare's *Much Ado About Nothing*? Consider the role gossip plays in both works, as well as the festive settings, the status or fame of the characters, and the use of costumes and deception. Please don't consider the talent discrepancies between the authors.

9. Do you believe the author intentionally mimicked the Bard, or was he influenced by his Muse? How does the creative process work? Is it different in different media?

Made in the USA
Middletown, DE
07 November 2023

42139904R00159